CONTRA

(Hellion Club: Book 2)

Aiden Bates

Disclaimer

This is a work of fiction. Names, places, characters and events are all fictitious for the reader's pleasure. Any similarities to real people, places, events, living or dead are all coincidental.

This book contains sexually explicit content that is intended for ADULTS ONLY (+18).

Chapter One

Ty yawned and glanced over at the clock. He had about as much interest in the final case report for the Fletcher case as he had in undersea fauna. He hadn't agreed to take on the Fletcher case. In fact, he'd argued vociferously against taking on the Fletcher case. "They're guilty as sin," had been his exact words. "And Lena Fletcher is her own worst enemy. She'll damage our reputation and give us a loss."

The problem with being the youngest partner at Clarke, Watts, and Wilcox was that his voice didn't count for much in the partner meetings. *Wait until you're older, you'll understand. Wait until you've been around the block a few more times, you'll get it. Listen to us, we get how this works.*

Lena Fletcher had embarrassed the firm. They'd lost the case. The attorney they'd put out there on trial had faced off against an uneducated chef from the Bronx and came out on the bottom. No one at the firm wanted to talk about it. It would have been like Ali going up against a sixteen year old girl and losing.

And now, because CWW policy demanded another partner review the case file and look for "opportunities to excel in the future," he was sitting here in his office at eight o'clock at night instead of being at home.

He frowned down at his report. There was absolutely no reason he had to be at the office reviewing the stupid file. He could take it home. He was a partner now. He'd been a partner for three months. He didn't have to *be seen* working his ass off. He could go home and work his ass off, under a blanket and with his cats. Maybe he could even put the TV on for background noise.

He packed up and left, as quickly as he could. Getting the train back to Murray Hill didn't take long, and grabbing a take-out salad for dinner was just a blip in the road. He headed up to his apartment and locked the door behind him, already taking his tie off.

"You know, taking your clothes off in front of your brother is considered weird."

Ty jumped and turned around. His brother Keegan stood in the doorway to his bathroom, dressed in khakis and a button down shirt in so many shades of orange Ty had to look away.

"Keegan. How are you even here?" He scratched his head.

"I stole your key and made a copy of it, of course." Keegan flung himself down onto the couch. "I was in the neighborhood, and I thought I'd drop in."

"You weren't in the neighborhood, Keegan. You're never in the neighborhood. That's one of the reasons I got a place here."

"You got a place here because it's cheap." Keegan waved a finger. "Compared to Fifth Ave, anyway. Okay, you're right. I'm on my way to the Hellion Club. And I figured I'd stop off and talk to my baby brother on my way there."

Ty wrinkled his nose. "Aren't you getting a little old for that place?"

"Not really. As long as you're an alpha and you can afford the membership fees, you can be any age you want. It's not just Hooters for alphas, Ty."

Ty shuddered. "Tell that to the ex-husband in the case I just had to review."

Keegan made a face. "Eew. Is it the Fletcher case? Look, whatever's going on there, Sol Delaney's a good guy. You'd like him. I was going to introduce you, but for the whole flamingly psychotic ex-relatives thing."

"I don't need a set-up, Keegan."

Keegan screwed his face up and spoke in a high-pitched voice. "*I don't need a set-up, Keegan.* Says the guy who hasn't had a date in eighteen months. My god, you know your plumbing's going to back up...like whoa."

Ty pinched the bridge of his nose. "Keegan, you're forty. Try to remember that and not talk like a fifteen year old street girl." He put his briefcase down and went into the kitchen. He tried to grab a beer from the refrigerator, but the only glass bottle he found was empty.

"Did you drink all of my beer, Keegan?"

"Yup." Keegan put his feet up on Ty's coffee table.

Ty rested his head on his freezer door for a moment. "Why did you put an empty bottle in the fridge?"

"Well, I didn't want you to reach for a beer and find nothing there."

Ty closed his eyes and tried to remember he was not allowed to punch his brother in the mouth. Punching his brother in the mouth would get him disbarred, and all of the work and sacrifices to make partner would be so much wasted time. "Okay. Okay. Anyway, I'm not getting fixed up with anyone from the Hellion Club, so maybe just let me live my life and...uh...go ogle the bartender or something."

"I'm actually going for a very important finance committee meeting."

Ty looked Keegan up and down. "Dressed like that? You look like a traffic cone that went through a wood chipper."

Keegan flipped him off. “Look. You’re evading the issue. You haven’t had a date for eighteen months, and that’s just not healthy, bro.”

“I’m fine with it. It’s a choice.”

“Well, yeah, it’s a choice. I know it’s a choice. You’re not bad looking, when you’re not standing next to your awesome oldest brother with the incredible fashion sense. The thing is, bro, your choice makes no sense.” Keegan gave him a big, cheesy grin.

Ty sighed. “Look. Even though you’re the last—absolute dead last—person I want to talk to about my sex life, I’m fine with it. I have cats. I have my job. It’s enough for me. So, maybe you could just be on your way to your alpha strip club.”

“There’s no stripping going on. Sure, they don’t wear too many clothes, but that’s okay. The human body is a beautiful thing. It should be worshipped and celebrated, Ty. And you are not fine with that. You tell yourself you’re okay with it, but you’re not. I know you. I’ve been your big brother since the day you were born. And you’ve read every book about babies and child development since you were able to read.

“We knew you were an omega long before any stupid tests, okay? You wanted babies. You wanted lots of babies. And you’re not getting any younger.”

“Thanks for that helpful reminder, Keegan. I’d forgotten I’m thirty-one already.” Ty spoke through clenched teeth.

“Look, bro. Obviously you’re working through some stuff, and that’s fine. But if you want to have a kid, you’re going to have to get there sooner than later. I’m just saying. It just hasn’t worked out yet. And that’s fine.”

It wasn’t fine. Keegan could say it was fine, because he wasn’t the one who had to live with it. Ty had to put up with everyone's pity, or worse, their scorn. Keegan could be a forty year old bachelor and get away with it. Ty was already over the hill. "And there's nothing I can do about it. Even if I go out and screw random guys until I catch, I can't get away with that. A guy from this kind of firm who carries out of wedlock? No way."

"So get married, dumbass. Although, maybe don't work for that kind of firm anymore. Just a thought." Keegan shrugged.

"I like what I do. Except the reviews," he added, glaring at his briefcase. "I like the kind of law I practice."

"Look." Keegan threw his arm around Ty's stiff shoulders. "What you'll have to do is get married. And you can do that. You might have to give up the whole long courtship and princess carriage thing, but you're a big shot lawyer now. You guys don't do that crap."

"Criminal law does tend to kind of tarnish the tiara a bit." Ty gave his brother a dark look.

"So skip it. We've got some guys who are in particular positions who could stand to get married. You know, they need to reform their images and stuff, or they need the money. And, you know, our dads are willing to drop a pile of cash on you and your husband whenever you get around to getting hitched."

"Because that's not humiliating."

"They're old fashioned. What are you going to do?" Keegan spread his hands wide. "Anyway, you let me fix you up with one of them. You guys get married. You get your baby, either with him or through whatever means you negotiate. You went to school for that crap, it's up to you. And then when you've filled whatever needs you both have and our dads' deposit clears, you guys can get a divorce. Just like that." He snapped his fingers. “I can think of five different guys from the Hellion Club who’d jump at the chance.”

“Now there’s a ringing endorsement.” Ty rubbed at his face.

The whole idea of a fake marriage just to get a baby made him want to throw up. He didn’t want to have sex with strangers. For all that his experiences had made him cynical, he still thought he was worth a bit of romance. He still thought he was worth actual love.

Keegan’s idea would destroy that last little bit of hope.

He took a deep breath and tried to force himself to look at things rationally. “I guess for all that’s appealing about the idea of love and romance, it’s not something that can happen for everyone.”

“Nope.” Keegan’s voice was cheerful. So was his grin. “Personally, I think it’s all a lie. This is the way it should be. It’s a transaction. Your expectations are laid out clearly in black and white, along with the consequences for failing to live up to them. There’s no fuss, no hand-wringing. Everyone gets what they came for, and they leave happy. It’s a thousand times better than all of this pissing and moaning everyone does. *Does he love me? Does he love me not?*”

Ty bowed his head. He didn’t want this. He didn’t want a temporary marriage. He didn’t want to marry a stranger. He didn’t want to marry anyone from the Hellion Club or anyone his brother knew at all. He wanted someone who loved him, treasured him, and wanted to be with him.

But he also wanted a baby. He’d been holding out for true love for thirty-one years, only to become more disappointed with each passing day. Maybe Keegan was right. Maybe this was the only way. And he’d have a baby. The baby would love him. It wouldn’t be the same kind of love, but it would be love.

"Fine." He clutched at his stomach as it turned. "Come up with a list of candidates, and I'll look them over."

Keegan clapped his hands. "Finally! Let Operation Get My Brother Laid commence!" He all but danced out the door, leaving nothing but the smell of his atrocious cologne in his wake.

Ty poked at his salad, but he wasn't hungry anymore. He couldn't stomach looking at the Fletcher report, either. All he wanted to do was go to bed.

His cats climbed into the bed with him, curled up against his side, purred. He scratched them under their chins and behind their ears, just how they liked. Maybe he could call Keegan and tell him to cancel. This was a stupid idea. He should just be content with his cats and be done.

But he couldn't. The whole world seemed to want him to get married, and he wanted to have a baby. He couldn't do one without the other, and this was the only way. He'd have to hold his nose and cope. He was definitely writing the contract so he didn't have to spend much time with the groom, though.

***

Carter's knees ached as he walked into the Hellion Club. Thank god for winter. If he'd had to go someplace in shorts or something everyone would have seen the huge bruises on them. It was a good kind of bruise, because he knew exactly how he'd gotten them, and last night had been fun as hell, but it had been a private kind of fun.

He walked up to the bar and ordered an Old Fashioned. The omega behind the bar grinned at him and made sure to brush his hand with his own as he handed him his drink. "Pitchers and catchers must be starting up soon, huh?"

Carter grimaced. “You bet. Should be a good year, too. We made a lot of good trades in the off season, did a lot of good moves, and I’m just glad I’m still in New York, you know?” He sounded like he was giving a media sound bite. He felt like he was giving a media sound bite, too.

“Well, that’s good. I can’t wait to see what you guys come up with. You’re always fun to watch. I love to see the way you handle your bat and balls.”

Carter opened his mouth to reply. He liked his omegas forward like that. He didn’t like to have to work too hard to get a rise out of them; it felt like their consent was at best grudging and no one liked to feel like they were pushing someone into sex. The bartender was hot, had an incredible body, and Carter would cheerfully spend a night with him.

Unfortunately for Carter, Keegan Cunningham inserted himself into the conversation. “Carter Bowman, just the man I was looking to see.”

Carter’s grin tightened, and he turned to the bartender. “Hold that thought,” he said. Keegan Cunningham was the last person Carter wanted to hear from right now. He was a badly dressed alpha who came from old money, forty years old, and still acted like a frat boy.

Unfortunately, he sat on the financial committee. And if Carter wanted to stay in the Hellion Club, he needed to stay on Keegan’s good side.

“Keegan, my man.” He clapped him on the shoulder. “How’s it going?”

“It’s going, bro. It’s going. Come on and take a little walk with me, would you?” Keegan didn’t wait for him, but guided him toward the library.

Carter followed him into his least favorite room in the club. He hated the quiet of the space. He hated all the books. They felt creepy to him, menacing. They passed Sol and Alden Delaney conversing quietly in one of the many little alcoves. It was too quiet to hear what they were talking about, but neither of them looked thrilled with the other.

Carter ignored them. Their conversation looked private.

Keegan took a seat a discreet distance away from the Delaneys. "So, Carter, I've just come from a finance committee meeting. And the subject of your dues came up."

Carter closed his eyes. "Look. I've got a long term contract. I'm a little strapped right now, but I'm coming out of it in a few months when I get paid again. It's a temporary blip."

"Hey, I know, man." Keegan pressed a hand to his chest. "That scam artist hit a lot of guys hard. I mean, you could have maybe not put all your eggs in one basket, but as it happens I know a lawyer who might be able to help you get some of it back. In the meantime, there's the matter of your dues."

Carter swallowed. It wasn't like he'd die without the Hellion Club. It was just good to have. It was good to have a place to go in every major city, a place to be social. A place where he could find like minded people. "Look, just a few months."

Keegan nodded. "The Club understands there are times when members need more time to come up with the fees. But, ah, we can't do that for everyone. I have a proposal for you."

Carter's palms broke out in a sweat. "A proposal?"

"Marry money."

Carter laughed. It sounded hysterical to him, but he couldn't hold it in. "Just like that."

"Actually, yeah. I've got an omega who comes from money, scads of it. He's also a partner with a major white-shoe law firm, even though he's only thirty-one. And he's looking to get married."

Carter frowned. "What's wrong with him?"

Keegan blinked. "What do you mean, what's wrong with him? Nothing's wrong with him."

"A rich omega's still single at thirty-one? Something's got to be wrong with him." Carter crossed his arms over his chest. "What is it? Ugly? Squeaky voice? Too bossy? Too bitchy? What is it?"

Keegan winced. "Ouch. I think he's perfect."

"So, why haven't you married him?"

"One, I'm a permanent bachelor. No one can nail this fine ass down. Two, there are about a bazillion city, state, and federal laws against it. He's my brother."

"Oh." Carter shut his mouth. "Shutting up now."

"Don't worry about it. I can see where you'd be concerned. Ty is pretty driven, and he's had some not so great relationships in the past. When it came down to choosing those guys or his work, he picked work. Which, I guess you could say he got what he deserved, but he's my brother so I won't.

"Anyway. I'm not talking marrying him forever. He needs a husband for a certain period of time to get his share of our grandparents' estate. He wants a baby in the worst way—he wants a baseball team, really, but he'll be happy with one. You guys can negotiate how that happens, and how long you stay together." Keegan waved a hand. "At the end, you get a cut of the inheritance, and he gets the baby."

Carter buried his face in his hands. "What did you major in at college, man? Pimping?"

Keegan did a double take. "Excuse me?"

"You're trying to pimp me out to your unmarriageable omega brother for money. That's what it boils down to. I mean the payout is long term, but it's not...it's me, having sex with your brother, for money." He rubbed his face and looked at Keegan through his fingers. "The worst part is, I'm thinking about it."

"Okay...I guess I can see your point. It is a little bit like pimping." Keegan sprawled out in his chair and laughed. "But let's face it, man. You need the money. And you'd probably make a cute kid, too."

Carter rubbed at the back of his neck. "I'm not sure I'm ready to be a dad, either. You know what I mean?"

"No one's asking you to be a dad, bro. All you'd be, at the end of the day, is a donor. A very well paid donor, you understand what I'm saying? You wouldn't even have to live together once the baby's on the way." Keegan leaned forward, elbows on his knees. "Just don't get caught on camera with dudes in other cities, you know? That looks bad. He'd totally understand, but it looks bad."

"Right." Carter sighed. "Shouldn't you want better for your brother than a ball player who's only with him for the money?" He scratched his head. "Shouldn't I want better for your brother than a ball player who's only with him for the money?"

"Maybe. But he's not going to get better than that." Keegan's jaw tightened. "It might be nice, but let's face it. That kind of sappy, romantic BS is for poor people who don't have to worry about estate planning and that kind of crap. Once you're at our level, you can't afford to waste your time on that kind of frivolous nonsense. It's all transactional. You marry him, you put up a good show in public, and when the time comes you part amicably. No fuss, no muss. Are you in or not?"

Carter bowed his head. "I guess I'm in." What choice did he have? He might not die without the Hellions, but he needed them. "God help me, but I'm in."

"Awesome. I'll tell Ty the good news." He pulled out his phone and snapped a picture of Carter, then he typed on his phone. Carter's phone beeped with an incoming message a moment later.

It was a biography page from Clarke, Watts, and Wilcox, a major law firm headquartered downtown. The guy staring out from the page was hot, in an intense kind of way. Carter wouldn't want to go against him in court. Carter wasn't sure he wanted to go against him anywhere. "You're sure he's an omega?"

"Oh, yeah. Trust me on this. Anyway, look forward to hearing from him in a few days. Between the three of us we can make a date and head down to the Justice of the Peace or something."

"Sounds...well, it sounds miserable, but what are we going to do." Carter shook Keegan's hand. "What does he like? What's he into? What does he do in his spare time?"

Keegan grimaced. "He hasn't had spare time since he left law school. He has cats. He's fond of the little bastards, I think. They keep biting me every time I go to his apartment." He shook his head. "Anyway. You'll have a chance to ask your questions at the wedding."

"I don't even get to meet him beforehand?"

Keegan made a face. "Why would you want to? Anyway, I've got to run. I've got a date."

Carter stared at his drink after Keegan left. He wasn't sure what to make of the encounter. Part of him thought he'd just secured his future. The rest of him thought he'd just made the biggest mistake of his life, even worse than the time he'd let the catcher take him to a local bar in San Juan during winter ball.

Well, he hadn't signed any contracts yet. His soul was still intact, so to speak. But would it stay that way? He could still back out of this mess, but he'd have to give up too much. The Hellion Club had come to mean too much to him. He couldn't give it up.

There weren't many alphas in pro sports. There weren't any omegas at all. Carter was on the road for weeks at a time during the season. He needed to be able to be among friends, people who understood him. It wasn't even about sex, although that was nice. It was about family, about companionship.

Funny. He'd always figured marriage was supposed to be about family and companionship too.

Chapter Two

Ty looked down at the stack of case files on his desk. There had to be a reason the firm hadn't moved to electronic files, right? Oh sure, they had to use paper for archival purposes, but surely they could move information internally without killing an entire forest each time they needed to say something.

One of the other partners stuck his head into Ty's office. "Any chance you'll have those done by tomorrow morning?" The partner asking was Spada, never one of Ty's favorites. A network of fine red lines had broken out across his nose at some point in the past few weeks. Spider angiomas, they were called. Everyone knew Spada kept a bottle of whiskey in his drawer and changed it more than once a week. Well, his drinking problem had only gotten him thrown out of court once. Ty shouldn't judge.

"None, I'm afraid." Ty checked the clock on his laptop. "I'm getting married in two hours. I'll be out of reach for the rest of the evening."

Spada frowned, blinking. "Getting married? That seems unlike you, Cunningham."

Ty sighed, but only a little bit. Spada was right, after all. "I suppose it is. Everyone needs a change at some point, you know."

Spada stepped a little further into Ty's office. "You know," he said, propping himself up on Ty's desk, "this is a good step for you. Depending on your husband, of course. I don't know who you're marrying, but the firm tends to think well of family men."

And what do they think of guys who walk into arranged temporary marriages for the sole purpose of getting pregnant? Ty schooled his face into seriousness. Spada wasn't exactly known for his sense of humor. "That's good to hear. We're definitely hoping to start a family."

"Well, good luck to you. A couple of hours, you say?"

"Yeah. It'll just be down at City Hall, no big deal." It certainly wasn't the formal wedding he'd dreamed of as a kid, with flowers and champagne, but there would be a marriage license and everything. "I'll be back to work tomorrow."

Spada gave him a quizzical look. "How does the husband feel about that?"

"Fine. Fine. He gets it. We both have demanding jobs, so neither of us is really in a position to object." He straightened his back. He had no idea how C. Bowman, 2B, NY, felt about it. They hadn't communicated directly with each other at all. It bothered him on some level, that C. Bowman hadn't reached out, but then again Ty hadn't reached out to him. He didn't even know C. Bowman's first name.

"Okay." Spada paused just long enough for the silence to be awkward. "I guess I'll see you tomorrow."

"Bright and early." Ty faked a smile. "We've got that intake meeting at eight, and then we're talking about the Delaney estate audit at noon."

"You're sure you don't want to take some time off? It's your first wedding, isn't it? That's usually a special time for a couple."

"We'll be fine, I promise. We don't need a lot of fuss."

Spada left the office with a weak little smile, probably to hit the bottle again. Ty gave some real thought to joining him. There was still time to call this whole thing off. No contracts had been signed. He could still retreat to his own apartment after work, play with his cats, and maybe even get a good night's sleep.

He picked up a case file and looked at it, pretending to read it while his stomach tied itself into knots. Keegan came up with some stupid ideas sometimes, but this one took the cake. What had Ty been thinking, anyway, taking his brother up on this idiocy? Here he was, about to go say yes to a stranger—sleep with a stranger, on purpose! And promise to pay him, to boot!

He cleaned up his desk and packed up his briefcase. He shouldn't look at the situation that way, like some kind of weird prostitution contract. Ty was a go-getter, a doer. He always had been. He'd never been content to just sit back and wait for things to come to him. He'd wanted independence, so he'd gone to law school, found a job with a top firm, gotten his own place, and now he was the youngest partner in the firm's history. He was the only omega partner, too. He'd wanted a career, so he'd turned away from alphas who wanted a society husband.

He'd always wanted a family. This might not be the way he'd wanted to go about it, but he was getting the job done. Ty would be a dad, and if he had to marry some guy his brother had dragged out of the Hellion Club's men's room—

He stopped himself. Those were the wrong kind of thoughts to have. Who knew what Keegan had told this guy to get him to go along with this crazy scheme? What was his name again, Carson? Chris? Channing? Carter? Whatever. Ty took a deep breath and grabbed his coat. Whatever Keegan had told him to get him to go along with this mess, he deserved better than Ty's resentment or contempt. He was doing Ty a favor—*and being paid well for it*—and Ty needed to remember that fact.

It was snowing as he stepped outside. He stood and caught a few flakes on his arm, marveling at how they looked under the streetlight. Then he shook them off to hail a cab. Once upon a time, about a million years ago, he'd been a skier. He'd been on the ski team, in fact. He hadn't been on the slopes since undergrad, but he missed it. Maybe someday he could head back out there, take a vacation and enjoy the rush of a good downhill slalom again.

Then again, he was thirty-one now. He'd probably wrap himself around a tree or something. He hadn't had a vacation in ten years. It had been worth it, but he probably shouldn't think about doing those kinds of dangerous activities now that he was so out of practice.

The ride to City Hall took all of ten minutes. Ty tried to pretend he wasn't nervous, but his chest was tighter than it should have been. He figured that was normal, under the circumstances. Most people were probably nervous on their wedding day, right? They probably didn't hope their vehicle got caught in a ten hour traffic jam on the way to the venue, but he'd get over it eventually.

Ty headed into the office building and made his way to the justice of the peace's office. He normally had a typical New Yorker's speed when he walked, but now he trudged along like a Southerner strolling through molasses. This was a mistake. He'd done the wrong thing here.

He opened the door to his destination and pulled himself upright. He couldn't show this kind of weakness, not in front of his brother and not in front of his soon-to-be husband. He needed to start things off with this unknown alpha—Carl? Cosmo? Crispin? on an equal footing, and Keegan was like a shark. If he sensed weakness, he'd be all over Ty in a second.

The City Clerk sat at his desk. Ty knew Fred Rodriguez, the City Clerk, comfortably well. Rodriguez had told Ty more than once that performing weddings was his favorite part of the job. He smiled broadly when Ty walked in. "Ty Cunningham! When I saw your name on the schedule I almost fell over in shock. I thought you were married to the firm, bro!"

Ty ducked his head and grinned. If he focused on Fred, he wouldn't have to think about the other men in the room. "Ah, come on, Fred. All new lawyers are married to their firms. Otherwise they don't get past that 'new lawyer' smell."

"What, greasy takeout and unwashed bodies, because they haven't left their desks for three days?" Fred raised his eyebrows at Ty.

"The smart ones wash up in the bathroom." Ty grinned at him. "How are you doing?"

"Can't complain. Can't complain. The super in my building just quit, so of course that's when the heater goes out, right?"

A deep, almost rumbling voice spoke up from the other side of the room just outside of Ty's vision. "If you want, I could stop by and take a look at it tomorrow. My dad's a plumber back in Nebraska. I'm not an expert, but I can probably get it running again until your landlord can get the right guys to come out."

Ty turned around slowly. He'd seen pictures of his fiancé, of course. He'd done his due diligence. C. Bowman, 2B NY, was maybe six foot three. His dark suit was tailored to his thick, muscular frame, and made his green eyes stand out. If Ty had met him in a bar, he wouldn't mind getting to know him better.

Those hands, the ones sticking out from under the end of his jacket, were huge. Ty pretended his mouth wasn't watering. He was a lawyer. He wasn't supposed to have those reactions, damn it.

Fred, of course, was oblivious to C. Bowman, 2B NY's huge, strong hands. He was immune to his stirring, deep voice and his intense green eyes had no effect on Fred whatsoever. "That's...kind of awesome. How come that's not something that comes up on the sports shows, huh?"

An older Hispanic man standing beside C. Bowman, 2B NY swatted at Bowman's arm. "Because if word gets out that he's out there messing around with heaters and boilers and what the hell ever, it would invalidate his contract." He scowled up at Bowman, and then smiled over at Fred. "Don't worry. I won't tell the big boss—but you'd better not get hurt." His accent reminded Ty of Puerto Rico.

Keegan popped up and put his hands on Ty's shoulders. Ty hadn't seen him in the room, not anywhere, and so he jumped. Keegan seemed to find this hilarious, because he cackled like a hyena. "Dude, the look on your face, bro!" He doubled over, clapping his hands. "If you could see it! Anyway, did you bring the contract?"

"Right." Ty sniffed. "Keegan, have you been at the bar?"

"I had one drink, bro. And then that prick Hannigan tripped and dumped his entire glass of whiskey onto my shirt." Keegan straightened up. "Not that there's anything wrong with a celebratory drink or two. My baby brother's getting married! How exciting is that!"

Bowman grimaced. Ty couldn't fault him for it, although he could have wished he'd kept it to himself a little better. Then again, if Ty wanted guys to not wince about marrying him he should probably have worked harder at becoming husband material, instead of partner material.

He pulled the contract out of his briefcase to hide his distress and passed it to his fiancé. Bowman looked it over. His hand shook as he read it. "Are you sure you want to go through with this?" he asked. He didn't look directly at Ty, and Ty guessed he could understand that. He probably wouldn't have looked directly at someone who had to pay someone to marry him, either.

"If you're uncomfortable, we can always call it off." Ty had lots of practice keeping his tone neutral and he needed every bit of it now.

"Of course he's uncomfortable." The man standing next to him, Bowman's witness Ty supposed, snapped and stepped between them. "You've basically got him over a barrel, don't you? He's marrying a stranger, he has to sign a contract to do it, I mean this is all just the dumbest thing I've ever heard—and I've been in baseball since I was seventeen; I've heard a lot of dumb shit. Only a monster wouldn't be uncomfortable with that. Which begs the question, what the hell is wrong with you, anyway?" He pointed a finger at Ty.

Ty took the contract out of Bowman's hands. "And we're done here." He slipped it into his briefcase and headed for the door. His cheeks blazed with shame and humiliation. He hadn't wanted to do this in the first place, damn it.

Keegan jumped to keep him in the room, all but tackling him in the process. "Hey, hey. You wanted a baby, this is the only way for you to get a baby. It's okay, little bro." He kept his voice low and soothing. "The mean guy doesn't have to come around to your place. You don't have to see him after you leave this room."

He turned to Bowman and the nasty guy. "Look, Belmonte, I get that you're trying to look out for your boy here. And I get that this isn't the most conventional arrangement. But Carter here's getting something out of this deal too. He's getting money he needs, thanks to that financial advisor scam thing. He's hardly being exploited. You can take a look at the contract if you want. There are no expectations on him that will take away from his on-field performance. And if nothing else, it should keep him away from any off-the-field shenanigans for a good three years. Am I right?"

Belmonte held out his hand and tapped his foot. Ty stared him down, but Keegan elbowed him. “Don’t be difficult, Ty. Christ, it’s not like you ever have to see the dude again.”

Ty passed the contract over. He didn’t have to see Belmonte again, but he did have to deal with Fred. Fred seeing him like this was downright degrading. If the other partners found out about this, he’d never survive.

Belmonte pursed his lips as he scanned over the contract. “Well, I can’t see how you’d be getting screwed in this, except in the whole custody department. But if you don’t want the kid anyway, that shouldn’t be an issue.” He handed it over to Bowman to sign. “I still say there’s something deeply wrong with you, Cunningham. Paying people off to marry you. If you can’t find someone to do the job the right way, you should just be happy with what you have.”

“The thought had occurred to me,” Ty told him, through gritted teeth.

Keegan stepped on his foot while Bowman signed the contract. “Hey. Shut up. And as for you,” he continued, looking over at Belmonte again, “lay off my brother. This whole thing was my idea, not his, so if you want to bitch at someone about it bitch at me. You have no idea what’s behind it all, and you could never understand, so just back off.” He took the contract, signed it at the witness position, and slammed it onto Fred’s desk.

Fred was startled into action. He duly signed and notarized the contract and cleared his throat. “So, ah, after all of that, I’m guessing you don’t want the flowery speech or stuff about love and romance, huh?”

Ty looked away. He couldn’t meet Fred’s eyes. “I’m thinking it’s a little out of place here, yeah.”

“All right then. Just, uh, sign in the appropriate places, I guess. All four of you.” He tugged at his shirt collar while the wedding party signed. “Okay, then. Do you have rings?”

Ty sighed and reached into his briefcase. He’d gotten wedding bands. He already wanted to take them back.

Belmonte snorted. “What kind of omega goes out and buys his own wedding bands, anyway?”

Bowman picked out the larger ring and slid it on to his own finger. Ty slipped the remaining one onto his.

“And you’re married. Congratulations.” A thin sheen of sweat had broken out on Fred’s high forehead. “I’m going to hit a bar.”

Belmonte stormed out, with Bowman close behind. Keegan followed. Ty made ready to follow, but Fred put a hand on his arm. “Are you really okay with all of this, man?”

Ty bowed his head. “Not really. But Keegan was right. There’s a lot at stake here that I can’t really explain, or hope anyone else understands. I just...“

“If you need anything, let me know. I don’t like it, Ty.”

Ty licked his lips. “Me either. But it’s what I have to do to get where I want to be.” He made a face. “I’m trying to pretend it’s like law school, you know?”

Fred patted him on the shoulder and chuckled. “Here’s hoping it works out just as well.”

Ty wasn’t going to hold his breath on that.

***

Carter hadn't ever been the kind of guy to sit around and contemplate his wedding day. He'd figured he'd get married someday, but only after baseball was over. Baseball had been his life for so long there hadn't been time for real love or romance, only casual flings. He'd been to a few of his friends' weddings, though, and even the hastiest and most last-minute events hadn't featured any grooms who looked like they were showing up to their own funeral.

Tyler Cunningham hadn't smiled once. He'd walked in the door with his face as white as a sheet. He'd looked over at Carter, he'd gotten *even paler*, and Carter had only gotten that reaction once. It had been from a September call-up rookie pitcher with the bases loaded, when Carter had been in the middle of a scorching hot fifteen game hitting streak.

He'd thought he was being kind when he'd asked if Tyler was uncomfortable. The guy had taken the contract by the corner, like the thing was tainted or something, and stuck it back into that briefcase. Carter hadn't asked to back out. He hadn't tried to call it off, even though he had to admit this was the most pathetic thing he'd done for money in the history of time.

It was worse than the nude calendar he'd done in A-ball.

Now it was done. After Tyler's attempt to bolt and Tracy's vicious outburst, Carter and Tyler were married. They had shiny rings on their hands, and they stood in the City Hall vestibule in a little awkward quartet. What, exactly, were they supposed to do now?

Keegan—damn the man—clapped his hands once and rubbed them together. "Okay. I'm starving. Who's up for a celebration? Steak dinner, my treat."

Tyler gave his brother the oddest look. It was somewhere between *I want to carve your heart out* and *I can't believe I'm related to you.* His skin had taken on a bit of a greenish cast.

Tracy curled his lip. "Are you for real right now? Do you seriously see anything here worth celebrating?"

Keegan favored Tracy with a steely glare. "Now that you mention it, yes. Yes, I do. If you don't want to come with us, Belmonte, go home. Don't sit there and be a gloomy Gus and bring the rest of us down."

Tyler looked away. Something had to be going on here. Carter couldn't make himself believe that Tyler was here voluntarily. Keegan had made it sound like he was on board and excited, but Carter hadn't actually spoken to Tyler before today. And maybe that stunt with taking the contract away hadn't been Tyler being easily miffed—maybe he'd just been looking for an excuse.

"Um, sure. Maybe we'll all relax after a nice dinner." Carter smiled blandly and played up the stereotype of the Big, Dumb Jock. Surely Keegan would let more clues slip if he thought Carter didn't have two brain cells to rub together than he would otherwise. And if not him, maybe Tyler would.

Tracy looked up at the ceiling and muttered in Spanish. Carter wasn't a hundred percent sure what he was saying—his Spanish wasn't the best—but he got the impression it wasn't very complementary toward his new husband. Something about "skinny short boys who have to buy husbands don't make good company," but Carter wouldn't swear by that translation.

Tyler, though, maybe there was more to him than it looked like. He just blanched. He stuck his hands in his pockets, looked up at the ceiling, and said, "You know what? I'm going to pass. I'm not—I just don't feel comfortable with that right now. You all can go to your Hellion Club or whatever. Have a good night." And he took off down the hall with his head down, walking fast enough someone would have had to at least jog to catch up with him.

"I can see why he can't find a husband on his own." Tracy glared down the hall.

Keegan grabbed Tracy by the collar. "He speaks Spanish, you son of a bitch." He dropped Tracy. "Damn it. Ty!" He chased off after his brother, who ignored him.

Carter turned to Tracy, who at least had the good grace to look ashamed of himself. "Sorry, Carter. I shouldn't have said it. I didn't think he'd speak Spanish, but that's on me. I know better than to assume that kind of thing."

Carter rubbed the back of his neck. He hadn't been married for an hour, and already his marriage was on the rocks. If the marriage weren't fake, he'd be pissed about that. "Yeah, well. It is what it is, right? Come on, let's find a place to get a beer or something."

They headed out into the night and looked around for the brothers. Not seeing them, he hailed a cab. They headed to a bar near Carter's apartment, where they got normal pub food and beer. Carter signed a handful of autographs, and then they were left in peace. "Something about this whole arrangement stinks," Tracy said, once their food had been delivered. "What does Tyler get out of it, anyway?"

"According to Keegan—and it's Keegan, so you have to kind of wonder—his brother's always wanted kids, but he wasn't willing to give up his career. To get to where he is, and he's the only omega partner at his firm and the youngest partner they've ever had, he must have been pretty darned focused. So, I guess he must just be feeling that whole biological clock thing."

"Still. This isn't a real family." Tracy shook his head and took a gulp from his drink. "Someday you're going to retire. And you're going to get married for real, and you're going to have kids for real. And they're going to want to know about their big brother or big sister. What are you going to tell them? Sorry, I sold them for cash?"

Carter squirmed. "It's not like that."

"It's exactly like that, Carter. It's exactly like that, just spread out over a little bit more time. And if a guy can't put his career on hold or prioritize a husband and family, he probably shouldn't have kids once he's gotten to that point, you know? It's one thing for you. You're a pro ball player, and you're not the one who's got to carry the child. But staying pregnant—it's not so easy as all that. You really think he's going to be willing to just put his feet up? You think he's going to be okay with feedings at three in the morning when he's got a meeting at seven the next day? No. No way."

"I don't know. I'm sure he's already thought of all these things, Tracy. I just...Look. I needed the money. And I went through with it because a man should follow through on his promises, and now I'm just uncomfortable with something that's going on there. Okay? It's not even about having the money to get me through anymore. Once I saw him, and I saw how he reacted to things, I knew there was something else going on there."

"Oh, sure, there's something going on there all right." Tracy made a face. "I'm sorry. I just don't understand what you think he's getting out of this. And I'm not sure this is what marriage is supposed to be. It shouldn't be a transaction. It should be about love. That guy there, he's not someone you can love. I'm not sure he even wants to be someone you can love."

"I don't know. I don't know anything about the guy. I know he's had some not so great relationships, I know he's got cats—"

"Oh, my God, he's a crazy cat omega, that's even worse!" Tracy buried his face in his hands. "He's going to wind up feeding your kid from the cat dish."

Carter laughed. He couldn't help it. "Okay, now you're just being silly. He's going to be fine. He strikes me as the kind of guy who does whatever he sets out to do, and does it well. If he's set out to start a family, he'll raise the kid just fine. According to Keegan, I'm just the donor." He shrugged. "A well-paid donor."

Tracy pinched the bridge of his nose. "You shouldn't have to be a donor. You should be able to be your own person, living the life you want."

"Look, I got Madoffed. What are you going to do?" Carter clenched his jaw and waited for his anger to subside. "It is what it is. This will tide me over, and who knows, maybe he'll turn out to be the kind of lawyer I can use sometime down the road."

Tracy finished his beer in one gulp. "Well, I hope so, but it's not looking good." He stood up. "Anyway, I'm going to have to head down to Florida soon. Hopefully things look better soon." He patted Carter on the shoulder, threw some cash in for the bill, and took off.

Carter's phone buzzed with an incoming text just as Tracy walked out the door. It came from Keegan's phone. *I'm guessing you and Ty never exchanged contact info.*

Carter blushed. Fortunately, the bar was dark and no one could really see. *No.*

Keegan replied with an address in Murray Hill. *Your husband's apartment. Bring something boozy.*

Carter rolled his eyes. Was he supposed to get the poor guy drunk? He signaled the server, paid the check, and left. Fortunately, there was a liquor store near Ty's apartment that had some decent wines. Champagne might not be entirely appropriate here, but a little bit of something red could be okay.

He asked the doorman to call Mr. Cunningham and got only a raised eyebrow. Seriously, who did this guy think he was? "Could you tell him it's Carter Bowman, please? He's expecting me."

The doorman picked up his phone and somehow managed to convey enough scorn with the gesture that Carter wondered if the guy was somehow psychically projecting it right into his brain. After a moment's conversation, the doorman turned back to him. "Mr. Cunningham will see you. He's in Apartment 4-D."

"Thank you." Carter headed over to the elevators, and silently gave thanks that their contract precluded the need for them to cohabit. Selling his condo would give Carter some badly needed money, but he'd rather drink poison than live here. Sure, the pre-war building was nice, but dealing with the doorman on a daily basis would be misery. Finding that the elevator had an actual elevator operator did not make the place more desirable.

He found his way to Tyler's apartment and knocked softly on the door. Keegan answered the door, and a small black cat tried to make a run for it. Carter dropped and caught the critter before he could get far, resulting in angry mewling and fierce struggling.

"Little bastard likes you," Keegan said, letting him in and shutting the door behind him. "If that had been me I'd already be bleeding from three places." He looked Carter over. "All right. You listened when I told you to bring the booze, anyway. He's in the living room, wine glasses and corkscrew are in the kitchen, you're welcome. Have at it." He patted Carter on the shoulder and headed for the door. "Hey, lock up behind me, would you? I've got a date."

Carter gaped at him. "You've got a date? Dude, you're not staying?"

"It's my little brother. This is his wedding night. No, I'm not staying. That's screwed up." Keegan made a face at him and left. Carter caught the little black cat just in time.

He locked up behind Keegan. The little black monster turned his back on him, chatting crossly as he stalked out of the room. Carter was now alone with his husband...and his cats.

He wasn't afraid of cats. He wasn't.

He headed into the kitchen and opened the wine. After a second's work, he found two wine glasses in the pristine kitchen and walked around until he found Tyler. There wasn't much on the walls. Most of what there was looked like it related to ancient Egypt somehow. *Great. The guy's obsessed with cats and into ancient Egypt. He's going to sacrifice me to their cat god or something.*

He found Tyler after a few seconds' wandering, with the help of the chatty little black cat. Tyler was folded on one of the couches in what looked like an uncomfortable position. He wore sweats and a plain white tee shirt. One cat sat on his hip, and another was pressed up against his belly. He looked up at Carter.

"Hey." His voice was soft, and his hazel eyes downcast. Then he folded his lips together, exhaled, and straightened his back just a little. "I figured you'd gone out."

"I got a bite to eat, and then Keegan clued me in on where you live, so." He held out a glass of wine. "I didn't know if you were a drinker or not."

Tyler took it. "I'm not, typically. Don't really have the time." He sipped. "Thank you."

Carter took it for as much of an invitation as any. "So. This is weird. A little awkward."

Tyler huffed out a little laugh. "That's one way of putting it."

"We don't have to do anything tonight, man. I get that there's an end goal in mind, for you. And that's fine. But I also..." He trailed off as he saw Tyler's shoulders stiffen. "I'm going about this all wrong. I don't want anything to feel forced or anything on your end. We're basically strangers, and you don't strike me as the kind of guy who's used to random hookups. So, if you'd rather not take that step at this point, I won't be offended. I promise." He ran his hand through his short hair. This whole thing was awkward as hell.

Tyler looked down for a second, and then he shifted. The two cats scattered, and Tyler stood up. "I think the sooner we get through it, the better. Don't you?" He moistened his lips. "I know this isn't exactly your idea of a picnic either. The sooner we get the baby out of the way, the better and less awkward it will be for both of us."

Carter bit his tongue and tried to decide if he should be offended by that statement or not. After a second, he decided that he didn't need to be. Tyler really was just here to make a baby. He wasn't necessarily thrilled about it, but he did want this, in his way. "Okay then." He put his hands on Tyler's shoulders. "Is it all right if I kiss you?"

Tyler nodded, slowly. It took a second or two for him to warm up, but once he got going he wasn't a half bad kisser. He responded well enough to Carter's touches, and his skin showed heat as Carter touched it. When Carter tried to slide his hands under Tyler's shirt, though, Tyler insisted that they move to a bedroom.

Whatever. Tyler was the one driving the bus here.

In here, with only the glow from the streetlight to light their way, Tyler livened up still further. He found lube in the nightstand, made sure Carter could find it, and he definitely knew what he was doing when he worked Carter up to full hardness.

Carter worked him open as gently as he could, trying to pay attention to his husband's little cues. Unlike most of his partners, Ty was not a talker. He didn't make much sound at all. He seemed to be enjoying it on some level—he got harder as Carter moved along, and he gave little sighs and choked-off moans—but he fought against any expression of it.

Carter wouldn't have minded watching Tyler's face as he entered him, just to get some feedback, but Tyler wanted to be taken from behind. He buried his face in his pillow, so he could hide his pleasure even more.

Carter didn't understand that, and he wasn't sure he liked it, but he didn't let it stop him. He sank himself deep inside of Tyler. Tyler's body felt amazing around him, hot and tighter than anyone Carter had known in a very long time. He thrust into him again and again. Tyler might not want to show his enjoyment, but Carter would give full voice to his.

When he'd finished, he pulled gently out of his husband, and went to go get a washcloth to clean them up. He worried, as he fumbled around in the darkened bathroom, that he'd screwed it up somehow. Had he managed to leave his husband unsatisfied on their first night together—their only night together, if Tyler caught?

But no. Tyler had come, the evidence clear on the sheets. Carter cleaned him up and stood, awkward for a moment. With a normal hook-up, he'd wrap his partner up in his arms and hold them for at least a little while. Tyler wasn't normal. What did he want?

“Er, we should probably exchange phone numbers or something.” He scratched at his beard.

Tyler sighed, and sat up. He picked his phone up off the nightstand. “Yeah. Yeah, that’s probably a good idea. What’s your number? I’ll text you, and that way you’ll have my number.”

Carter rattled it off. “At least this way we won’t have to have your brother running messages back and forth for us.”

“Yeah, I don’t see that happening ever again.”

Carter pulled his clothes on. “I guess we’ll talk tomorrow or something?” He slunk out the door, a strangely unsettled feeling in the pit of his stomach.

Chapter Three

Ty woke up at six the morning after his wedding. He was sore, in a good way. It was the kind of sore he tended to get when he pushed himself a little harder at the gym. It had been a very long time since he'd had sex at all, and even longer since he'd so thoroughly enjoyed it.

What kind of a person was he that he enjoyed sex with some guy he didn't even know?

For a moment, he thought about calling in sick. He'd never done that before, and he figured he had a few weeks of sick time accrued. At the same time, he'd promised Spada he'd be there. He'd even brought up the intake meeting and the Delaney estate meeting. And there was no way Ty was going to miss the Delaney estate meeting. That was a mess and no mistake. Someone's head was going to roll over Alden Delaney's estate, and Ty wanted to watch it happen. He'd gone on record about the guy's shady dealings, several times.

Sometimes it was nice to be proven right.

Besides, if he called in, everyone would assume he was at home sleeping in with his new husband. If Ty was actually at home sleeping in with his new husband, it would be one thing. As it was, he would just be sitting at home crying, and Ty refused to be the kind of guy who sat home and cried.

He snarled and threw on some workout clothes. He headed downstairs and hit his building's workout room. Half an hour on the treadmill later, he still felt like sobbing, but he could at least focus on putting one foot in front of the other. He was doing what he had to do, damn it. And maybe, just maybe, there was already a baby deep in his belly to show for it. He could release poor Carter from his contract early, and they'd never have to do that again.

Not that Ty would necessarily mind having sex with Carter again. As Ty washed up and got ready for his day, he had to admit that truth about himself. Objectively speaking, the sex had been good. He didn't even hate Carter. With the exception of the Hellion Club connection, he seemed like a nice enough guy. Under other circumstances, he wouldn't mind talking to him, getting to know him a little better, maybe exploring the little bit of attraction he already felt for him.

It wasn't going to happen, though. For one thing, Carter would be leaving soon. He was a baseball player, or whatever sport it was that had people running off to Florida in February. He'd be gone until April at least, and then gone more often than not until October. And the firm handled enough high profile divorce cases to know how it was. He'd have a different guy in every town, nothing to hold his interest.

Lord knew Carter's friend didn't think he should have been there in the first place. It was one thing to be a single omega at thirty-one and have to pay someone to marry you. It was something else to have another person, a complete stranger, point out that you were a single, over-the-hill omega who had to pay someone to marry you.

He turned his thoughts away from that. He wasn't going to have to see the dreadful Belmonte again. With any luck, he was already pregnant. He'd pay Carter off, and he'd be able to forget that any of this had ever happened.

He got dressed and headed out, travel mug in hand. He walked to his office.

He loved that he could walk to work. It was a huge privilege, and he understood that. When the baby came, if the nanny needed something, he could just run right out the door and be home and back in minutes. If he needed to be home to meet a school bus or something, he could do that too. It would be perfect.

The only people in the office when he got there were two first-year associates. He greeted them with a smile, because even if his life was sad and pathetic and a cautionary tale he didn't need to bring everyone else's day down too. One of those first-years, a tiny redhead by the name of Sophia MacCrum, had been getting here early and leaving late every day since she started. He made a mental note to sit down with her and have a chat about goals outside of work. Some things were worth it, some things were not, but it was important to know all of the risks before going too far down a path.

He spent his first hour drinking coffee, although just to be on the safe side he mixed his regular strength coffee with decaf. It was vile, and he hated it, but it was best for the baby. It would be a minimum of two weeks before he knew if he'd caught, but he wanted to do everything right to make his body safe and inviting for a fetus.

Years ago, a school counselor had told him he had "obsessive tendencies" that he should probably keep an eye on. As he carefully mixed his coffee with decaf for the fourth time before heading into the intake meeting, he wondered if she hadn't had a point. Maybe while he was on family leave he'd look into it.

He went through the intake meeting, and he spent the time between that meeting and the one at noon over the Delaney estate calling clients and reviewing their cases with them. The Delaney meeting went well, except for the fact that he wound up getting stuck with the wretched case. The firm's managing partner, Madison Clarke V, would take no other suggestions.

"Cunningham's the only one who noticed something was up with the old man, and he turned out to be as dirty as they come. We're in the business of defending everyone, but we have to have all of the information. The bastard was even lying to us. Cunningham's the only one who got suspicious. He gets the case, and that's final."

Ty would have been more gratified by the nod if he wasn't expecting to have to go out on family leave halfway through the process, but he smiled and faked it anyway. It was a prestigious appointment, restoring the firm's honor in a way. He'd have to find a way to pull it off.

After the meeting, he retreated to his office to review the estate records. The estate had just been frozen by federal authorities due to Alden's suspected crimes. The heir, Solomon Delaney, had piles of money of his own and didn't need to access it, so Ty had little to do on that front. He called Sol to offer his condolences and to check in.

Sol—who was apparently a friend of Keegan's from the Hellions—asked for a meeting at his new place up in the Bronx, but he was otherwise civil and cooperative. He said he wanted his fiancé to be part of the discussion, and Ty guessed he could understand that. It was nice that the whole true love thing existed for some people.

He set an appointment for the next day at six, which seemed like a reasonable time for a man of Delaney's position to be free, and turned to his next task. That was when his phone buzzed. He picked it up and found a text from an unknown number. *You free for dinner tonight?*

Ty blinked at it for a minute. Who would possibly want to grab dinner with him? Was it a wrong number? He opened the message, though, and saw it was a number he'd texted last night. Late last night.

Oh. It must be Carter.

What time? Could he actually make himself face Carter again, after being so wanton and desperate last night? He'd barely been able to force himself to leave the house today, after everything.

Whatever time works 4u.

Ty frowned at his phone. It took him a few seconds to puzzle out "4u." When he got it, he groaned. He hadn't ever gotten the hang of text shorthand, and he never would. What was the right answer here? He should stay here and work. He'd left early to go get married yesterday. He should stay late and delve into the Delaney estate, damn it. All of the ins and outs were going to take some teasing out.

Except Sol Delaney was a member of the Hellion Club. And Carter was a Hellion. Alden Delaney had been a Hellion. It would hardly be goofing off or personal time if Ty went and spoke to someone who'd been a member of the same social circles as the people he was trying to serve, and whose estate he was trying to disentangle.

Maybe eight? We can eat at that Italian place across the street from me.

OK. Dress code?

Business casual.

See you then.

Ty quickly made reservations before he could chicken out. Why would Carter want to do this? Had he just gotten some kind of terrible test result back from the doctor?

He slogged through the rest of his workday as best he could with all that anxiety in his gut. He wanted to think the butterflies in his stomach were from the baby, but he wouldn't feel anything at this point. He still had enough good sense to know that. He was afraid of whatever it was Carter had to say.

At least the Delaney case was interesting enough to read, all by itself. Money laundering, tax evasion, murder, attempted kidnapping—it read like a thriller, but in the complex mixture of Latin and English known as Legalese. There was no way that the estate was going to emerge unscathed. At least Alden's latest spouse would get what was coming to him, according to the terms of his prenup. That account had been fully funded at the time of his marriage and couldn't be touched. His previous spouses weren't so lucky.

Maybe Keegan was right. Maybe love, at a certain point, stopped existing.

His alarm went off at seven thirty. He'd gotten lost enough in his work that he'd managed to forget the mess that was his personal life. He had to give himself credit for that, at least.

He checked himself out in the men's room mirror and cleaned up a little. Carter already thought of him as pathetic and in need of pity. Ty didn't need to make it worse by showing up looking like a mess. Once he managed to make himself look presentable again, he headed out to the restaurant he'd suggested.

Carter was waiting for him there. "Hey." He didn't hug him, or kiss his cheek, but then again Ty was unreasonable for expecting it. "How's it going?"

"It was an interesting day at work. They, ah, they assigned me to a pretty complex case. It's going to take up a lot of my time and energy, but it's a good sign. It means they trust me with this stuff."

"Hm." Carter raised his eyebrows. "Congratulations! Anything you can share?"

Ty stared at Carter's huge hands. He contemplated Carter's lush lips and his barely-there beard. "Probably not in a public place. But you might know some of the players better than I do. I'd love to get your thoughts about them before I go to meet with them tomorrow."

Carter preened. He absolutely preened when Ty asked him about people he knew. Tyler understood people, better than most. It was part of his job as a lawyer. Was Carter intimidated by Ty's position? By his education? By his background? "I'd be happy to. Maybe stopping by your place? I'd like to see that little kitty of yours again."

"Amun? The escape artist? He's a funny one. He's got a major hate-on for Keegan. None of them like him, but Amun bites him every time he sees him. I'd try to train him out of it but it's funny."

Carter snickered. "Wow. Something he said yesterday makes so much more sense now."

Ty froze at the mention of yesterday. "Look. About yesterday..."

Carter slumped his shoulders. "Tyler, I get that it was awkward. I do. I'm not entirely sure what's going on between you and your brother, but I'm getting the impression that this isn't a hundred percent voluntary on your part."

Ty shuddered. Had he really come off that badly? "I said yes, okay? It was Keegan's idea, but I said yes. I do want a baby. I always have." He stopped and considered the wisdom of proceeding. It wasn't as though Carter could have a worse opinion of him, after all. "I was upset by what that guy said, but it's not like it wasn't true. I've always wanted kids, a bunch of them. Would I have preferred the traditional way? Sure. It didn't work out. That doesn't mean that I don't want a kid, okay? I can afford it, and I think I'll be good at it. And when Keegan pointed out that this was the only way it was going to happen, I realized I was holding out for too much."

"Ah, crap, Tyler. You deserve better." Carter turned his head away.

"Don't you dare feel sorry for me, Carter. I may be worthless when it comes to being husband material, but I'm a damn fine lawyer. I'm smart, I'm tenacious, and I've got the strength to do what I need to do. And if that means marrying a stranger to get the family I want, then I'll do it."

Carter reached across the table and took Ty's hand. "I ain't feeling sorry for you, okay? You sure as hell don't seem to be feeling sorry for yourself. A lot of guys wouldn't do any of the things you have. They'd just linger, you know? I'm just...I guess I think it's too bad. I think you've got a lot to offer."

A large part of Ty wanted to know exactly what basis Carter had for that argument, since he hadn't known Ty for more than a day and hadn't had any conversation with him whatsoever. The rest of him basked in the praise. He ignored both parts. If they wanted to fight it out, he would let them do it on their own time. "So," he said instead. "Why don't you talk to me about baseball?"

Carter did a double take at the change in subject. "Um, how do you mean?"

"Your bio, which I did look up, says you're '2B.' Is that a *Hamlet* quote?"

Carter gaped at him, slack jawed. Then he gulped his water down. "It's going to be a long night, isn't it? You really don't know anything about baseball?"

"Nope." Ty sat up a little straighter. "I know there's a ritual that takes everyone down to Florida in February, but that's about it."

"Hoo boy."

Ty grinned in relief as Carter spoke.

***

Carter made a face at his trainer, Dave, but he did another thirty reps with the stupid medicine ball. The guy was a sadist, and that was all there was to it. Only a true sadist could have come up with all of this crap, with the twisting and the turning and the straining. It was torture, and he was absolutely getting off on seeing Carter in pain.

"You almost ready for Spring Training?" Dave checked something on his tablet. It was probably another way for him to torture Carter, because why would he want to do anything else?

"I'm getting there." Carter couldn't speak in more than grunts at this point. His core muscles were too sore for him to draw much breath. Dave would be coming with the team. Carter paid extra for Dave to train him in the off season, because apparently Carter was a masochist.

"You should be in decent shape. It won't be too bad for you. Not like Ortega. I hear he got married in the off-season, and his wife's a fantastic cook. He gained something like fifty pounds we've got to somehow peel off of him in the next six weeks." He winced. "Coach tells me you got married too."

"Uh, yeah." That was rep thirty, thank God. Carter put the medicine ball down. "He's a lawyer, though. Not a cook." He tried to imagine Tyler working a stove, and he shuddered.

"That's a good thing. It's funny, though. I didn't know you were seeing anyone."

"Well, you know. The spirit just moved us." Carter stretched his back to hide his discomfort. "He's a nice guy. I'm friends with his brother."

"Ah." Dave nodded. "Well, congratulations. Is he coming down to Florida with the rest of the WAGs?"

“No. Like I said, he’s a lawyer. He’s got a bunch of work to do here. It’s cool. We’re not the kind of couple that needs to be together every second, you know?” They didn’t really need to be together *any* seconds, but Dave didn’t need to know that.

“Huh. Okay. As long as you guys are happy, I guess. Anyway, I’ll see you tomorrow for Leg Day.” Dave clapped his hands, and Carter staggered off to the locker room.

He hosed off in the shower and got dressed. Maybe he should reach out to Tyler. They’d exchanged a few texts over the past week, and they’d gotten together one more time for dinner, but that was about it. Even that seemed to have been something Tyler squeezed in. Maybe Tracy had been right. Maybe Tyler shouldn’t be trying to raise a kid if he didn’t have time to meet up with his husband.

He sent a text to Tyler. *It’s Friday night. U busy?*

Tyler responded after five minutes. *I should be free after seven. Why?*

Seven. Carter hadn’t known Tyler long, but he knew Tyler would be working the whole time. *Thought u might want 2 get 2gether.*

OK?

Carter stared at his phone for a second, trying to figure out exactly how to respond to that. Did Tyler want him to suggest an activity? Did he want Carter to explain why he wanted to get together? Okay, so they weren’t a traditional couple, but they were still married. They could still get together and spend time together or something.

I’ll meet you at seven at your place, he said finally.

That was where Tracy found him; still staring at his phone. "It only works right if you call someone," his manager told him. "Although that's not advised in the locker room. It's weird."

Carter rolled his eyes. "Thanks, Tracy. Believe it or not, Nebraska isn't quite so isolated as that. I'd figured it out for myself."

Tracy sat down on the bench beside him. "Trouble in paradise?"

Carter hesitated. He shouldn't bring his troubles to Tracy. Tracy didn't like Tyler. At the same time, Carter didn't have anyone else to talk to about this. "I'm trying to get together with Tyler, and it seems to confuse him." He showed Tracy his text conversation with his husband.

Tracy curled his lip. Then he took a deep breath and sighed. "So, my first instinct is to say he's being stuck up and just doesn't want to hang out with you. But you've been getting together, right?"

"Exactly." Carter beamed at Tracy. He was a good guy. He might not like Tyler, but he was capable of pushing past his personal dislike. "He's seemed open and stuff when we were together. Just, you know, a little confused. I like the guy. And I feel kind of bad for him."

Don't you dare feel sorry for me, Carter. Tyler's voice came back to his mind, unbidden. It was hard not to feel sorry for him. Tyler had so much going for him, but for whatever reason no one wanted to be part of his life in that way. No one would ever think twice about an alpha having a career and a family, after all.

"I don't feel bad for him. The guy's rich enough to go out and buy himself a husband. Whatever else is going on, it's got to be some consolation that he can just buy his way out of it, right?" Tracy chuckled. "But you're a good guy, Carter. You like to help people. I get it. And it's not a bad idea to try to be friendly with your future ex."

Carter flinched from the term. "Can you maybe not put it quite that way?"

"It's the truth, Carter. You signed the contract yourself. You wanted it that way. You're not in love with the guy, and he's not in love with you." Tracy gave Carter a hard look. "Go on, enjoy his company, go hang out with him. But don't get all hung up in solving his problems, okay? Solve your own."

Carter couldn't argue with Tracy. He still had plenty of his own issues to deal with. He didn't need to pile Tyler's problems on top of his. "Yeah. And who knows how Tyler wound up this way. Maybe he's got some serious personality flaws or something that I'm just not going to see. I should focus on baseball and getting my own finances back on track."

"Right?" Tracy patted him on the back. "Good man. I'll see you Monday, okay?"

Carter nodded, and Tracy headed into the clubhouse while Carter took off. He didn't have anyplace else to go, so he headed in to the Hellion Club to kill some time.

Only two kinds of people came to the Hellion Club in the middle of the day. Older alphas who'd left their jobs a long time ago came to enjoy the time they had left, and guys in fields with odd hours came to socialize and be seen. Carter wasn't the only professional athlete in the bar when he arrived. He saw a couple of football players he knew, and he waved to them. He saw entertainers—rock stars, actors, directors, that sort of thing—and he saw a few politicians.

And, of course, he saw Keegan.

Keegan sauntered over to Carter as soon as they made eye contact. "Bro!" He put an arm around Carter's shoulders. "Hey man, how's married life treating you?" His loud voice got the bartender's attention better than anything else could have. "A drink for my brother-in-law here, would you?"

The bartender brought them both dark liquor drinks garnished with cherries. "Married, huh?" He gave Carter an appraising look. "That's a shame."

Carter's cheeks burned, but Keegan just laughed. "Yeah, well, he's just your type, isn't he? Don't worry, Irv. He'll be back on the market soon enough."

Carter cringed. Keegan wasn't wrong, but still. "Thanks for the vote of confidence, man." He sipped his drink.

"What, it's true. It's no knock on you. Ty is just Ty, you know? There's no changing him. He's going to be himself. That's just the way he is." Keegan winked at the bartender, who blew him a kiss and pranced off to go serve another customer. "He's about as interesting as wallpaper paste."

"He's not that bad. He doesn't talk much about himself, but he does listen. And he's been handed a pretty big job at work, so that's something, right?" Carter took a gulp from his drink. "I don't know how to get him to open up."

"Why do you want him to? Even if he was your real husband, someone you picked, it's not like you'd be with him for the lols, right? No one picks a husband for someone to pal around with. You don't want to talk to them. They're there to run the house and make babies." He laughed. "I don't think I ever saw my parents spend time together that didn't involve talking about us, the household, or something like that."

"Huh." Carter hadn't grown up with money the way the Cunninghams had. He guessed it was a different world. Obviously Tyler—Ty—had different expectations of Carter than he had of himself. Still, it didn't sit right with him. "He just seems, I don't know. Lonely, maybe. Like no one's reached out to him in a long time. Who are his friends?"

"Who knows? He doesn't do friends. He works. He's got the cats. Seriously, Carter, you're looking for depth that isn't there." Keegan patted him on the back. "Come on, bro, if you're looking for an omega to be your new best friend, pick one of the omegas around here. They've all got lives, and things like that. Ty's just not going to be what you're looking for." He snorted. "Christ, if I'd known you wanted an actual husband I wouldn't have suggested this arrangement. I wouldn't put you through dealing with Ty."

Carter forced a smile and changed the subject. He'd have to try another angle, if he wanted to get to know his husband better.

A few hours later, he met up with Ty over near his place. The wind had picked up, and it bit right through his coat. Ty didn't look any warmer. "It's freezing out here. Is there any place in particular you want to go?"

Ty gave him a quizzical look. "I don't have any place in mind. I thought you did."

"I just thought it would be a good thing for us to get together." Carter set his jaw. "Sorry. Maybe it's a bad idea. I'll just go." He stuffed his hands in his pockets.

Ty hesitated, and Carter's heart beat a little faster. Would Ty really just let him walk away?

"Wait. Let's go...grab dinner, I guess, and we can talk about your expectations. Okay? There's a seafood place about a block away, and they don't usually need a reservation."

Carter grinned. "Let's go. This wind is going to peel my skin right off." He offered his arm to Ty, who took it after looking at him like he was an alien for a full three seconds.

They only had to wait for a minute or so before they were seated, and Ty leaned forward. "So, is everything okay?" A little line appeared on his forehead. "Do you need anything? Money, legal help, spare cat litter?"

Carter stared at him for a long moment. "Is it that weird for people to just call you to hang out?"

Ty raised his eyebrows. "It's not something that happens all that often, no." Carter opened his mouth to say something, but Ty raised a hand. "We talked about not feeling sorry for me, Carter. It's okay. I work a lot of hours."

"Sure. I know that. But I'm sure everyone in that office has a social life." Carter busied himself tearing up the napkin for the place setting beside him.

"Maybe." Ty glanced away for a second. "There was a guy I used to date, for a while. He, ah. We had a lot of friends in common, but when we split up they chose to stay his friends, and I was working too many hours to rebuild a new social circle from scratch. Which is fine. I have some college buddies from undergrad, but we mostly stay in touch through social media. We're all over the world, not all in one place where we can get together for beers after work or anything. Not that I'm drinking right now anyway."

"I'm sure it's too early to know if you're pregnant yet." Carter frowned at him.

"It is, but I'm not drinking because I don't want to risk it. I get one shot at this, Carter. I'm not going to blow it." Ty grimaced briefly. "Anyway, I said it mostly as an example of what's realistic and what isn't."

"Right." Carter ducked his head as his cheeks blazed. "Sorry. It's just...I don't know. It just feels like I'm not doing what I'm supposed to be doing here, you know? I mean, yeah, I know it's an arrangement. But we are married. I shouldn't be ignoring you. I should at least try to treat you decently, right?"

Ty blinked. It looked for all the world like the wires in his brain just weren't making a connection. "Okay," he said after a long moment. "And I...appreciate that. But you didn't sign up for that. You signed up to make a baby and get paid."

Carter slouched down in his seat. "Sure. And that's fine. I can do that. I just—it feels weird, okay?"

Ty relaxed his shoulders. His face softened, and he reached across the table to take Carter's hand. His hand was soft, with long, thin fingers. He'd never done manual labor, never built up a blister. "Carter, screw outside expectations. Okay? We're already so far outside of what ninety percent of the rest of this country would ever do that it's laughable. What do you feel is right for you? What do you *want*? I promise, I'm not going to be offended. I'm not going to go running to the press and tell them their sports hero is a big jerk or something. You don't have to impress me. I'm already grateful to you for helping me out with this whole thing."

Carter looked into Ty's hazel eyes. "Ty," he said after a second, "I'm not a hundred percent sure what I want. We kind of did things in a weird order. I don't have any expectations. I do want to get to know you better, okay? I want to know who you are. Even though this is temporary, even though it's a means to an end for both of us, I still want to know you. I want to know who you are, what you like, what you do for fun. I don't want to look back and say, 'Oh, well, I was married to a stranger for however long.' You seem like a good guy, and I want to know more. Is that okay?"

Ty chuckled. He dropped Carter's hand, which sent a disproportionate wave of disappointment crashing into Carter's gut until he realized their food had just arrived. "It's not a bad thing," Ty told him. "I'm afraid there's not much more to me than work and cats, but it's not like hanging out with you is a bad thing." He lifted his water glass in a kind of toast. "So. How much longer before you have to go to Spring Training, and what's it really like down there?"

Carter was halfway through describing the grueling Spring Training regimen before he realized Ty had deflected the subject away from himself, yet again.

Chapter Four

Ty's hands shook as he unpacked the test from its pink box. He'd have been embarrassed to buy a box like this in the store. There wasn't anything inherently shameful about being an omega or being pregnant. Every omega wanted to be pregnant and wanted a family. Buying a pregnancy test was a sign that the omega was on his way toward making that dream a reality.

But pink?

Pink was one more way of trying to feminize omegas. The tests weren't the same tests they ran on pregnant women. The hormones weren't the same hormones women had, not exactly, and the people using them weren't women. They were men. Why try to lump omegas in with women? It might save money on packaging costs for the manufacturers, but it created more problems for the omegas who had to use the tests.

He was getting distracted, and he knew it. He shouldn't let himself do that. What kind of father would he be if he let himself get distracted by every little thing? The packaging wasn't the important thing, and maybe it would have been shameful to buy it fifteen years ago but he had the internet now. The test had been delivered today, and no one needed to see him carrying around a stupid pink box.

He filled the cup, added the dipstick, and set the timer. Then he sat back to wait.

He knew he shouldn't get his hopes up. He wasn't young anymore. He wasn't old, exactly, but he wasn't young. Guys' fertility declined after their mid-twenties, and he needed to keep his expectations realistic. He shouldn't count on being able to get pregnant right off the bat like that, not from one sexual encounter.

Of course, how many other guys had managed to do just that? How many little "accidents" did his brother have running around out there somewhere? Why couldn't he be that lucky? If he's pregnant he could start making his plans right away. He could convert the guest room into a nursery, he could start looking for a nanny, and he could of course tell Carter. Then Carter could stop coming around and trying to hang out with him.

Not that Carter was unpleasant company. In fact, the thought of Carter backing off gave Ty a pang somewhere in the middle of his chest. That was why it was better for Ty to be pregnant, and for Carter to back off now, than to sit around waiting for Carter to get bored with him later. He'd rather get it over with now than wait for him to do it later on, when it would hurt more.

The timer pinged. Ty approached the counter slowly and took out the stick.

Not pregnant. The words couldn't have been clearer.

Ty wiped away tears. He'd tried not to get his hopes up, but he'd done it anyway. It was kind of what he did. He threw the test away and retreated to his bedroom. He'd been stupid to even think of getting married anyway. He was well past his prime, he hadn't been someone anyone would want when he'd been young in the first place, and what if he was sterile?

He should just call Carter and release him from his contract. Once Ty got his share, Carter would get paid, and they could get divorced. Carter didn't need to waste his time coming around anymore. A nice guy like him didn't need to stay tied to a bland, boring omega like Ty anyway.

He crawled back to bed. He wasn't completely useless. He was a damn fine lawyer. He'd found four loopholes to protect parts of the Delaney estate already. He'd kept several clients out of prison, and he should be proud of that. Some guys just weren't destined for a family, and that was okay. At least it was going to have to be okay, because Ty was going to be alone for the rest of his life, and that was just all there was to it.

He pulled the covers up over his head. He'd let himself throw a pity party until the afternoon, because he guessed he was allowed on a day like today. Once the clock ticked over, though, he was going to make himself get up and do some work. Sure, he felt awful. Awful wasn't productive, and no one cared.

He would have to break the bad news to Carter, though. He wasn't looking forward to that.

His alarm went off again at one, at which point he peeled himself out of bed and made himself some coffee. His cats followed him into the kitchen, and he gave them some treats. At least someone should get some happiness out of today.

He put on sweats, headed for his desk, and got to work. The Delaneys weren't his only clients right now, and he had plenty of people he needed to keep happy. He lost himself in contract law until his phone buzzed with an incoming text at four.

It was from Carter. It was always from Carter. *Hey. Did you take the test?*

Ty flinched, and he forced himself to reply. *I did. It came back negative. I'm sorry.*

Ty's phone rang then, and he almost didn't answer it. The only people who called were from the office, and he wasn't up to dealing with any of them today. When he checked, though, it was Carter. "I'm really sorry, Ty," he said. "I know how much you were hoping."

Ty hung his head. It wasn't his job to sit around and bring his husband down, damn it. "It's okay," he murmured. "It was probably an unrealistic expectation anyway, you know?"

"Most people don't catch right away, I guess. Still, I know it's disappointing. I can hear it in your voice. You want to get together? We can hit a bar."

Ty's first instinct was to decline. He didn't want to hurt a potential baby by drinking alcohol. He punched himself in the thigh. There was no baby, potential or otherwise. "You know what? I'd like that. Let's go to a bar. It's been a long time since I've had a Manhattan."

Carter gave a delighted laugh. "Awesome. I'll pick you up just as soon as I can get there."

Ty caught a reflection of himself in the window. If Carter was coming over, he needed to clean himself up.

By the time the doorman let him know Carter was there, Ty had found something decent to wear and he'd shaved. He met Carter downstairs, and they headed out to one of the local bars. "So you like Manhattans, huh?" Carter linked arms with him without hesitation as they walked down the sidewalk. Ty thought about pulling away, but he decided he liked it. Sure, it wasn't going to last, but he needed the comfort today.

"I used to." Ty managed a little bit of a grin. "After law school it got to be a little harder to get out and let my hair down, you know? I was too tired most of the time. That would be a laugh riot, right? Go out and your buddy passes out before he's finished his first drink, blowing bubbles in his cocktail."

Carter chuckled. "I hear you. Believe it or not, Spring Training isn't much different. Or the season, now that I mention it. You're not allowed to drink at all during Spring Training, and you're not supposed to drink much during the season. Your whole diet is monitored very closely. Can't let anything slow you down. So then November hits, right? And your friends are all like, 'Hey, it's party time!' And you're like, 'Yeah, I'm going to sleep through till Valentine's Day, it'll be a party all right." They ducked into a bar that didn't look too trendy or too seedy and found a table near the back.

"Ugh. Yeah, I think some people think baseball is still like it was when Babe Ruth played the game, and you could still eat sixty-seven hot dogs in one sitting and perform." Ty smirked. "They don't think about what kind of toll it takes on the body to perform the way you guys are expected to today."

Carter narrowed his eyes at Ty. "I thought you didn't know anything about sports." Their server approached, and he ordered Manhattans for both of them.

Ty blushed. "I might have done some research."

"Might have?"

"If I'm going to be married I shouldn't be completely in the dark." Ty squirmed. "I mean, I do want to know something about what you do."

Carter smiled. "I'm glad." He reached across the table and took Ty's hand. "I like that you actually want to know me. It makes me feel like we're more of a couple, and less of a fraud."

Ty made himself laugh. "Okay," he said, and looked away. "That's an interesting way of looking at it. I mean the whole ceremony was legal and everything."

"I know. I know." Carter took his hand away, and Ty tried not to show his disappointment. "I just—never mind, I'm being weird about it."

Ty wanted to ask him what was weird about it, and what he would consider actually being a couple. What he wanted from

Ty. The arrival of another patron, however, put a stop to their conversation. "Ty Cunningham?"

Ty couldn't see the speaker, because the low light inside the bar and the brighter light outside hid his face. He'd know the speaker's voice anywhere. Sebastian Britton's honeyed tenor had haunted Ty's dreams and nightmares for years. As Seb approached the table, Ty knew he couldn't get away. He'd already been seen. He couldn't pretend Seb had mistaken him for someone else.

Besides, Carter had already confirmed his identity. "Do you know Ty?" He turned to face Seb, face open and pleasant enough. He stood up and offered his hand for Seb to shake.

Seb ignored the hand, although he did turn to face him. "Yes, yes, I was his fiancé years ago." He waved a hand, dismissing their relationship like it had been casual. After so long, Ty supposed it probably had been. "I'm Sebastian Britton, with Allemani Bank. Ty, I can't believe it's really you. I didn't think you did the bar thing anymore."

Ty frowned and gripped his cocktail glass. "It's been a while. Seb this is Carter Bowman—"

Seb rolled his magnificent brown eyes. "Right, the ball player. I've heard." He dropped a hand onto Carter's shoulder. "Shame about that financial advisor. I heard you were more or less wiped out, right? Let that be a lesson to you, there, Carter. Never put all your eggs in one basket. Someone who tells you to do something like that is pretty much always a fraud." He fished for his wallet and pulled out a few bills. "Be a pal, would you, and go order another round. My treat."

"Seb, he's not the houseboy." Ty sat up straighter.

Carter smiled at Ty. "It's okay, Ty. I don't mind." He took the bills and headed over to the bar.

Seb snorted. "Why do you even know baseball players, Ty? You don't care about sports, not even a little bit. You never did."

"My brother introduced us." Ty glared at his ex and sipped from his drink.

Seb proved immune from Ty's censure. He always had been. "Oh. Keegan." He shuddered. "He always did know some of the most...interesting people. I thought you were more discriminating than that, but I guess beggars can't be choosers."

Ty closed his eyes and bit the inside of his cheek. "So, were you meeting someone here, Seb?" He'd spent seven years wondering what he'd do if Seb ever came back to New York. At first, he thought he'd embarrass himself by flinging himself into Seb's arms, or maybe quit his job and run off to someplace Seb would never go. Stabbing him with a cocktail skewer had never been on the list, but it was an increasingly appealing option.

"No, no, I was just looking for someplace to get out of the wind for a little bit. I just moved back to New York this week. The bank promoted me and sent me back, so here I am. I wouldn't have thought things would have changed this much in seven years, but here we are. New buildings, practically new streets, and here you are being seen in public with a football player."

"Baseball, actually." Ty gritted his teeth.

Seb waved his hand. "So, I did drop by to see your parents. I was surprised to hear you were still single. I know you'd been keen to get married, start a family, and all that."

"Well, you know. Work and all. But as it happens, I am married."

Seb blinked at him, face blank. "No, no you're not. Your parents told me you're not, and they'd be the first to know."

“Not so much, as it turns out. We didn’t invite them.” Ty sipped from his drink. “They were less than enthusiastic when you left, and things have gotten a bit strained. We didn’t make a big deal out of it. Carter values his privacy. He doesn’t want his personal life distracting from team business.”

If Ty hadn’t gotten very used to hiding his emotions and reactions in court, he’d have fallen over laughing at the look on Seb’s face. “You married...that? He’s a jock. A sports player. He’s never even been to college. He barely graduated high school.”

“He has an Associates, I believe. And I don’t require my husband to have an advanced degree. I need someone who’s compatible with me, who wants to be with me, and who cares for me. That’s all.” Ty kept his face bland and glanced up toward Carter, who was returning with their drinks.

“Okay, but Ty, he doesn’t care for you. He cares for your money. You know that. Even someone *like us* wouldn’t be interested in an omega who can’t entertain them, but a guy like him? You have nothing to hold him to you.” He spread his hands wide. “I’m not trying to be hurtful here, Ty. I’m a realist. I’ve always respected you enough to tell you the truth, no matter what.”

Ty looked up to see if Carter had heard Seb, but he hadn’t gotten within earshot yet. “Seb,” he said, and picked up his drink again. He was going to need a few more of them if Seb insisted on sticking around. “Seb, I don’t know that ‘respect’ is the word I’d use.” He smiled as Carter set the drinks down on the table. “There you are, Carter. I was getting worried.”

Carter took his seat with an affable smile. “I just had to sign an autograph for a fan. You know how it is.”

Seb schooled his face into something slightly less contemptuous. “You know, you can do some of these signings and conventions and things and you'll make a killing doing autographs. You don't have to do them for free."

"I know. My agent's always trying to get me to do them, but the thing is being nice to fans when I meet them in the street like this pays off in the long run. Tickets cost a fortune, and they can't always make it to a game. They still watch the games on our network, they buy our merchandise, and all that good stuff. So this benefits the team as a whole. They're already paying me good money, and of course there are endorsements and things like that. I don't need to be going out and gouging the fans."

"Yeah, I got taken for a ride by that scam artist. I'm not proud of it. But I also know I'm still getting paid. I'll be okay, in the long run." He shrugged, still self-assured. "Thanks for the advice, though."

Seb looked at Carter like he was an alien. He'd never understand an attitude like Carter's. For Ty, that just made Carter even more appealing.

***

Carter thought he might be making some progress with Ty. It might have been a big assumption, given that they seemed to come from different planets as far as marriage was concerned, but Ty let him hold his hand in public and even pouted a little bit when he stopped. It was something, right? It meant they were getting somewhere?

But then the world's worst human being showed up, in a three piece suit even though it was Saturday. God, his suit even had that stupid little fake handkerchief in the front pocket, who did that? Carter had only seen that in weddings before now.

Whoever this guy was—and he'd been engaged to Ty before, so he must have been someone—he rubbed Carter the wrong way before they'd exchanged more than a handful of words. Maybe it was the suit on Saturday. Maybe it was just the way his face was built, with a heavy mouth permanently stuck between a pucker and a pout. Maybe it was the way he dismissed Carter like he was staff.

It probably had a lot more to do with the fact that Ty's walls all went back up as soon as he heard Seb's voice.

After Seb finished delivering his unsolicited advice regarding autographs, he filled them both in on where he'd been for the past seven years. When he'd left, he'd been promoted to a "highly prestigious" position with his company's London office. "Only a fool would refuse to take it, of course." He looked over at Carter. "You understand. It's not like you'd refuse a trade to, I don't know, San Francisco, if they paid you more money and gave you a better position besides."

Seb clearly didn't understand how sports worked, but Carter didn't feel compelled to change that little detail about him. It would mean having to talk to him longer. "I went over to London, and it was simply a fantastic experience. You were so foolish not to come with me, Ty. It would have been right up your alley. Plenty of shopping, so many old bookstores. Anyhow, I got married about six months after I landed."

Carter risked a glance over at Ty, but it wasn't like Ty was going to show any reaction to that. He just toyed with his cocktail glass. "Did you bring your husband back to New York?"

"Ah, no, he passed away about a year ago." Seb's tone didn't sound like a grieving widower. He might have been talking about a neighbor, or a neighbor's gardener. "I don't mind telling you, I was happy to be promoted out of London. Truth be told, I was eager to get back to New York. I liked my work in England, don't get me wrong, but culturally it just wasn't what I'd expected." He shrugged. "So, I've been back for a few days, I've only just moved into a new apartment, and I'm looking to settle back in. Carter, Ty tells me the two of you are married?"

Ty had admitted it? Carter didn't know why that surprised him, but it made his insides glow a little. "We just got married a few weeks ago, but yeah. We tied the knot. We couldn't be happier."

"But he hasn't brought you to meet his dads yet." Seb's full lips curled, just a little bit. "Isn't that interesting?"

Ty rolled his eyes. "It's like I told you, Seb. They were pretty pissed when you left. We don't exactly spend much time together."

Carter glanced over at Ty. Something was going on here, and he would get to the bottom of it sooner or later, but he needed to have Ty's back right now. They were on the same team. "It's not like Keegan spends much time with them either."

Seb scoffed and downed a good portion of his Manhattan. "Keegan. Is he still an ape?"

"He's a little rough around the edges, but he's got his good points. You know, he's open minded about a lot of things. He's supportive of Ty, in his way. And he's the one who introduced me to my husband, so all things considered I'd have to call him a friend." Carter had to work hard to keep his tone affable. He didn't want to make a scene, but Seb's patronizing tone would have gotten him plunked in baseball.

"Oh. Well, you know. I suppose you're a little more tolerant of rougher behavior, with all of those locker room antics we see on television." Seb's smile didn't reach his eyes. "Honestly, I'm surprised the man made it through undergrad. He's illiterate."

Carter stared, and he didn't bother to hide it. He'd never dare to say anything like that about a partner's family, especially not in public. And maybe he wasn't Keegan's biggest fan, but it wasn't right to let this Seb guy sit there and trash him.

“Keegan has his strengths,” he said, even though he couldn’t think of what they were. “Just like all of us. So, I’m sorry about your husband. You must miss him very much.”

“Of course, of course.” Seb sat up a little straighter. “So, Carter, when does Spring Training start for you?”

“I leave on Friday.” It wasn’t like Carter could hide it. Seb could look it up and find out. “I’ll be back in time for opening day on April 6.” He was being paranoid, and he knew it. Seb wasn’t going to make a move on Ty, for crying out loud. He was a widower, and grieving. He’d already had his chance with Ty. Carter and Ty weren’t even a real couple, for crying out loud. They had the right to go outside their marriage for happiness or satisfaction, if that was what they craved. He had no right to be jealous.

“Ah. Aren’t you worried, leaving your new husband alone so soon after the wedding?” If Carter hadn’t known better, he’d have sworn Seb was reading his mind.

“Actually, I’m not. Ty knows I trust him, and I know Ty trusts me. We’re adults, and we have a solid basis for our relationship.” He smiled, showing teeth. Maybe Seb would ask him to step outside, recognizing the challenge for what it was.

Seb did not. He sniffed and tossed his head a little, but he looked away. “That’s really fantastic. I’m glad you’ve found someone you can trust so thoroughly.” He drained the rest of his glass. “Enjoy the rest of your evening out, boys. I’m sure I’ll see you around.”

He left the bar, and Carter was left with Ty and a boatload of questions. Finally, he picked up his drink. “So,” he said slowly. “You were engaged to that?”

He regretted the words as soon as they left his mouth, because they were rude. They were almost insulting. He didn’t like this guy, and he didn't think much of him, but he didn't have the right to disparage Ty's ex to him.

Ty just laughed. It was the first genuine, belly-busting laugh he'd given since they met, and it transformed his whole face. Carter had seen him as hot, and he'd seen him as good looking in an intense kind of way. He'd never seen him as beautiful, until now. "Right? Oh, my God, I thought I was in love with him!" He doubled over with laughter, and more than a few people turned to stare. He wiped tears away and tried to catch his breath. "I saw him just now, and all I could think of was how much I couldn't wait to take a shower and wash the slime away."

Carter relaxed and took Ty's hand again. "Seriously? Why did you agree to marry him if he's so slimy?"

Ty blushed. "I guess he reminded me of my dad, a bit. His family is pretty close with mine, you know? They'd been trying to set us up for years, but they couldn't make it work. Then they did, and it was okay. At least, I thought it was okay. I didn't know better, you know?" He shook his head and looked at the door. "What a pompous ass."

Carter snickered. "What broke you two up?"

Ty stopped laughing. He turned red, and he looked down. "I'd love to be able to tell you I woke up, saw what a jackass he is, and kicked him to the curb. It wasn't like that at all." He took a deep breath. "I'd worked my ass off to get through law school. Top of my class, right? And I got the absolute best job offer I could, from the firm I'm with now. And he turns around and tells me, 'Well, you can't take it, because I've got a job offer in London. And you're just going to quit your job when we have kids anyway.'"

"So, you left?" Carter rubbed his thumb against the back of Ty's hand.

“No. He did. I told him I was willing to do the long distance thing. It’s not like it mattered, because I was going to work so many hours over the next couple of years we wouldn’t see each other anyway. And I pointed out he’d known that when he proposed. So, he called off the wedding, more than half of which was already paid for, and all of our friends sided with him. And that’s all she wrote.” He folded his lips into a grim little line.

Carter almost couldn’t believe what he’d just heard. “What a dick.”

“Well, you did meet him. Did you expect he’d ever been a nice guy?” Ty managed a laugh. “It’s funny. I know we’re not...you know. I know we don’t expect eternal bliss from one another or anything like that. I know this is a transaction, and our expectations of each other are set accordingly. But I have to say, Carter, you’ve already taught me to expect so much more from people.”

Now it was Carter’s turn to blush. He hadn’t done much for Ty. He’d shown up, confused him, hung out with him a few times, and married him for money. “Seriously?”

“Seriously.” Ty bowed his head and took his hand back. He wrapped it around the stem of his cocktail glass. “Anyway,” he said with a kind of brittle cheer. “I apologize for the way he behaved to you. He should know better, but he doesn’t.”

Carter smirked. “You’re not responsible for his bad behavior. But I will admit that he was not my favorite person. I did pocket his cash, though.”

Ty’s eyes widened. “Wait, what?”

Carter leaned forward and lowered his voice. He didn’t want to brag, but he did enjoy getting reactions out of Ty. “Come on. I’m the starting second baseman for the local favorite team. I don't ask for free drinks, but I usually get them." He winked and sat up. "I won't tell Sebastian if you don't."

Ty grinned again, and he relaxed a little more. Carter couldn't tell if he was relaxing because he was learning to trust Carter more, or because the Manhattans were working their magic. He was going to have to assume that it was both. "My lips are sealed," he said. His eyes twinkled.

Carter chuckled and moved his seat, so holding hands didn't feel quite as physically awkward. "So you and Keegan aren't all that close with your parents." He had to admit he'd been curious before, when he and Ty first got married. He'd expected to have some kind of "meet the parents" night or something. Ty hadn't shown much curiosity about Carter's parents, though, and Carter hadn't exactly wanted to call them up and tell them he'd gotten paid to marry someone. He hadn't wanted to push the issue, but Seb's comment made him wonder.

"No, not really." Ty made a face. "I mean we were both in boarding school as soon as we could be, so it's not like we ever had much of a relationship with them to begin with. And that was our normal, you know? Everyone else we knew was just like that, until we got to college." He turned his head. "They pushed for me and Seb to get together, and they were really upset when I wouldn't go to London with him. They tried to fix me up with a few alphas after that, but they were all basically Seb clones, and I wasn't about to quit the job I'd worked so hard for. Yeah, I wanted a husband and a family. I didn't want to lose everything I'd been and done to get there. My dads didn't get that. Don't get that, I guess."

"I see." Carter didn't see, not really, but it wasn't any fault of Ty's. He couldn't quite make himself understand parents who tried to restrain their children like that, especially based on something so simple as whether or not they could bear children. "When's the last time you spoke with them?"

"I don't know. I think I sent them a Christmas card." He scratched his head. "I don't want to make it sound hostile, because it's not. It's just...we're not close. We don't seek each other out, and it's fine. I'm a lot closer with Keegan."

"Obviously." Carter smirked and lifted his glass in salute. "That's too bad, though. Do you plan to tell them you got married at all?"

"Well, I'll have to. If I want to free up that portion of my trust fund for you, I have to tell them. I was just hoping to wait until there was a baby on the way." His face melted a little, reminding Carter that they hadn't decided to go out tonight just because it was fun.

"Hey. It's okay. We can try again before I leave for Spring Training." He squeezed Carter's hand.

"Really?" Ty blushed. His skin was so fair it was easy to see when he blushed. "I hate to put you through that again."

Carter felt his jaw drop. "Ty, I'm sorry if I gave you the impression that you *put me through* anything the last time, okay? I enjoyed it. It was a little bit weird because we didn't know each other at all, but I liked it. I like you, and I'm sure as hell not going to complain about doing it again. All right?"

Ty nodded, mute. Had he not enjoyed it? He'd been responsive, at least. He'd gotten off. It must have been a little galling, under the circumstances, but Carter hadn't gotten any complaints before. Ty wouldn't look at him, though.

Carter remembered Seb, and the way he spoke to Ty. He wouldn't have been at all shy about any shortcomings or complaints. He'd have made any issues he had perfectly clear. "Look," he said, trying to catch Ty's eye. "It was good for me, okay? I hope it was good for you, and next time will be even better. I promise."

Ty managed to grin a little bit at that, and Carter had to be satisfied with that. He didn't try to force the issue, but he knew Ty had a lot more going on under the surface.

Chapter Five

Ty's omega dad, Beau, called on Sunday afternoon. Ty almost didn't recognize the number. "Hello?"

"Tyler, this is your father." Beau's thick Georgia accent hadn't lessened during his long decades in New York. On the contrary, Ty sometimes suspected Beau of laying it on even thicker simply because of New York. "I assume you're well?"

"Of course." Ty minimized the open window on his laptop, so no cat could change the document he was working on, and went to get himself some more water. "How about you and Dad? Everything okay?"

"Oh, we're just fine. Just fine. Don't you worry about us. We just got back from a nice long stay in Texas, so we avoided the worst of the cold weather. And we had a visit from that nice young man, Sebastian Britton. You know, the boy you were supposed to marry but were too stupid to hang on to."

Ty rolled his eyes and tapped the mouthpiece on his phone. "What's that, Dad? You're breaking up. Sorry, terrible reception here."

"Hush, Tyler. We both know you're sitting at home alone, and you get perfect reception. Now, you listen to your father. Sebastian stopped by yesterday, and then we saw him again this morning. He's a good boy, making sure we're doing well and all that. He told me you went off and got married."

Damn it. What kind of stupid game was Seb playing now? On the one hand, it spared Ty the necessity of having to tell his parents about Carter himself. On the other, now he couldn't tell them on his terms, when there was a baby on the way. Well, the cat was out of the bag now. He couldn't do anything about it but get through it. "That's right."

“We didn’t give our permission or our approval. We haven’t even met the boy yet!”

“He’s twenty-eight, Dad. He’s hardly a boy.” Ty headed back toward his desk. Isis was already sitting on it, right next to his laptop, batting at the keyboard with one little white paw.

“We still haven’t vetted this man. We haven’t given our approval. If you think we’re going to free up the rest of your trust fund after a stunt like this, you’re sorely mistaken.”

“Fortunately, the terms of the trust aren’t written in such a way that it’s at your discretion. The terms are that I have to be married, and stay married, for one month. We’ll pass that threshold in a week, by which point I’ll submit a copy of the marriage license to the trustees, and it will all be taken care of. You won’t have to worry about a thing, Dad.” Ty smiled. Smiling softened his tone, but he also couldn’t really help it.

“This is an outrage. Sebastian says he’s only using you for your money. He’s going to take you for everything you have and leave you with nothing, and then where will you be! We set up that trust specifically to make sure that didn’t happen, but we didn’t think we’d raised you to be so stupid as to marry without our permission!” Beau had gotten so angry he managed to pronounce “our” with three syllables, a rare feat.

“We have a prenuptial agreement in place. Sebastian didn’t mention it because we didn’t discuss it. Sebastian and I aren’t friends, Dad. And he didn’t exactly endear himself to Carter, either. Look, I’m sure you’ve got a lot to say about it—”

“I do have a lot to say about it. I’m deeply disappointed in you, Tyler. You’ve gone from being forever alone, which was just sad, to going off and being profligate which is worse. All the money we wasted on your education, and you’re wasting it on some big, dumb athlete without a dime to his name!”

"He's a charming man, Dad. And Keegan knows him. He introduced us. He's known Carter for a while, actually. For all I know Dad's met him too. He's a member of the Hellion Club. So, maybe it would be a good idea to withhold judgement until you actually meet him?" Ty wouldn't hold his breath on that, but he figured he'd get the words out there. "Anyway, what's done is done. I'm married, I'm pretty fond of the guy, and I'm working on a big project at work right now. Is there anything useful you wanted to talk about?"

"You'll regret this, mark my words."

"Not half as much as I regretted getting engaged to Sebastian Britton. You and Dad have a good day, all right?"

Beau hung up without another comment. Ty chuckled and sent a text to Carter. Technically, he didn't need to text him. A conversation between himself and his dad didn't need to involve Carter, but he wanted to make sure he was being as transparent as he could be.

So, Seb told my dads.

Carter texted him back almost right away. *Why do I doubt he was being helpful?*

Ty just grinned and chuckled. *Is there a good time to see you before you leave for Spring Training? I don't want to be in your way or anything or interfere with your routine. I know baseball players can be superstitious.*

You did do your research! :D Ty had to grin when he saw Carter's little emoji. *I've put all of my superstitions into a box until I get on that plane. I'm at your disposal until Friday at noon.*

Maybe dinner? Ty held his breath. He'd never been the one to suggest getting together before. It had always been Carter. Was it too much? Was it too forward of him? His heart beat faster as he waited for a reply. Maybe Carter would just want dinner.

Maybe Ty would be okay with that. He wanted to have sex again, of course. He wanted to have sex because it was the only way to get pregnant, and he wanted to have sex with Carter because sex with Carter felt good. If Carter wasn't up for it, though, Ty could accept it. He could completely understand not wanting a guy like him. He had to admit, he liked spending time around Carter.

Good God, he wasn't starting to love his husband, was he?

Does Thursday work for you? We can get together earlier than that if you want, but I want to spend my last night in New York with you. Carter followed that up immediately with *Sorry, I don't mean to make it uncomfortable.*

Carter had no way of knowing Ty was sitting on his bed hugging his phone or staring at the screen with what had to be the dopiest look in the world on his face. It was ridiculous, and Ty knew he needed to watch himself. He shouldn't get too attached to Carter, however good Carter made him feel right now.

You're not. I'm looking forward to seeing you Thursday. Ty held his thumb over the keyboard. He wanted to invite Carter over for more than just Thursday, but he held back. He needed to be smart. He needed to protect himself. *I'll get us takeout?*

Sounds good. I'll be there at 7.

Ty made an entry on his calendar. He was now officially too keyed up to work, so he headed downstairs to hit the gym. This was all about making a baby, nothing else. He needed to remember that.

He fought to keep his wits about him for the rest of the week. He had plenty of work to keep him busy, but through it all was the unending reminder on his calendar. Thursday, seven o'clock, meet Carter. He could hardly sleep. His bed felt too big, too empty. What was wrong with him? He'd never been like this before. All this for a guy who was going to be leaving for six weeks, for crying out loud.

Thursday finally rolled around. Ty got through his day on autopilot. He ducked out of the office and ran home at six, just to get an extra shower in. Carter probably wouldn't care, but Ty wanted to make the extra effort. He wanted to be well groomed for his husband. He wanted to smell good. He wanted Carter to go off to Florida with a good impression.

He ordered delivery from a nearby restaurant, although truth be told he was too nervous to eat. All he could think about was Carter. Would Carter just want to get the job over with, or would he want to spend time with Ty too? Would he think of Ty at all while he was in Florida, or would he be completely absorbed in baseball and flirty little omegas?

Carter showed up at exactly seven o'clock. He didn't need to be buzzed up anymore. Ty had given him a key not long ago. He still jumped up when he heard the key turn in the lock. "Carter. Hey." He smiled and gestured to the dining table in the kitchen. "Thanks for coming by."

Carter grinned at him. "I wouldn't have missed it for the world, you know. I've been looking forward to this all week." He hung his jacket in the closet and bent down to pick up Ra, who was squeaking mercilessly at him. "I'm just using you for your cats, you know."

Ty locked the door behind him and used the chain too. He wasn't going to let his brother interrupt. "It's a reasonable thing to do. They're my greatest asset. Come on, I've got dinner ready and waiting." He'd even broken out real plates and everything.

Carter definitely seemed to appreciate the food in front of him, but he still looked around the kitchen with curiosity. "Tell me something," he said. "Have you ever cooked a day in your life?"

Ty sat back and wiped his mouth. "I'm not exactly a professional chef, but I can keep myself fed if I have to. I made myself learn in undergrad. Why?"

"I'm surprised, I guess. I know where you come from, I see this fancy kitchen, and I was just wondering if it had ever been used." Carter hung his head sheepishly. "I shouldn't make assumptions, though."

"Well no, you shouldn't, but hey. In this case, it was reasonable." Ty would have been pissed if someone else said it, but this was Carter. He must be falling hard, because Carter was getting a lot of passes as far as he was concerned. "I'd be ashamed to cook for someone else, though. It's been a while since I've had time, and I'm not very good."

"I want to decide for myself." Carter stood up, cleared his plate off, and helped Ty to his feet. "When I get back from Spring Training, I want to try something you cooked. Even if it's super simple, okay?"

Ty ducked his head. He'd never had a partner who wanted him to cook before. "I'll try. I'm keeping the delivery place on speed dial, though."

"Fair enough," Carter laughed. "Can I kiss you?"

Ty's breath caught in his throat. All he could do was nod. Last time Carter had kissed him Ty had felt like he was waking up from a coma. He hadn't been prepared for that, but he wanted it again. It wasn't what he got, though. This time, it was like he was seeing the stars out in the countryside for the first time. Everything felt clearer, brighter, and *more* than it had before.

He cradled Carter's face in his hands and breathed in his scent. He tasted like dinner, but he smelled like soap and a little bit like pine trees. It was a good scent, strong and masculine, and Ty didn't want it to fade or wash away.

Carter steered him toward the bedroom, still locked to him at the lips. Ty walked backwards and hoped the cats had the good sense to get out of the way. He closed and locked the door, just in case Keegan decided to let himself in despite the chain.

Ty knew his brother well.

Carter pulled back for a second, and then he stepped over to the bed. "I know this is going to sound weird, Ty, but I want to see you. I want to leave the lights on, and I want to look at you while we make love. I want to see what you look like, what's making you go wild, and what's just not doing it for you. You're a beautiful guy, a lights-on guy. Can we do that? Please?"

Ty bit his lip. He'd never been a lights-on guy before. Was Carter messing with him? All he could see in his husband's eyes was perfect sincerity.

He backed away from the light and took his shirt off. Then he pulled his undershirt over his head. Carter's eyes lit up, and he parted his lips beautifully.

Ty took a deep breath. He could do this. His pulse raced, and his palms were slick with sweat, but he could show himself off for Carter. He could make Carter happy. He already knew Carter would return the favor. He stepped forward and helped Carter off with his shirt, and then he kissed his way down Carter's chiseled chest and abs.

He didn't stop to think about all of the younger, better-looking omegas who'd had this privilege before him, and who'd have this privilege once he was gone. He could enjoy himself now and worry about the rest when Carter's incredible scent had faded from his memory.

He got to Carter's waistband and hesitated. He could feel the heat just below and the strong bulge. That amazing cock had been in him once before. He wanted it again. "Is this okay?" he asked, looking up at Carter.

Carter's eyes were already a little glassy, but he shook himself out of it. "Oh, my God. My God, Ty. I want to, I do. But I also want to come inside you, and I know you want that too." He stroked Ty's cheek. "Next time, if you're up for it."

Ty let Carter help him up, and he moved over to the bed in a kind of haze. He almost didn't believe there would be a next time. If he got pregnant, would Carter touch him again? Right now, seeing the desire in Carter's eyes, Ty had to say yes.

He moved to roll over and then remembered himself. Carter wanted to see him, for some unholy reason. He lay back and watched as Carter got rid of his pants and grabbed the lube out of the nightstand. "I've been looking forward to this all week," Carter told him, slicking up his hand.

Ty smiled as the first finger breached him. "Me too," he said, and ran his hand along the long line of Carter's back. He couldn't get enough of touching him. He had to get it all in now, because tomorrow Carter would be gone.

Carter worked his way into Ty patiently, and it was the best thing he'd ever felt in his life. The last time he'd still been a little tense, but now he'd worn himself down until he was nothing but desire and need. He moved when he was ready, so full and focused he couldn't form the words. Every thrust from Carter sent him closer to the edge, and it was all Ty could do to keep from crying out with joy as Carter sank into him over and over.

“Come on, Ty.” Carter bent his head and touched his forehead to Ty’s. Both of them were sticky with sweat, but Ty didn’t care right now. “Let me hear you. Please, Ty.”

Carter wanted to hear him? Ty would have to think about that later on. For now, all he could do was obey. He let out a loud moan as Carter dragged across his prostate, and another one as he slammed home again. Each cry Ty let loose seemed to only encourage Carter more, and soon he wrapped a hand around Ty’s heavy cock. “Let go, Ty. Come on, let go. Let it all out.”

Ty came with a shout, sending thick ropes almost up to his chest. The sound, the sight, or maybe just the feel of Ty clenching around him, was all Carter needed, and he lost the rhythm and came hard inside Ty.

He half-collapsed on top of Ty for a moment. Then he gently pulled out and came back to clean them up. Ty was glad. He didn’t think he was ready to move yet. “Are you staying?” he asked. He tried not to sound too plaintive.

Carter climbed back into the bed, a broad smile splitting his face. “If you want me to.” He took Ty into his arms without waiting for confirmation, though, so apparently he’d figured out Ty’s answer for himself.

***

Carter left Ty’s house when Ty did. He had zero interest in getting out of bed that early, but he also had zero interest in hanging around Ty’s empty apartment that was probably haunted anyway. The cats were cute and all, but they didn’t make the best conversationalists. Plus, they got to fool around a little bit in the shower, and Carter didn’t want to miss out on that.

Ty seemed sad when they parted, but he didn't say anything beyond promising to text. He didn't go so far as to say he'd call. If Carter had a little bit less self confidence, he'd be offended by that. As it was, he figured Spring Training couldn't have come at a more awkward time. He was just starting to get somewhere with his new husband, and now he had to leave.

Oh, well. Maybe they could keep the momentum going. Ty definitely seemed to have loosened up and to have gotten more comfortable with Carter. That was good. He'd been enthusiastic about their encounter last night, and he'd been ready to go down on Carter. Carter had been ready to let it happen, too, but he remembered just in time that he wasn't there to get his rocks off like that. He was there to make a baby.

Would Ty still want him if they'd succeeded?

He pushed the intrusive thought out of his head. He'd made his bed, he had to lie in it. Maybe he could talk Ty into trying to stick it out and seeing where it led them, maybe not, but he wasn't going to agonize about it.

He collected his things and headed to the airport. Ty had gotten him a ticket, thankfully. He hadn't had to go with his hat in his hand to the team and ask for help. When he checked in at the kiosk, he found that Ty hadn't just gotten him a ticket, he'd gotten him a ticket in first class, and he didn't know what to think about that.

Was he horrified that Ty thought he was some kind of prima donna who needed to be pampered like that for a flight down to Florida? Was he terrified that Ty just thought first class was the normal way to fly? Or was he pleased, warmed even, that Ty thought well enough of him that he'd done something so generous for him?

He decided to go with option three. He didn't know why he liked Ty so much, but he did. Ty probably did have flaws and ulterior motives here and there, but not in this particular case. Ty had shown he wanted to be kind and helpful to Carter, and this was just one more example of that.

His flight was smooth and pleasant, leaving him nothing to complain about. He landed and collected his luggage, and it only took him about five minutes to find the car the team sent him. Once his things had been loaded into the trunk, he settled into the back seat, and he was ready to go.

The Spring Training facility looked a lot like the actual stadium back in New York, with the exception of player housing facilities. A lot of the guys, especially veteran players, liked to complain about housing during Spring Training. "I'm paying how much to have a house down here and a house up in New York so I can live doubled up like a college kid?" They'd fume, and Carter could kind of see their point.

At the same time, living communally with the big leaguers had helped him more than anything else when he'd been in the minors. It had helped him to keep his head on straight when he'd come up to the bigs, and when he'd gotten his first big contract too. He welcomed the chance to pay the favor forward, even if it was as a cautionary tale the way it was now.

He checked in with Spring Training staff, got his room assignment and key, and went inside. He had a decent room assignment, although the bed was narrow and nothing at all like the one he'd been in last night. The team spared no expense when it came to the players' comfort, but a narrow single bed had nothing on a king sized bed with a warm, affectionate omega and a couple of cats.

He snapped a picture of the bed and sent it to Ty. *Not quite as nice as home.*

Ty replied fifteen minutes later. He must have been in a meeting. *You're making me blush.* He included a smiling, blushing emoji, so he'd apparently figured out how to use those. Maybe his meeting had involved his secretary teaching him how to find the emoji keyboard.

Training didn't start until the day after, but once they'd checked into the facility they were under staff control. People who read about the strict training regimen in articles or who saw spots about it on TV shook their head and muttered about how draconian it was, and how these guys must be stupid to let themselves be controlled like that, but they didn't get it. Carter got paid a lot of money to get out there on the field in April and perform his best. He needed to be in peak condition to do that. If they took pride in their jobs, shouldn't he take pride in his?

He knew some basics about nutrition, but he didn't have a master's degree in sports nutrition. He'd take the expert's advice on how to best fuel his body, instead of going with guesswork. He knew what felt good to his body and what put him in pain, but he wasn't a doctor or physical therapist. Those guys had the expertise to squeeze the most performance out of his body without injuring him. The players would push themselves too hard or they'd develop bad habits that wouldn't become problems until they turned thirty and blew out joints and disabled themselves for life.

He went to the cafeteria and ate the dinner the staff had prepared for him. It had been precisely calculated to his dietary needs, as an alpha of his age and weight. It smelled bland and boring. It kind of tasted like cardboard, but it was what it was.

Tracy showed up about halfway through Carter's meal. He sat down with his own dinner, which smelled a thousand times better than Carter's, and looked him up and down. "Well," he said after a moment, "it doesn't look like your weird lawyer guy ate you or anything. Maybe he's not a serial killer after all."

Carter laughed. “Not as near as I can tell, no. He’s just a guy. A nice guy, actually. I kind of like him.”

Tracy rolled his eyes. “We call that Stockholm Syndrome in Puerto Rico.”

“No, really. He’s just a really nice, sweet guy. His family’s a little screwed up, and I think his ex needs to spend a little time fielding line drives without a cup, but Ty himself is nice. I like him.” He ducked his head. “It’s weird, you know? I know we’re supposed to just be in it for the contract, but I keep finding I want to protect him. I want to help him. We went out last weekend, and he smiled for real, and it was like the sun coming out after a snowstorm.”

“I’m calling the team shrink. I don’t know if they have a pill for Stockholm Syndrome or if they just keep you apart and make you go to church or something, but there’s got to be a treatment.” Tracy made a face at him. “I mean come on, Carter. This guy’s own brother will be the first to say he’s boring. He’s however old he is, and he’s all set to just bribe someone into marrying him, and he only wants to be married long enough to have a baby. He doesn’t even want you around long enough to help him raise it.”

“That’s not because of him, though.” Carter stiffened his back. Okay, so he and Ty wouldn’t have even met if it weren’t for the contract, or for their arrangement. The fact was, they were actually pretty compatible. “That’s the other people in his life who’ve convinced him this is how it has to be.”

“And he couldn’t go on one of eight gazillion dating sites and try online dating like a normal human being?”

“No, Tracy, I told you. People convinced him he couldn’t do that. And you know what? I believe it. The kind of guys his parents kept setting him up with wouldn’t want a guy like him. If they’re all like Asshat McGee there, they all want someone who’s going to reflect them, not be his own person.” He shrugged. "I'm secure enough in myself that I don't need my omega to reflect me. I want him to be happy, to have a life of his own, and not always to be snooping around in my stuff and making himself nuts while I'm on the road."

Tracy grimaced and rubbed the back of his neck. "Okay. I might have lost a spouse that way." Carter pursed his lips and gave his coach the stink eye. "Fine, two wives and one husband. But that doesn't mean you won't have those issues with a guy who's so desperate he's got to buy a husband, man."

Carter gritted his teeth together and tried to make himself relax. Tracy was just looking out for him, like his own father or uncle would. "It doesn't guarantee anything, I know. But Tracy, you know we don't even have fidelity built into our contract, right?"

Tracy started choking on his mouthful of whatever it was he was eating that smelled so much better than Carter's dinner. Carter jumped up and slammed his hand down between his shoulder blades, and Tracy managed to breathe again.

"What the hell? Of course you've got fidelity built into your marriage contract! You're married. It comes with the territory," he said when he'd caught his breath.

Carter smirked. "Actually, it doesn't. Our contract, the one we signed before we officially got married, states very clearly that there is no expectation of fidelity on the part of the alpha so long as any relationships are conducted with all due discretion for the duration of the contract period." He flexed his hands. "I thought it was a little weird when I saw the contract written out, but I guess I get it now. He literally just wants to have the baby. He doesn't expect me to want to be with him at all, and he accepts that. Now, I have no intention of actually being unfaithful."

Tracy wiped his mouth. "Of course you don't. You were raised better than that." He slumped in his seat. "You know, with these other guys, I have to worry about them getting into all kinds of trouble. I worry about PEDs. I worry about other drugs. I worry about their tempers, I worry about them getting hurt. I worry about them beating up their wives and going to jail. I worry about all kinds of knuckle headed things, you know? After that Aaron Hernandez mess, I worry about even more than that."

"I know that, Tracy." Carter took a mouthful of his cardboard gruel. "You're a good coach."

"Shut up and listen to me for a minute, would you? With you, Carter, I worry that you're in over your head. I'm not worried that you're going to do something stupid, because you've got a good head on your shoulders and you're old enough now you're not going to get caught up in all that bullshit. But I am worried your heart is too big for your head." He shook a finger at Carter.

"I'll be fine, Trace. He's not going to hurt me. He's a good dude, he wouldn't hurt a fly." Carter grinned. "The hardest thing with Ty is going to be convincing him that someone wants to be around him."

"And do you? Or do you just like the idea of playing protector. Because Carter, let me tell you, it's not as easy as it sounds. I did meet him. And I met that brother of his. There are plenty of obstacles right there."

"There are plenty of obstacles, Tracy, but one thing's taken care of already." He winked at his coach. "I don't have to figure out the right way to propose."

Tracy had to laugh at that. "Go on, get to bed you giant goofball. There's no reasoning with you when you're like this. I'll see you tomorrow bright and early for drills."

Carter grinned and left the cafeteria. His roommate still hadn't showed up, which wasn't a good sign for the guy. Ah well, it happens. He liked paying his own good luck forward, but he didn't mind having the time to himself either. He took out his phone and dialed Ty.

Ty picked up right away. "Carter? Is everything all right?"

Carter chuckled. "Of course everything's all right. I just felt like calling my husband, that's all. Is that okay?"

He could hear the shy smile in Ty's voice when he replied. "Of course it's okay. It's a little unusual to get used to, but I kind of like it." He cleared his throat. "So, ah, how's it going? I noticed they're generous with your housing down there."

"Well, I will say this. It's good to get back to the routine. And it's nice to get out of the cold weather, too. It was in the low eighties when I landed here today. As opposed to, you know, the thirties, when I left."

"Yeah, yeah." Ty sighed. "Too bad you've only got that narrow little bed. Otherwise I could sneak down there, and maybe weasel my way into your dorm or whatever, and maybe I could enjoy the sunshine too."

"Ah, geez, Ty. Now you've got me all hard again and watch my roommate walk in right now." Carter was only half joking. "Tell me the truth, though. Would you ever actually come all the way down here?"

Ty hummed. "Well, the Delaney estate does have some property down there. I could probably find an excuse." Then he sighed, and his tone turned more serious. "But, I wouldn't want to take away from you doing what you needed to do down there or anything like that. There's a reason they take you away from your families and everything, right? They want to make sure you're getting the right food, the right amount of sleep, all that."

Carter groaned. “There you go being all logical on me. I mean, it’s only six weeks, right?”

“Yeah.” Ty sounded about as enthusiastic about that as he would about a root canal. “It’s weird, though. You’ve only been gone for a day, and I miss you.”

“I miss you too, Ty. Believe that. I’ll talk to you in the next couple of days, okay?”

“Okay. Talk to you soon.”

Carter went to bed. Yeah, he was in trouble, all right. He was more than halfway to falling in love with his husband.

Chapter Six

March came in like a lion in New York, dumping a full foot of snow onto already saturated streets. The city was already efficient with its cleanup and did their usual best with what they had, but that didn't change the fact that millions of people had to commute through a slushy mess to get to where they were going. Even though Ty only had to go a couple of blocks to get to or from the office, he wasn't immune from the crankiness caused by wet feet or cold wind.

He couldn't think of Carter down in Florida with anything like equanimity. He knew Carter was working hard, and doing arcane rituals to prepare himself for the baseball season instead of sitting around in the sand watching the waves. Still, he couldn't help but imagine Carter in a pair of swim trunks, sitting on a towel and smelling of sun block. In his better moments he could even imagine himself beside Carter.

It had been too long since he'd taken a vacation, of any kind, with anyone. Carter wouldn't be available for a vacation until November, of course. If Ty had any kind of luck at all, he would be pregnant by then. Unless he was sterile, of course, in which case he would just have to deal with it.

He'd been getting daily updates from Carter about Spring Training, updates that helped Ty to feel like he was part of whatever was going on down there. Sometimes he got a picture of the guys doing all kinds of weird exercises to strengthen themselves and get ready for the season. Sometimes he got pictures of individual ball players, being serious or goofing off. Once he got a picture of a grumpy looking Tracy Belmonte, arguing with something that had to be the other team's mascot. At least, he hoped it was the other team's mascot.

He responded, of course. Trying to think of ways to reply only reinforced all of the ways in which Keegan was right. Ty was boring, and his life was boring. He liked what he did, but he could hardly send a picture of himself reviewing laws about the estates of people under investigation.

Not that he expected to hold Carter's interest for long anyway. Carter seemed interested now, and Ty appreciated that. He loved the way he felt when he was around Carter. He hated that he'd needed Keegan to fix him up with some guy, and to have what amounted to a fake relationship. When he was with Carter, it didn't feel fake. It felt more real than anything he'd had with any of the jerks his dads had fixed him up with.

Maybe he just didn't know how to tell the difference.

He pushed his doubts aside as he kept up his communications with Carter. He found things to text Carter about. Weird little law foibles that popped up during the day weren't likely to be of much interest, he'd learned that much over the years, but he took pictures of funny scenes at the courthouse when he had to go. He took pictures of his cats, too. Carter seemed to have a special fondness for Amun, so he sent a few extra pictures of his most rascally cat.

He went out once with Keegan, because Keegan insisted he wasn't going to let him be some kind of hermit. Ty sent pictures of that, too, even though he stuck to water because of the potential for pregnancy. That alone made Keegan roll his eyes. "You get that most people don't know they're pregnant for at least a month and they drink like fish, right? And the kid turns out fine?"

Ty made a face at his brother. It was juvenile and ridiculous, and it felt good. "It's not like I get any do-overs. I want to do it right."

"Suit yourself, Captain Buzzkill." Keegan ordered two drinks anyway and informed their server he was Ty's designated drinker. She just gave him an exasperated look and turned to Ty. "Is he driving anywhere?"

"Hell no, ma'am."

"That's fine, then." And she left to bring them their orders.

"So," Keegan said, sitting up a little straighter, "I got a visit from an old friend of yours."

Ty let his head fall back until he was looking up at the ceiling. "Let me guess. The eternally charming Sebastian Britton."

Keegan toyed with his fork. "Good God, that guy was always such a douche. Remind me why you were going to marry him again?"

"I'd tell you but I don't know. I can't think for the life of me why I thought that was a good idea." Ty covered his face. "Did he turn into a bigger jerk while he was in London, or was I just too dumb to see it?"

"Both. And he was not complementary about Mr. Bowman, not even a little bit." Keegan shuddered. "He's totes jealous, bro."

Ty tried to translate Keegan's words. "No. He's the one who left, remember? And he was never that into me. It's our dads he liked, and their money."

"Mmm-hmm. But now you've got money of your own, your trust fund, and the money you'll get when they kick off. And my estate, because you know I'm never tying myself down." He stretched his back out and scratched his belly, a proud smile splitting his face.

"Right. Right. But he can't honestly think I'd take him back. He made his feelings about me pretty clear when he left." Ty almost reached for one of the glasses the server delivered when she showed up, but he remembered himself just in time.

The thought of Seb coming back for him would have been all he wanted seven years ago, or even six.

He was older now, and wiser.

"Well, it's not like this thing with Carter's a long-term deal. But, I wouldn't if I were you." Keegan shrugged. "It's up to you, and obviously our dads would be thrilled. Beau has been jawing my ear off about it for three weeks now."

"Ugh." Ty slumped down. Maybe the baby—if there was a baby—would be okay if he had a drink after all. When did the fetal brain develop again? Better not chance it. "The great part about hanging up on him is that he won't do that to me anymore."

"You hung up on him? For reals? Sweet, bro, sweet." Keegan clapped his hands loud enough for the whole bar to hear. "That explains why they want us over there for brunch on Sunday, but they made me be the one to tell you."

Ty closed his eyes and counted to ten. "You're choosing now to tell me this?"

"Well, yeah, dude. Anyway, we should be there at ten. Hangovers are optional, but it's probably best to not have one. You know how Beau can be."

"Oh, yes." Ty managed a tight smile. "I do know just how much fun Beau can be."

He mentioned the upcoming ordeal in his text to Carter that night. Carter called him up, concerned. "Are you going to be okay? I know you and your dads don't have the greatest relationship."

That was the amazing thing about Carter. He thought about things like that. "I'll survive. Keegan will be there. He's kind of an ass, but he's never hesitated to go toe to toe with... well, anyone when he felt he needed to. He's funny that way." He licked his lips. "Do you think you'll want to meet them?"

"I'm a little worried about mouthing off at them myself, but you know what? I've already got your approval. I don't give a good goddamn about theirs." He chuckled. "It's funny. I know we're doing everything backwards, but it's kind of freeing in a weird way. We don't have to worry about whether or not our parents like our choice, or anything like that. We're already married."

Ty laughed as the tension ebbed out of him. "It's true. We are." One of the cats pounced his finger, attracted by the ring. "You'll have to forgive me if I'm looking forward to April, though."

"Oh, me too, Ty. Me too."

Sunday arrived. Ty took a Lyft to his parents' place. He could have walked, but there was still enough snow and salt on the ground that he didn't feel like it. He dressed up a little, even including a tie, because that was who his parents were.

He timed his arrival to happen five minutes late. Normally, Ty abhorred lateness. It was Sunday, and they hadn't even bothered to tell him to come over on their own. He didn't feel compelled to be all that punctual, and this way he was a little more likely to have his brother there to run interference for him. Just as he'd planned, Keegan was waiting for him when he walked in the door.

His alpha father, Ed, handed him a mimosa without preamble. Keegan was sprawled out on the couch, with a mimosa in hand and an empty glass on the table in front of him. *Ah, good. It's going to be one of those get-togethers, I see.*

He tried to push the glass away. "Thanks, Dad, but I'm trying to avoid alcohol these days. It's early to tell yet, but I don't know if I'm pregnant or not, and I'd rather not risk it."

Ed's face darkened, and he pressed the glass into Ty's hand. "Nonsense. Your father drank while he was pregnant with you, and you turned out just fine."

Ty stopped resisting. *Sure, if by "fine" you mean "has to pay someone to marry him" and "so boring his own brother thinks he is "hopeless."* Maybe it was for the best that Carter was safely in Florida. He shouldn't have to see Ty like this.

"Now that we're all here," Beau drawled, "maybe we can *finally* eat our brunch before it all freezes over." He stood up and swept off into the large formal dining room.

Keegan caught Ty's eye and rolled his. Ty understood his brother without having to hear words. Apparently it had been a long morning already. If Beau's behavior was any indication, those two mimosas were definitely necessary.

They seated themselves at the ridiculously long dining table. No one needed a table this long in New York, not anymore. Ed had inherited it from his grandfather, who'd inherited it from his, and so on and so forth. They would keep the stupid table in the family until the end of time, or until some descendant finally wised up and shipped it out of the city. For now, Ed took his proper place at the head of the table. His husband sat at his right hand, his alpha son at his left, and Ty sat beside Keegan. His proper place was beside Beau, as the omega son. He knew it, but he made the choice to sit next to his brother.

Keegan didn't react, other than to burp loudly. Beau's eyes blazed, and Ed put his own mimosa down to stare at Ty from under his bushy eyebrows. "You're out of place, Tyler."

"Usually." A servant, dressed in a gray dress, approached and filled his coffee cup. He picked it up and sipped from it, while his fathers sputtered.

"What's gotten into you, Tyler? You've never been this openly defiant before. I mean yes, you defied us when you let Sebastian get away, but that was different. This is just you needling us to be petty. Why are you needling us, Tyler? You've already gotten what you wanted. You wrested control of the trust fund, against our better judgement." Ed's rumbling voice even made the servant nervous.

Ty just sat calmly and waited for someone to pass him the eggs. "It's hardly needling to sit in a different space, Dad. I haven't been here in two years. It doesn't seem all that important to sit on one side of the table versus another. This way Keegan and I can pester each other without having to risk kicking Dad in the process."

Keegan elbowed him, lightly, to help him prove his point. Then he passed the eggs.

"It's disgraceful is what it is. We made a mistake sending you to college in the first place." Beau narrowed his eyes at Ty. "What does an omega need with college anyway? It wasn't like you were going to have to get a job. You could walk away from that foolish thing tomorrow and be perfectly fine for the rest of your life. It's ruined you for a husband."

"Now dad," Keegan said, and slugged down the rest of his mimosa. The servant appeared from out of nowhere with another one as he continued. "You know Ty's already got a husband."

Ed waved a hand. "Poppycock. Everyone knows that isn't a real marriage. They didn't make an announcement, they didn't go on a honeymoon. Tyler didn't even take the next day off from work, and they're still living in separate apartments." He pointed at Ty. "That cornfed cretin is using you for your money."

"Every guy you tried to set me up with was using me for your money." Ty shrugged. "And who says poppycock anymore?"

Beau gasped, dropped his fork, and covered his mouth with both hands.

"Carter and I have an understanding. We know what to expect from each other. We have a prenup in place so that, in the event of a divorce, he knows exactly what he'll receive in terms of compensation. He can't be using me for any more than that, unlike—oh, Keegan, what was his name?"

"St. James." Keegan grinned, wolfish and a little sloppy. "Who names their kid St. James?"

"Their family is a very old Connecticut family," Beau informed them, standing up.

"Canonizing your child before they've figured out how to open their eyes seems a little silly to me." Tyler sipped from his coffee again. He'd have to remember to send his brother a present. "Anyway, he wasn't even shy about using me for your money. He wanted me to sign the trust fund over to him outright before he'd even kiss me. That's why I dumped him, by the way."

"Nonsense." Ed scowled at him. "I know the boy well."

"Apparently not, because he's also got three illegitimate children to support and his parents won't contribute a dime toward them." Keegan yawned. "The guy's a scumbag. He honestly thought Ty was just going to put up with it."

"And why wouldn't he? They're a respectable family." Beau crossed his arms over his chest. "All alphas have their foibles. I've raised you, Tyler, to be tolerant and understanding of your alpha. They have their needs, and they're important men. You can't expect them to devote themselves entirely to you."

Ty held up a hand. "I don't want to hear any more. It's making me think very differently about you and Dad, and that's just not someplace I want my brain to go right now." Wow, talking back to his parents was feeling pretty darned good. "I've found an alpha I like, who likes me. We've agreed to what we expect from the other, and that's all there needs to be to it. What's done is done. Why don't we just enjoy our brunch in peace and have a very pleasant day?"

Beau sat down, blinking like he was starting to doubt his reality. Ed set his jaw, but forced a smile to his face. Tyler knew that look. His father might have lost the battle, but the war wasn't over.

***

Ty called on Sunday night. Carter had been waiting on pins and needles for that call. He had a half-formed idea in his head that Ty's parents, who bore some resemblance to aliens from *Star Wars* or something but also wore tuxedos to breakfast, might have eaten him. According to Ty, they hadn't, and they probably wouldn't have. "They hate me too much for that," he said bluntly. "They were pissed because I sat in the wrong seat at brunch, never mind the rest of it. Apparently at thirty-one I can still be 'defiant.'"

Carter leaned back against the painted cinderblock walls of his assigned room. "Yeah, well, at this late date you're not likely to change them. Thankfully it's only three weeks until opening day. Can you hold out that long?"

Ty sighed. "I don't know, Carter. I might just need to run away from home. You know, at thirty-one. Leave the cats, leave my job, and come pout on the beach until you come find me."

"Why do I get the impression that you wouldn't make it easy for me, either?" Carter chuckled.

"Are you kidding me? I haven't been on a beach since, um, hoo boy. Junior year of undergrad? Must be. Yeah, I mean I did an externship with a firm in San Juan the summer between first and second year of law school, but there wasn't a lot of time to go to the beach then."

Carter gaped for a moment. "And that's why you speak Spanish."

"Actually, I double majored. But yeah, I speak it. I'm not holding a grudge against your coach or anything." He took a deep breath. "Anyway, when I get to that beach you can bring me a daiquiri or something, because I took another pregnancy test and I failed it."

Carter licked his lips. He could hear the frayed sound of Ty's voice, even though he was doing his best to sound strong. If he was in New York, he could just get a cab over to Ty's place and hold him for a while. He could try to show his support without trying to come up with words when no words could ever really do the trick. Instead he was all the way in Florida, where he could be about as useful as a frog on the Space Shuttle.

"Okay. Okay, first of all, sweetheart, you didn't fail. It feels like it, especially to a genius like you who's never actually failed a test, but that's not how it works. No one has worked out the timing on omega fertility. We just don't know. But we haven't been trying for very long, and it's okay if we have to keep trying for a while. At least, it's okay with me." He made himself smile. He didn't have to work very hard, because he wasn't lying here. "I'll be the first to admit to how much I enjoy the trying."

Ty scoffed, but when he spoke he sounded more shy than scornful. "You can't really mean that."

"Oh, but I do. I'm not a kinky guy, Ty. I don't need a lot of bells and whistles and weird accessories and all that. I like being with you. I have fun with you in bed, and I have fun with you out of bed. I'm looking forward to seeing you. Not fulfilling my side of the bargain, but seeing you and spending time with you. And yeah, I want to give you a baby because you want a baby, but I get it might not happen right away, and I don't mind one bit."

Ty took a deep breath. "I don't want to make you do anything. I know there are plenty of younger guys out there, livelier guys or whatever—"

"So? Maybe I would have noticed them before we got married. I don't now. I'm telling you, Ty, I like you. It's silly to tell you to calm down about making a baby. It's something you want, something you've wanted for years, and you're pretty worried about it. But Ty, we'll get there. We've got three years, and we have the option to revisit that agreement. Okay? I'm not in a rush to cut you loose."

Part of Carter felt like he was talking to a frightened animal. The rest of him felt like he was standing in an airplane doorway. He had his chute on, and he was pretty sure it would work, but he wasn't ready to jump. Not yet.

Ty was silent for a good thirty seconds on the other end of the line. Carter knew he hadn't hung up, because he could hear the cats mewling. When Ty did speak, he sounded a little more solid, a little less on the edge of a breakdown. "I don't want you to feel pressured, Carter."

"I don't. I'm good. I'll let you know if that changes, I promise."

He could hear the little smile in Ty's voice. He could almost see it, if he closed his eyes and relaxed enough. "Thanks, Carter. I sometimes wonder how it's possible for you to be real. You're amazing, you know that?"

Carter snorted. "I booted the ball like six times today in our split squad game."

"I know. I recorded it and watched it to cheer myself up."

Carter smiled so hard his face hurt. "Was that the first baseball game you ever watched?"

"Maybe...okay, yes. But it won't be the last. I promise."

"That's probably the sweetest thing anyone's said to me." Carter wondered if he could explode from pride.

They finished their call with some basic small talk and hung up. It was late, and Carter was tired. Working out in the off season wasn't the same thing as playing a game, even an early split-squad game when he got pulled in the sixth inning so Tracy could see what an eighteen year old kid could do.

He heard from Ty a few more times that week, which wasn't unexpected. He also heard from Keegan on Wednesday, which was less expected. "Dude. We gotta talk." Keegan sounded like he was hiding in a bar bathroom or something, which considering that it was Keegan might actually be the case.

Carter closed his eyes. Whatever it was that had Keegan calling him was probably important. "Hey, Keegan. What's going on?"

"Well, I guess my first question needs to be, 'what are your intentions with my brother?' Because I'm not really sure right now. I thought I knew, but I can't say I do now, and as his big brother I kind of do need to have the answer."

"Are you drunk right now?"

"I've had like three martinis. I'm fine."

Carter looked up at the ceiling. He'd had nothing but water since he got here. "Okay," he said, and tried to keep his temper in check. "I like him more than I thought I would. I like him a lot, actually. It's a little ass-backwards considering that we're already married, but I'd say we're still in the getting-to-know-you stage. That said, I'm not seeing anyone else, I'm not looking to see anyone else, I'm faithful—"

"Yeah, whatever. I didn't ask about that. I asked about your intentions."

Carter touched his lucky jersey, which was hanging out of his laundry hamper. Maybe it would give him strength. "Spend more time with him? Back him up when he needs it? Give him what he wants—the baby, whatever? Be a decent husband?"

Keegan let out a little sigh. Carter couldn't tell if it was a sigh of relief or frustration. "So Seb's been coming around. A lot."

Carter fought down a wave of jealousy. If he punched the wall he'd have to explain his broken hand to the media, then he'd die of shame, and that would just be bad all around. "He's pestering Ty?"

"Not for the most part. He stopped by Ty's office once, Ty chased him off, that was the end of it. He tried to get friendly with me, like, three or four times."

"Dude, no, he hates you." Carter covered his mouth. "I'm sorry, it's been a long day—"

"Don't apologize, bro. It's demeaning. Besides, it's true. The dude's looked down his nose at me for decades, just because I never wore an ascot and didn't prance around with my nose in the air. He can take his decorum and his protocol and shove them up his—"

"Anyway, you said he's been coming around?" Carter had to wonder just where Keegan was going with all of this, if he had to down three martinis just to bring it up.

"Right. He's been getting all buddy-buddy with me. I send him packing, so he goes and hangs around with my dads. And let me tell you, he's finding a much more receptive audience with them." Keegan sniffed, loudly. "You know what he wants."

“He wants Ty back.” Carter scratched his head. “Why? Don’t get me wrong, I think Ty’s pretty much perfect, but Seb there showed loud and clear that he does not share my opinion.”

“Exactly. And come on, bro. Perfect? He’s my brother, and even I wouldn’t go that far. But, anyway. I was wondering to myself, ‘Self? Why would your little brother’s asshole ex, who broke his heart into a million pieces, start sniffing around again? Is he just a sadist or does he have a deeper motive?’”

Maybe Keegan wasn’t as drunk as Carter thought. “I’m back from Spring Training on April second. My game should be done at around five. I can get away with bringing a bat home. Tell me where he lives, and I’ll go take care of the problem.”

“Dude. No. You’d be the first suspect, and you don’t want to go out like that for a guy like him. Okay? We play this smart or we don’t play it at all. Besides, I want to know what’s really going on here. I don’t get the impression that he’s gotten any better with age. Not at all.”

“No.” Carter shook his head, even though Keegan couldn’t see him. “He was talking about a promotion at work and said his husband died.”

“That’s a perfect place for me to start, bro. And thanks. You told me all I needed to know about your intentions with my brother.”

“I did?” Carter scratched his stubbly chin.

“Yeah. When I suggested he might want to hurt Ty, you were ready to go beat him down almost as soon as you got off the plane. You’re a good man, Carter. A good alpha.” The line went dead.

Carter stared at his phone for a moment. Keegan was one weird guy.

And, of course, because the universe just worked that way, someone knocked on his door just then. "Lights out was twenty minutes ago, Bowman." Great. It was Tracy, and he was in a mood.

Carter got up to answer the door. "Sorry, Coach. Family call."

"Your actual family, or that pack of freaks you married into?" Tracy crossed his arms over his chest and scowled.

Carter opened his mouth to object. He shouldn't let anyone talk about Ty's family that way. The only problem was that Tracy was right. "Er, the latter. Come on in."

"Look. I get that new marriages carry a lot of drama," Tracy said, letting Carter pull him into the room. "I do. Especially the first, because everything's so new and delicate, and you just don't know all the rules yet. But if I let you sit there and talk to your honey man all night then I have to let Oscar talk to his wife all night, and then he winds up beaning six guys and it's all on me. Okay?"

"Er, Oscar's the catcher, Tracy. And it wasn't Ty I was talking to." Carter explained the situation with Seb, Keegan, Ty, and the parents as best he could without getting too wordy. Tracy couldn't tolerate unnecessary words. He claimed they gave him heartburn.

"Oh. Okay. That's...still not a reason for you to have your lights on. Holy crap, Carter, I don't care. The guy's got an ex who wants him back? Great! That means you don't have to stay married to him!" Tracy threw his hands up into the air.

"Tracy, this guy's bad news. For one thing, Ty doesn't want to be married to this guy. For another, if his brother's calling me up three sheets to the wind to make sure I'm ready to protect Ty from this guy, he's probably not someone to whose tender mercies I should be abandoning Ty."

"Ugh." Tracy rolled his eyes back into his head. "Fine, okay. Do you really want to get into this crap? Because it sounds like drama. You've got enough to worry about during the season without having to worry about whether or not some creeper is trying to chat up the guy you don't want anyway."

Carter ground his teeth. "It's not that I don't want him, Tracy. I do. Okay? I like him. And I wouldn't want to abandon anyone to this guy. Something about him is really making me uncomfortable. Ty's parents were desperate for him to marry Seb all those years ago. They've barely spoken to each other since the breakup—him and his parents, I mean. Now that I'm here, Seb's all buttering up the parents again. Do you see where I'm going with this?"

Tracy pouted. He actually pouted. Then he scowled. "Didn't you say his husband died?"

"Yeah. Yeah, he said the guy died about a year ago."

Tracy's scowl deepened. "So, we've got these scouts. Some of them are a little bored right now—the guys we had them watching washed out. Note your lack of a roommate."

"I've been noticing that, Tracy."

"Well, part of what they do is look into a guy's background. I can't promise they'll find anything. There probably isn't anything to find. But if there is, they'll find it for you, or at least they'll give you a good starting point. They're pretty good. They're the ones who found out that pitcher was actually ten years older than he said he was."

"I remember that. Okay." Carter rolled his shoulders. "Thanks, Tracy. That's a load off of my mind."

Tracy grinned at him, and then he pretended to scowl. "Well, you know, we can't have you thinking about that kind of thing when you're supposed to be playing. It affects performance, you know. I don't like this whole contract marriage thing, but we're friends, and if you're worried about it I'm going to help you." He patted Carter's shoulder. "Lights out, buddy. I'll see you in the morning."

Chapter Seven

Ty shook the FBI agent's hand. "Thanks for all your hard work, Agent Duffy. I really do appreciate everything you've done to try to make this all go so much more smoothly."

Duffy, an older agent who could have doubled as a funeral director, looked surprised. "I don't get many attorneys for estates under investigation thanking me, Mr. Cunningham."

Ty huffed out a little laugh. "Trust me, Agent. My firm is just as outraged by the senior Mr. Delaney's activities as you are, and his son is. We all want to make sure that any illegal activity is thoroughly investigated and pruned from whatever is transmitted to his son. That way the younger Delaneys and their growing family can start their married lives with a clean slate."

"I can respect that." Duffy grinned. "Hopefully the next time we meet it will be under equally benign circumstances."

"I hope so too, Agent. I really do." He let his gaze fall to the calendar. Only a few more days until April 2, opening day at the stadium. He had a ticket to the game, ready and waiting in his nightstand drawer where the cats couldn't run off with it. "I can't think of an estate case that involved law enforcement that didn't wind up going to court but it's absolutely something I could get used to."

Agent Duffy agreed and headed out, and Ty wrote up his meeting notes for the record and for his final message to Sol Delaney. Delaney had been remarkably nonchalant about what happened to his father's estate, which only made sense. He'd been frank about how the senior Delaney had tried to use his money like a leash, and how it had backfired. It was nice to have, sure, but Sol didn't *need* it.

Ty could relate.

Somewhere in the back of his head, he concocted an elaborate fantasy. He, Carter, and the Delaneys would build a friendship together. It wasn't like they didn't have anything in common, after all. They'd get together for fun dinner parties, and to let their children run amok and play.

He didn't reach out. Sol's husband, Alex Cary, had gone through a terrible ordeal. He was pregnant again, but he probably wouldn't want to be associated with anything that reminded him of what he'd gone through. Ty worked for the same law firm that represented one of his attackers, for crying out loud. Besides, the only one they'd have any interest in was Carter, and they could speak to him at the Hellion Club.

Ty didn't have a lot to offer. He refused to use Carter as a crowbar to find him friendships. It would only make things worse when Carter left. He might say he was open to renegotiating their agreement when their term came to an end, but Ty wasn't going to count on it.

He looked through his list of active projects. The Delaney case had taken up a lot of his time, thanks to the intricate nature of the estate and the investigation into it. He still had the Bencivenni case on his plate. He'd managed to offload a lot of the leg work to junior attorneys, but he still had the trial coming up. He should probably get to work on that, if he wanted to keep the poor client out of prison. There was no doubt that she'd killed her husband, but Ty was holding out for getting her acquitted as a battered spouse.

It was risky. Juries didn't often accept abuse as a reason to justify homicide, and of course the victim's job at the consulate complicated things further. Ty figured they had nothing to lose by going for it. The DA wasn't offering any kind of plea deal, apparently at the request of the Italian ambassador. And Mrs. Bencivenni had plenty of evidence to back up her claims.

He settled in to review the case notes and lost himself in the details. People liked to claim he was a workaholic. Worse, they said he turned to work to fill up an empty and unfulfilled life. Ty loved what he did, and that was all there was to it. The younger brother in him loved knowing the rules so well he knew exactly how to get what he wanted from them. The good man in him loved finding a way to make things right. And the child in him, who'd always been less than adored, liked being able to look around and know he'd been successful on his own, without reference to his family.

The lights in his office came on automatically, when the ambient light outside decreased enough to make it necessary. He didn't notice, he was so immersed in his associates' findings. He didn't look up until a familiar voice cleared its throat from the doorway.

He narrowed his eyes and frowned up at Seb. "How did you get in here?"

Seb should have been put off by his scowl, and his prickly attitude. Instead he just smiled and strode right in. He threw his trench coat over the back of one of the chairs across from Ty's desk and sprawled in the other one, like he was at home here. "Some young kid let me in. Probably a first year, or maybe even an intern. Who knows? It doesn't matter. What does matter is that it's seven o'clock and you're still sitting here with your face in a file like you're a new employee trying to make a good impression. That so-called husband of yours isn't doing you much good if he can't make you take care of yourself."

"He's away." Ty pursed his lips at his ex. "Working." He lifted his folder, just a little bit. "You may be familiar with it?"

"Sweetheart, I'm an investment banker and even I've left the office for the day. Come on. I'll buy you dinner."

"I'm fine."

Seb jumped up, knuckles on the desk. “I told you to come out for dinner, damn it. I’m being nice, here.”

Ty rolled his eyes. He didn’t want to knuckle under and just do whatever Seb wanted. He also knew he was alone here, and he didn’t want to get Seb more worked up than he had to. Ty was no brawler. He heaved a mighty sigh, hoping against hope that Seb would get his subtle hint and leave him alone. “Fine. We’ll go to the Italian place in the lobby.”

“Wrong. There’s an Indian place halfway between here and your place.” Seb put his coat back on. “We’ll go there.”

Ty made a face, but he texted his brother. “What are you doing?” Seb crossed around the desk. “Who are you texting?”

“Keegan. I usually let him know when I’m doing something outside my usual pattern. It’s a safety thing.” Ty said the first thing that popped into his head. It was a lie, he pretty much never initiated conversations with Keegan, but he had to do something. Someone needed to know what was going on here.

“I guess that’s fine. If you were really married, of course, your husband would be taking care of you and you wouldn’t need to update Keegan.”

Ty put his laptop and his files into his briefcase. “And I’m sure you were always home when you were married? You never traveled?”

Seb’s face darkened with rage, but it passed. “That was different. I wasn’t faking my marriage to Niall.”

“Of course.” Ty meekly let Seb escort him from the office.

They walked up Park Ave together, heading toward Ty’s apartment. They didn’t speak. New York streets were loud streets, and Ty had nothing to say to Seb anyway. They weren’t friends, they weren't going to be friends, and Ty would rather be anywhere but talking to his loathsome ex. If Seb had something to say, he could come out with it and go home. It wasn't on Ty to draw it out of him.

Ty knew the Indian restaurant Seb meant, of course. He headed inside when Seb grunted and held the door for him. Had their relationship been like this when they'd been together? Ty didn't remember it that way, but he also hadn't known to expect better. Lord, he'd been a fool.

The host seated them and brought them menus, but Seb didn't need them. He ordered them wine, as well. Ty tried to decline, but Seb just ignored him as he ordered food for both of them. Ty tried to interrupt, but Seb kicked him under the table while talking smoothly with a self-assured smile on his face. When the waiter went away, he turned to Ty with a scowl on his face. "What the hell is wrong with you? You know better than to interrupt me when I'm speaking!"

Ty scowled at him. They weren't in an isolated and empty office anymore. "You were ordering for me, without even asking what I wanted. And I was telling you I'm not drinking."

"Yes, you are drinking. Don't be a drama queen, Ty. No one wants a drama queen omega, especially not one who's over the hill. And an alpha always orders for the omega. It's romantic."

"Believe it or not, it is legal for an omega to speak in public. I should know, I have a degree in this stuff." Ty glowered at him. "And even if that were a romantic gesture, which it is not, it wouldn't be appropriate for us because there's nothing romantic between us. I'm a married man. You're a widower who's not my husband. It's not appropriate. So don't do it."

Seb scoffed. "Your marriage is a sham and everyone knows it. I'm a member of the Hellion Club too, remember? Do you think I don't know about Bowman's financial problems? Do you think I'm not a hundred percent aware that you paid his membership fees this year?"

"So what? I didn't marry him for his money because I didn't need to marry him for his money." Ty made a show of examining his fingernails. It was an arrogant gesture, one he'd learned from Seb. It was also an excellent way to avoid having to meet Seb's eyes. "That doesn't make our marriage any less valid, or legally binding, or any of your goddamn business." Strengthened by his own words, he looked up and plastered a huge grin onto his face.

"Of course it's my business. We all know I'm your real alpha." Seb curled his lip. "This guy? He's nothing. He's no one! He's just some guy who lucked out in sports. His parents grow corn. That's exactly what they do. They're corn farmers, Ty. They dig in the dirt, they spread shit onto the dirt, and then they grow corn in it."

Ty sipped from his water. "So what? He's not asking me to become a corn farmer, and that's about the extent of my involvement. And if you want to turn up your nose at corn farming I'd recommend divesting from anything that depends on livestock, anything involving plastics, babies, or consumer goods like deodorant. Also popcorn."

Seb snorted. "I can use those products without tying myself to the producers, Ty. This is why you need to leave decisions about this kind of thing to alphas. We've got a much better head for dynastic considerations. You omegas would just breed with whoever suited your fancy at the time." He reached out and took Ty's hand. "You're very lucky I'm willing to be so understanding."

Ty yanked his hand back. "No touching." He put it down in exasperation. "Why did you drag me out here tonight, Seb? You know there's nothing between us. Even if I weren't married, there wouldn't be anything between us. I've never been the kind of guy who takes people back."

"Well, you should have been more accommodating at the time. I was always ready to marry you, Ty. You just couldn't compromise."

"You were demanding I give up my career so I could go and be a decorative plant in London. That's not a compromise. That's not even... you didn't even want *me*. You wanted an omega, and I was good enough to fit the bill. What I wanted, and what I needed, didn't make a bit of difference to you."

Seb rolled his eyes so theatrically he might have been on stage. "We knew what was best for you, Ty. You only thought you wanted to be some lawyer. And look at you. Still single all these years later."

"Married, actually." Ty wondered if he'd lost his voice, or if he was speaking in a register no one else could hear, when Keegan strode through the door.

His shirt was made of silk. It was silk, covered in a pig print. He wore it over hunter orange shorts.

Keegan walked right up to their table, which was a table for two. The lack of seating options didn't bother him. He grabbed a chair from another table, turned it around, and straddled it. "Ty! Little bro! Thanks for letting me know where you were. I'd have been pissed if I showed up for our dinner tonight and you were nowhere to be found, man." He swiveled his head, in slow motion, to give Seb the most disdainful look Ty had ever seen. "Sebastian."

"Keegan. Did you find that shirt in a thrift shop?"

"Nope. Stole it off your mom when I was leaving her house this morning." The waiter chose that moment to show up with the wine. Keegan grabbed Ty's glass and downed it in one gulp, then refilled it with the bottle the waiter still held. "Thanks, bro. You're a lifesaver. I'll have the samosas and an order of the lamb vindaloo. Thanks, my man." He turned back to Seb, who didn't even bother to hide his disgust.

"You're completely off your gourd." He picked up his glass and held it as far away from Keegan as he could, all but hunching around it. "What is wrong with you? Can't you see I'm trying to have a date here?"

"Well, bro, you might be trying to have a date, but Ty here, he's not trying to have a date." Keegan burped. "He's married, you perv. He's got a super hot sports star coming home to him in a few days and he doesn't want a dried up old frog like you hanging around stinking up the place."

Seb went red, and then he went white. "Ty, I'm afraid I'm going to have to cut our evening short. We can get together again sometime soon, when this ape isn't around to interfere." He stormed out of the restaurant in a huff.

Keegan straightened up, put his purloined chair back, and took Seb's seat across from Ty. "So that was exciting. How come you went out with him?"

Ty slumped where he was. "He showed up at work. I was alone in the office. When I said no, he got aggressive and I didn't want to push him further. I just..." He sighed. "I felt unsafe, so I texted you and agreed to go someplace public."

"Smart. Very smart." He pursed his lips and stared at the closed door. "Something about this stinks. As amazing as you are, little bro, I can't make myself believe he suddenly wants you back."

Ty scoffed. "You think?" He relayed his brief conversation with Seb to his brother. "It does stink. I can't trust any of it, and I don't want to. I like Carter."

"Well, I mean he's not really here for the long term."

"I know." Ty tried to pretend it didn't hurt to admit that. "It's fine, it is. But he's... if I can't have a guy like Carter, who treats me the way Carter treats me, I'd rather be alone. And Seb?"

"He's not capable of it. But there's a reason he's sniffing around, and I want to know what it is." Keegan scratched at his chin. "Well, we'll find out. In the meantime, samosas. Never underestimate the value of a good samosa, little bro."

Ty chuckled. Leave it to Keegan to salvage something from the night.

***

Carter stretched and smiled as he woke up. He'd almost forgotten where he was. He hadn't forgotten opening day in the stadium, of course. No one could forget that. It was the greatest day of an athlete's life. Everyone got to have opening day, the first day of a new season when every team started with the same even record. Not everyone got to start a new season with the most venerable, most renowned franchise in all of baseball.

No, Carter had come close to forgetting where he'd finished his night. He'd found a car waiting for him at the stadium after the game. Ty sat in the back of the car, waiting for him, with a huge smile on his face. "I watched the game," he said, with two spots of color in his pale face. It would have been his first time in a baseball stadium. "I had no idea what was going on, but I saw your home runs."

The car took them back to Park Ave, and to Ty's apartment. Ty had a nice little feast laid out for him, all set up perfectly in line with the team nutritionist's plans for Carter. Then he'd taken Carter back into the bedroom, shut the cats out, and shown him just how glad he was to have Carter home again.

Carter thought he could be forgiven for forgetting where he was, or for thinking it might have been a dream. It felt too good to be true. Ty lay in his arms, still sleeping peacefully. Two of the cats slept on top of him, while Amun swatted at Carter for daring to move and disturb his nap.

Ty must have felt Carter move, because his eyes fluttered open. "Good morning, sunshine."

Carter glowed. Today was an off day. He could spend the whole day with his amazing husband, if he wanted to. If Ty wanted to. "Hey there. I missed you when I was gone."

Ty blushed. "Did you really?"

Carter grabbed Ty's hand and kissed the knuckles. "As a matter of fact, I did. I know it's kind of weird, since I haven't known you long, but I really did miss you. You're nice to have around." He had to move carefully, so he didn't earn himself another scolding from Amun, but he wanted to make his point to Ty. "What've you got on tap for today?"

"I've got plenty of work I could be doing." Ty looked down, and then he looked up and met Carter's eyes. "But my husband's been away for six weeks. Think I'm allowed to take some time to wallow in having him back."

Carter laughed with delight. "Are you really going to blow off work to hang around with me?"

"I wouldn't call it blowing off work. I'd call it prioritizing my time. I've missed you too, you know." Ty's pink tongue darted out over his lips, and he blushed a little. "Like you said, we haven't known each other all that long. And I get that you're going to be traveling, for however long we're together. I accept that. But there was definitely something missing when you were gone, Carter."

Ty's phone buzzed, and he groaned. His cats hopped off of him, mewling angrily, as he rolled over to grab it. "It's my parents," he explained. "If I don't answer it, they'll just keep calling."

Carter raised his eyebrows as Ty answered. Ty didn't have a great relationship with his parents, so why would they call?

"Hello? Yeah. Really? I'm not sure what he has planned."

Okay, that didn't sound good. Ty sounded about as enthusiastic about whatever was going on as Carter would be about going to any bar in Boston on a road trip.

Ty muted his phone. "My parents want us to meet them for brunch. They say they invited Keegan, but I'll text him to make sure he's coming. Are you okay with this? If you're not, just say the word and I'll tell them to go to Hell."

Carter shifted Amun so he could sit up and still keep the cat warm and coddled. "On the one hand, you don't seem very comfortable with this. On the other, I definitely want to support you. And I remember how upset you were the last time you had to deal with your folks, so you know what? I'm here for it."

Ty's face softened. "You're amazing, you know that?" He unmuted his phone. "Fine. We'll be there. "

Carter would have thought there wouldn't be time for any fooling around before brunch, but Ty surprised him with a blow job in the shower. Afterwards, they got dressed in uncomfortably stiff clothes with ties and headed out to the elder Cunninghams' residence via Lyft.

Beau and Ed Cunningham lived in a huge old brownstone mansion over near the Natural History Museum. Most of these old places had been cut up for apartments years ago, but not this one. "You grew up here?" Carter whispered as they got out of their Lyft.

"Sort of. It's where I came back to on school vacations." Ty made a wry face. "If I couldn't avoid it, that is." He stopped and took Carter's hand. "We don't have to do this."

Carter hesitated. "Are you ashamed of me?"

Ty's eyes bulged. He looked like he was choking. "Are you insane? No. No, I'm not ashamed of you. I'm kind of ashamed of the way we got together, but you're amazing. You treat me like a prince and I'm proud to be your husband, however long we're together."

Carter hadn't wanted to be reminded of the temporary nature of their relationship, but he didn't think Ty meant it as harmful. If anything, Ty seemed to be feeling self-deprecating about it. "Hey." Carter squeezed his hand. "We're together for as long as you want to be, okay? If you're not ashamed of me, then why do you keep offering not to do this?"

Ty took a deep breath. "Because it's going to be terrible. They're terrible snobs. They look down their noses at anyone who doesn't come from money, going back generations." He licked his lips. "It's not that I'm ashamed, not at all. Not of you, anyway." He huffed out a little laugh and looked over at the window.

A curtain rustled. Were Ty's parents watching them? Good Lord. Carter kissed Ty's cheek. "We'll get it over with, and then we'll go home. Okay?"

Ty rolled his shoulders, trying to loosen up. "Okay. Good. Sounds good."

They walked up to the door, which a maid in a gray dress opened before they could ring the bell. She escorted them into a beautiful, opulent living room - Carter supposed people like this called it a parlor - and directed them to a couch that might have doubled as a torture device.

"It's an antique," Ty whispered. "They weren't big on comfort in the Victorian era."

"I guess not." Carter laughed and put his arm around Ty. He could feel the tension in his husband, and wished he could do something to soothe it away.

The maid returned with a silver tray bearing flutes of champagne, which both men took. Keegan showed up moments later. Carter had to admire his timing. He couldn't make himself admire Keegan's lime-green dress pants.

Keegan sniffed deeply when he walked into the parlor. "I love the smell of a set-up on a Sunday morning," he said, a nasty grin crossing his face. "It smells like drama. My favorite."

Ty couldn't hide his smile, although he seemed to be trying to give Keegan a disapproving look. "That's because it's not at your expense, Keegan."

"True. It gives me a certain freedom, doesn't it?" He waggled his golden eyebrows and turned to Carter. "Carter, my man! Two home runs yesterday, can't beat that! Keep it up and you'll go to the Hall for sure!"

Carter chuckled and shook his head. "I'm way too young to be talking about that. I've got a lot of baseball in me yet, assuming I don't get hurt or anything like that. Let's not jinx it, okay?"

Heavy footsteps interrupted their conversation. All three of the men turned to face the newcomers to the room. Carter recognized Ed Cunningham, although they'd never been introduced. He wasn't all that tall, but his broad shoulders and muscular stature screamed alpha. So did the way he carried himself, with his shoulders back and his head held high. His clothes screamed money. His hair was just long enough to look rakish, and it was a lovely shade of steel gray.

The man beside him, short and tan with big brown eyes, could only be his husband, Beau. His smile looked about as fake as a three dollar bill, but he moved with grace.

Carter already knew the third member of the party. He'd have been annoyed about his presence, but both Ty and Keegan looked just as shocked to see Sebastian Britton there as Carter. What kind of game were the Cunninghams playing? They knew Ty was married.

"So you're the alpha who decided to marry my son." Ed stepped forward, eyes and mouth flat. "It's interesting that you seem to be going about all of this ass-backwards, don't you think?"

Ty jumped in between Carter and his father. "Oh my God, Dad, were you raised in a barn?"

"You watch yourself, Tyler." Beau's words came out in a rarified Southern drawl, but Ty flinched just as much as if he'd snapped them out. "You know better than to cross your father. He's the alpha and you will treat him accordingly. What will potential suitors think?"

Carter cleared his throat and stepped forward. He could see the satisfaction in Sebastian's curled lip, and it was going to take everything in him not to punch it right off. "Hi. I'm Carter Bowman. I'm Ty's husband. He doesn't care what suitors think, because he's married. And as his husband, I can tell you that some alphas have no problems with omegas who have opinions of their own."

Keegan snickered. "I told you I smelled drama." He stepped in between Carter and Ty and the rest of the family. "Do I smell brunch? I'm pretty sure I smell brunch. How about if we go and sit down and pretend we're civilized adults who know how to behave around other human beings, hm?" He threw his arm around Sebastian with an audible smack that echoed from the walls and guided him into another room.

Carter gripped Ty's hand. "I think I see what you meant," he whispered.

Ty swallowed and squeezed back. "We'll make it through somehow."

The next room proved to be the dining room. The last time Carter had seen a dining room this opulent, he'd been watching a documentary about Versailles. He froze for a moment. He had no idea where to go or what to do, and who needed a sixteen-piece place setting for brunch anyway?

Beau sneered at him. "You'll be sitting next to Keegan over here." He indicated a chair on one side of the table. "Tyler, you're between me and Sebastian."

"Like hell." Keegan shook his head. He still had his hand on Sebastian's back. Now he jerked Sebastian over to the seat beside his own and plunked him down like a rag doll. "Seb here can sit next to me. We've got so much catching up to do, after that little misunderstanding about dinner. Don't we, Seb?" He squeezed the back of Sebastian's neck.

Carter took the opportunity to take the seat that had been previously assigned to Sebastian. He thought he knew what was going on here. He understood that Ed and Beau would rather that Ty marry someone who was like them, but he hadn't. It hadn't even been his fault. Now that Ty had gotten married, seven years later, couldn't they give up the ghost?

And why would Seb be party to their scheme?

He locked his and Ty's ankles together under the table. It might not be visible, but he could give Ty some support this way.

Beau flushed bright red. "The seating layout has been set for a reason, Keegan," he said through gritted teeth.

"Don't I know it, Dad." Keegan gave his father a thin smile. "So, Carter, why don't you tell us about Spring Training? How did that go?"

Carter saw both parents' eyes glaze over. Neither of them were sports fans. Keegan was just trying to change the subject. He could play his part, though, as this poor woman in gray served out the food. He spoke about dealing with the younger players, trying to set a good example and guide them through the process.

That might not have been the best way to showcase himself as a responsible young man who could be a good mate for their son. Sebastian pounced on the opportunity. "Are you really the best person to guide new players? You certainly can't teach them how to manage their money. It took you how long to lose everything?" He chortled, as though someone being wiped out by a con artist was the funniest thing he'd heard all day.

It was Sebastian. Maybe it was the funniest thing he'd heard all day.

"Yes," Ed purred, while Carter tried to get hold of his temper. "I'll admit to having some concerns on that end myself. Sebastian here is an investment banker. He just published an article about the warning signs with that fraudster and honestly, anyone should have been able to see that coming. Anyone, that is, who knows the first thing about finance."

Ty put his fork down. "That's very interesting. Of course, if anyone should have been able to see that coming, and didn't alert the proper authorities, one could argue they're guilty of a crime."

Keegan snickered.

Sebastian reached across the table and patted Ty's hand. "It's cute when you try to play lawyer, sweetheart, but it's not going to work here. I know the law pretty well when it comes to financial matters."

"Hm. You do know that I've successfully defended six fraud cases that went to court. And I've successfully sued twenty-five fraudsters for significant damages in similar cases." Ty's eyes lit up, but otherwise there was no outward sign of his enthusiasm. "I've won quite a bit of money for my clients on these cases, but I'll of course bow to your superior expertise." One corner of his mouth twitched upward. "You're with Allemani Bank, aren't you?"

Beau swatted him on the arm. "Hush, Tyler. He's an alpha. Omegas aren't here to show off and contradict, they're here to be pretty and make their alphas feel good."

Carter's stomach turned. "So yes," he said, to divert attention away from Ty. "I did get taken for a ride by a con artist. I'm recovering, thanks to a good contract, and I think it's good for young players to know what to look out for. I'd rather they learn from my mistakes than their own, wouldn't you?"

"Hm!" Beau sniffed and turned his attention to his quiche.

Ty leaned a little closer to Carter. Carter let him. It was going to be a long afternoon.

Chapter Eight

Getting used to the rhythm of baseball season was different from getting used to Spring Training. In most ways, it was easier. Carter was around more, and having him around made Ty's life better by several orders of magnitude. On the other hand, the times when Carter did have to travel or had too much to do to make it over to Ty's place, the loneliness hurt more than it had before, when Ty was just lonely all the time and he didn't know the difference.

Those were the times of Ty's greatest insecurity. Carter could have anyone he wanted, and Ty knew it. Why would he be with Ty, if not for the contract? He said he was willing to stick around, and he even played along, but Ty couldn't shake the nagging question of *why*. Why him? What exactly did he have to offer?

When Carter was around it was different. Ty could relax. He never felt insecure when Carter was right there in front of him.

They still lived separately, and that was what they'd agreed to in their contract. Ty hadn't been over to Carter's place. Sometimes he thought Carter was ashamed of him. Sometimes he thought Carter was just choosing the easier option, since it wasn't as though they had a lot of free time to go from place to place. Sometimes Ty figured Carter just wanted to hang out with the cats.

At work, life went on pretty much the way it always did. Ty worked hard and did the best he could for his clients. The firm had spent a lot of time and energy prepping for the Bencivenni case, but when the trial finally happened it took all of a week and a half. It started the week after Opening Day. The prosecutor got up and gave an impassioned speech about the rule of law, due process, and about all of the good the deceased had done in his community. He emphasized the good the deceased had done to advance women.

Ty got up and described his client's life with her husband. He described her hospital visits, incidents of abuse people had witnessed, long-term effects of abuse people had not necessarily witnessed, and her behavior after the incident. He showed images of her face immediately after the shooting, with all of its bruises.

The trial only took a week and a half because of the overwhelming amount of evidence Ty brought to the table. The jury took three hours to acquit. Ty's client, Mrs. Bencivenni, broke down in tears beside him at the defense table. He let her cry into his shoulder as the court adjourned. Media had followed the case because of the husband's prominence in the business world. He was acutely conscious of the photos being taken of them, but he tried to shield her. She'd always been a private person, and he hoped to help her keep her privacy as long as he could.

He got a call from Carter after the game that night. Carter was in Detroit for a game, not that he wanted to be in Detroit. Detroit was under a foot of snow at the moment, thanks to the helpful effects of the Great Lakes. They still had to play, though. "I have no idea how they're keeping the field clear, but they're doing it," he groused. "I'm telling you, it's impossible to field the ball when your fingers are frozen stiff."

"I can think of a few ways for you to warm them up, but that's probably not helpful right now." Tyler blushed at his own boldness, but Carter brought it out in him. "Sorry."

"Don't be sorry." Carter spoke quickly, warming Ty right up. "Please. I like it when you're enthusiastic. It makes me feel more confident, okay? I know I'm doing something right." He took a deep breath. "Anyway, I saw on the news that you won your case."

"It made the news out there?" Ty chuckled. "Well, I'll be. Huh."

"Yeah, well, that dirtbag was always being held up as some kind of example of guys who were Doing It Right, you know? Anyway, congratulations. I'm really proud of you."

Ty warmed under his praise. It wasn't like Ty didn't win court cases all the time, but this was Carter. His praise meant more, somehow. "Thanks. I appreciate that. Did I tell you I watched last night's game?"

"No, really? That's awesome. I know baseball isn't really your thing."

"It's getting to be my thing. I'm getting there, I promise." He laughed. "I've got someone to watch now, for one thing. You were totally robbed on that call at second."

"Right?" Carter's voice rose an octave. "That ump has had it out for me for years. I said something knuckle-headed to him when I was a rookie and he's never forgotten it. Never. I guess I made my own bed and I have to lie in it, but it still kind of sticks in my craw a little."

"It would bug me too. I've got a judge like that. The firm transfers me off cases that wind up in his court. It's wrong, his dislike of me shouldn't affect how he rules on cases, but he's also human." Ty shrugged. "We can plan around that, we're a big enough firm."

"I guess." Carter's scowl came through in his voice. "I'd be happy to go over and have a little chat with him, if you wanted."

Ty blushed. "You don't have to. I'm okay. But thanks." He toyed with a piece of paper on his desk. "You're a great alpha, you know that?"

"Me?" Carter laughed weakly. "Not so much."

"No, really. You are. You stick up for me. You make me feel safe, and taken care of." He bit his tongue. He didn't want to say too much. He didn't want to make Carter feel uncomfortable.

It was all true, though. Carter was a fantastic alpha. Ty couldn't remember a time when he felt so safe, so protected. Someone had his back. Someone was willing to stand by him, pick him up and support him when other people wanted to tear him down. Maybe it wasn't real, but it felt real and it would keep being real for the time being.

He tried not to focus on making a baby. He still wanted the baby, of course. He wanted to be a parent as much as he wanted to be a law partner. He just knew it came with a price now. Being a father would mean the inevitable end of his relationship with Carter. Carter was only here to give him the baby, and to provide "respectability" for Ty's single parenting in a deeply conservative field. He didn't particularly want children, or a husband. Once they'd covered their bases with prurient interests, he would leave.

At the same time, when he noticed he was feeling a little seasick in the morning, he couldn't help but feel a little hopeful.

He tried to hold back. He shouldn't get excited. It could just be a sinus infection. He went about his business for the next week, and then the next. He was already living according to early pregnancy protocols, so he didn't have to worry about hurting a baby if he was pregnant. If he delayed taking the test, he could hopefully avoid getting his hopes dashed if he wasn't pregnant.

Two weeks later, his symptoms hadn't gone away. Carter was back in New York, and he'd picked up on Ty's symptoms. It was time for him to take the test. Fortunately, he'd ordered them in bulk online, so he had plenty of them on hand. No reason to arouse pity in the lady who worked at the checkout counter at Duane Reade, after all.

He headed into the master bathroom while Carter sat in the living room with the cats. What was Carter thinking right now? Was he hopeful? Nervous? Worried? Was he hoping for a negative result? Was he hoping for a positive result so this whole long nightmare could be over? Was part of him, at least, hoping for a negative result so they could enjoy their time together a little longer?

The timer beeped, loud in the perfect silence of the bathroom. Ty crept up to the counter to check. Twice before, he'd done this only to have his heart shatter. What if the results were negative again? Would he be able to handle it?

He held his breath and looked at the tiny screen on the dipstick.

Pregnant.

He dropped it. Elation, like electricity, rose up from his feet. His fears about his relationship with Carter disappeared for the moment as all of his dreams came true. This, the little collection of cells coalescing in his belly, was the very thing that had been missing from his life all these years. He'd waited, and he'd hoped, and he'd dreamed. Now it was going to be his. Ty was going to be a father.

He cleaned up from the test and raced out into the living room. The only person he could think of to share his joy with was Carter, and all thoughts of their arrangement vanished from his mind as he flung himself into his husband's arms. "I'm pregnant!"

Carter paled, and his eyes widened. "You're sure?"

Ty nodded. “Those tests are the same ones they use in hospitals. They’re as accurate as accurate can be.”

Carter’s answering smile lit up his whole beautiful face. He pulled Tyler into his lap and kissed him, thoroughly. Ty couldn’t find any evidence of hesitation in his embrace, or his kiss. “I am so freaking happy for you, Ty,” he said when he pulled back. “So happy. We’re going to be fathers! This calls for a celebration.” He paused and looked down for a second. “Wait. Are you up for celebration sex? Or are you too, er, delicate or something?”

Ty laughed and kissed Carter instead of using words. “You don’t know anything about pregnancy, do you?”

“Not a thing. But I’m going to learn.” Carter tugged Ty’s shirt over his head. “I’m going to learn everything I can. And I’m going to be the best damn alpha husband the world has ever seen, Ty.” He picked Ty up in his arms and carried him back to the bedroom. “I want to make sure this is an amazing experience for you, every step of the way.”

Ty threw his arm over Carter’s shoulders and held on for dear life. Carter might be the single most amazing alpha to ever walk the earth. He didn’t really love Ty, but he faked it well. Ty would take it.

He reached for Carter when he put him on the big bed, but Carter stilled him with a kiss. “Hey. This is for you, okay? We’re celebrating you, and your dream. We’ve got all the time in the world for other stuff later.” He grinned and unbuttoned Ty’s pants. Then he pulled them down.

Ty had always been a little shy about his body. Carter chased any of those thoughts away. He parted his legs just a bit, giving Carter access to anything Carter might want. He wanted Carter to see everything, to have access to everything. Carter couldn’t share his joy in pregnancy, but Ty could do his best to make sure he felt something.

"I'm yours, Carter," he told him. "I'm all yours. I just want to make you as happy as you've made me."

Carter's eyes lit up at Ty's words. "Seeing you smile like this? That's what does it for me." He was already taking his clothes off as he spoke. Now he climbed on top of Ty and kissed him. As he kissed him, he dragged his lips down Ty's torso until he got to Ty's lengthening cock.

It wasn't exactly a surprise when Carter took Ty into his mouth. The hunger he showed in it, though, that was a little more shocking. He devoured Ty, sucking him right down to the root like a starving man. Ty could only grab the sheets as desire ratcheted up to need in a few seconds. Carter's mouth was soft and hot, while Ty was so hard now that he ached. He couldn't help but buck his hips a little, although he tried to hold back.

Carter took it all. His little laugh sent the most delightful waves up into Ty's body, and Ty cried out in his pleasure. This was incredible, and there was nothing else in the world but Carter's mouth, the bed, and the pleasure coursing through Ty right now.

He tried to signal to Carter before he came, but Carter kept at it until Ty exploded. He sucked until Ty had gone completely soft, and then he lay down beside Ty and pulled the covers up over them. Ty reached for him, but Carter just pulled him close. "I already finished," he said. "Watching you was the hottest thing ever."

Ty marveled at the amazing man beside him. "I have to be hallucinating you."

"Nope. I'm a hundred percent real, baby. Speaking of babies." He yawned and stretched his free arm. "Who do we want to tell, and when?"

Ty bit his lip. "I'm so excited that I want to tell the world, but I don't like to showboat like that. And I'm not sure we should tell much of anyone until the first sonogram, at least." He squirmed. He hadn't wanted to get into any negatives yet, but the subject had come up. "If there's anything wrong, I don't want to deal with people's pity, you know?"

Carter winced. "I hadn't thought of that, but you're right. We should probably tell Keegan, though. He's trustworthy."

Ty snorted. Keegan was generally about as trustworthy as a hyena, but he was probably viewing through the lenses of a little brother here. "If you want. I don't want to deal with Seb on the subject. He's creeping me out, and I don't think him knowing I'm pregnant will take away from the creep factor."

"Probably not." Carter shuddered. "I'll have to tell Tracy soon. He's my coach, and he's basically the second most important man in my life. I can't not involve him."

"Second?" Ty scratched his head.

Carter looked down at him. "You're the first, Ty. I know we didn't exactly plan for it, and we didn't get together the normal way. But I do care for you. I'm pretty sure I love you. I'll only leave if you want me to leave, Ty."

Ty blinked back tears. "Now I know I'm hallucinating you."

Carter chuckled softly. "Seriously?"

"It doesn't make sense." Ty shook as he spoke. It was all too much. "I love you too, Carter. I didn't expect to be as happy as I am with you. And I still can't quite believe it. But Carter, you've made me happier than I ever thought I could be."

Carter kissed him again, and they drifted off in one another's arms.

***

Pride beyond measure filled Carter when Ty told him the good news. He could feel good, damn good, about the pregnancy. He'd done the job he'd been hired to do, and technically his obligation was finished. More than that, he'd brought an immense degree of joy to his husband. Ty was a good man, a sweet omega who deserved happiness. Carter was proud to be the one to give it to him.

He knew Ty was insecure about their relationship, and there wasn't much he could do about it. He wasn't exactly feeling secure about it himself. They'd come together through odd means, and Ty could be forgiven for having doubts about their staying power. Carter hadn't intended to fall for Ty, but he had anyway. Ty would get it, eventually.

After they'd made love, they dozed in each other's arms for a little while. Carter couldn't stay forever. He had to get up and go to the game. Ty had tickets, of course. He had tickets to every home game, not that he was able to make all of them. Carter hated to leave, but Ty understood.

"The world doesn't stop because we're having a baby," he said with a shy little smile. "Go on ahead. I'll be in the stands tonight, watching."

"You won't be too cold?"

Ty laughed, little golden bells that lifted Carter's soul. "I wasn't last night."

Carter sat up, his mouth a perfect round "o." "You were at the stadium last night?"

"It was Friday, I had a ticket, and all of my cases were in good places to leave off for the night." Ty snuggled up closer to Carter, in contrast to his alleged understanding of Carter's need to leave. "I wanted to see you, even if it was only on screen."

Carter kissed him. "Thank you. It means a lot to me, you know? I know you're learning, and you're enjoying it, but it means a lot that you're learning about baseball for me."

Ty's cheeks turned pink, but he smiled. "You're worth it, Carter."

Carter wasn't a hundred percent sure of that. He was a good baseball player, sure, but he was also the nimrod who'd gotten caught up in a finance scam. Then again, he made Ty happy. That was worth a lot to him.

He got dressed and headed up to the Stadium. He wasn't the first to arrive, but he wasn't the last either. Tracy was paying attention, though, and he did pick up on the fact that Carter showed up later than he typically would. "What's the matter, Bowman, caught in traffic?" he asked, scowling.

Guzman, the shortstop stepped in. "Ah, coach, cut him a little slack, would you? He hasn't even been married for a year yet! He's still got a new husband at home and it ain't like he's late."

Tracy glowered at Guzman. "Yeah, yeah. Okay. Bowman, come see me in my office. Pretty please, oh you adoring groom, you." He rolled his eyes and stalked off toward his office.

Carter followed, a pit growing in his stomach. Was this what Ty felt like? No, the only thing growing in his stomach was joy. No one felt joy going into the coach's office, especially not right before a game. He couldn't get out of it though, and he wouldn't show weakness. He squared his shoulders and went where he was supposed to go, head held high.

He closed the door behind him and sat across from Tracy. "What's up, Coach? Is everything okay?" *Please tell me I'm not about to get traded. I don't think I can handle that right now.*

Tracy must have heard the begging in his mind, because he just scoffed. "Relax, Carter. You have a no trade clause, remember? You're too associated with this team for us to trade you away. No, I wanted to talk to you about the whole marriage thing." Tracy sat back and gave Carter a measuring look. "How are things going in that vein, by the way?"

Carter squirmed. "They're going okay, I guess." His face got hot. "I mean he's pregnant, so from that perspective they're going pretty well. They're going pretty great, actually." He tapped his foot against the ground, an absent-minded tattoo he barely even realized he was doing. He didn't care to talk about details like this with anyone, never mind someone he knew didn't like Ty much. "He's a pretty nice guy, you know? He's sweet. He's cooked for me a couple of times. He doesn't have to, but he called up the nutritionists here and asked what I was supposed to be eating. It was like a case to him. He just... wanted to do it. He wanted to make me happy."

"Huh." Tracy raised his eyebrows. "That guy, that ex of his. Is he still sniffing around?"

"Yeah." Carter bit down on the inside of his cheek. "He ambushed us at his parents' place. You know, they call guys like us rude and unmannered and whatever, but they do crap like invite Ty's ex-boyfriend over to the house for brunch. And don't tell him. And take the ex's side when he's unforgivably rude to the new husband. I don't get it."

"You don't have to get it. You're better off if you don't get it." Tracy made a face. "I did some digging. His parents, man. They're kind of, ah, unique. They shipped both kids off to boarding school when they were real young. I don't think there's much of a relationship there."

"No. There isn't." Carter pursed his lips. "Which is a good thing, really. Someone who desperately wanted Ed and Beau's approval would be difficult to love."

"Probably. Ed's been sued twenty-seven times for shoddy conditions in his rental properties, and his response every time was to jack the rents. The dude's a maggot. But the other guy, this Britton jerk, he makes Ed look like a saint."

Carter licked his lips. He hadn't thought about Sebastian all day. He certainly hadn't been thinking about Sebastian's many flaws, or his father-in-law's issues. It took a lot for Tracy to condemn how a man made his money, so Ed must have been a truly vile individual. And Sebastian was lower than that?

"What does he do?"

"Well, it looks like he was involved with some of the scam sales procedures that got Allemani Bank into so much trouble a few years ago. He got promoted into the job over in England just before the bank got busted for it, so he didn't have to face any consequences." Tracy curled his lip.

Carter mirrored the expression, unconsciously. "Wow. I wonder how many other guys at the bank did the same thing? Got promoted just in time and left the rest of those poor suckers to pick up their slack?"

"Probably a lot of them. Which is why none of my money is at Allemani Bank. I had one old account there and I transferred it yesterday. Not that any other bank is likely to be any better, but still." He took a deep breath. "But what has me worried is that husband of his. The dead one."

"The one he's supposed to still be mourning." Carter leaned forward. Sebastian didn't seem to be grieving at all, but who was he to judge? Maybe their marriage had already started to flounder.

"Yeah, that one. The one they pulled out of the Thames with blood underneath his fingernails."

Carter coughed. "Excuse me? Blood under his nails?"

"Yeah. According to reports at the time, which was only a few months before he came back to the States, the husband was alive when he went into the water. No way to tell if he was conscious, but he absolutely struggled with someone before he went in. And he's obviously dead, so there's that."

"Oh my God." He covered his face with both hands. "You think he had something to do with it."

Tracy smirked. "Well, I can't prove it, and neither could Scotland Yard. The bank promoted him again and brought him back to New York before they could do much to even try."

"Jesus." Carter flopped back into his seat. "I can believe almost anything about that dude, but murder? That's a lot. I mean it could have been anyone. London can be violent, and who knows who might have had a grudge against that asshole. They might have decided to take it out on his husband."

"True. But all the same, that still puts your man in some danger, doesn't it? He's someone in Assy's orbit, and he's someone Assy at least seems to think he's got a relationship with. If he offends someone and that someone decides to lash out at Assy's associates..."

"Then the end result is the same." Carter pinched the bridge of his nose. "I'm not a hundred percent sure what to do here. I can't be here all the time and keep him safe. I have a job to do, and he's not going to let me just lurk around like that."

"No. And neither will your contract. I'm sympathetic, but the front office will say things like 'you can't prove anything ' and 'we have police in this city for a reason' and 'you used baseball resources for what, Tracy?' That won't be helpful." Tracy looked away for a second. "Do you have anyone you can talk to about this? I know your boy's family's about as trustworthy as the average snake, but there has to be someone who cares about him."

Carter snapped his fingers. "He's got Keegan."

"Didn't he show up to your wedding in a fuchsia velour tracksuit?"

"It was supposed to be a proper suit, I think. Just, you know, special." Carter grimaced. "Okay. He's unconventional, but have you met his parents? I don't think he had a choice. He's definitely all in for Ty, though. He stood right up and defended his brother and no one was about to stop him, so there's that."

"Okay." Tracy tapped his pen on the desk. "It's not like we've got a lot of other options, I guess."

"No, we don't. Thanks for chasing this stuff down for me, Tracy. I appreciate it." Carter grinned at his coach. "How exactly do baseball scouts get access to all that dirt, anyway?"

"Ah, now that's a trade secret. But let me tell you, before we signed you, we knew things about you that you probably forgot." He winked at Carter. "Come on, let's get out there and get ready for the game."

Before they headed out, Carter sent Keegan a text. *We need to talk. Can you come to the game with Ty and stick around after?*

Not into threesomes, bro. But I'm more than happy to take in a game.

Carter shook his head at Keegan. The guy made a point of being absurd, every day.

He had a pretty good game out on the field, getting one home run and two doubles and only striking out once. His fielding was pretty spot-on too; he had nothing to complain about on that end. He couldn't see Ty in the crowd. He thought he caught sight of a guy dressed in a neon rainbow tracksuit, but that didn't necessarily mean it was Keegan. Surely, in a city of seven million people (not counting suburbs), Keegan couldn't be the only one who dressed like that.

After the game, Ty and Keegan met up with Carter and Tracy at the employee entrance. Keegan turned out to indeed be the man in the rainbow tracksuit. Ty held a hand up to his eyes between himself and his brother. "That outfit is bad for the baby," he complained.

Carter beamed.

Tracy just rolled his eyes. "You do realize that the baby doesn't even have eyes yet. It doesn't have a brain. It's just a bunch of cells." He turned to look at Carter. "Do they not have basic bio classes at these fancy private schools?"

Ty frowned peevishly at Tracy, while Keegan just guffawed. "You're hilarious, my man." He slung his arm around Tracy's shoulder. "What do you say we all go somewhere a little more private and talk things over?"

Tracy groused, but they all headed over to Keegan's place in Gramercy Park. Tracy even drove them in his huge Mercedes. Keegan's place turned out to be a penthouse in an elegant pre-war building with plenty of exposed brick, and it was nothing like Carter would have expected from Keegan. It was clean. It was almost too clean, with no clutter or messes visible anywhere. There weren't even dirty dishes in the dish drainer.

Keegan offered them all beers, except for his "preggo little bro, 'cause you know that's a no-no."

Carter would have expected Ty to bristle, because it was Keegan and because he didn't like being told he "couldn't" do things. Instead he just beamed, and rested his head on Carter's shoulder. Tracy's face softened at the gesture.

When Tracy explained the information he'd collected about the Brittons, all joy and warm fuzziness fled the air. "That's horrible!" Ty shuddered and folded in on himself. "I don't want to think of Seb as the kind of guy who could just up and kill someone."

"I mean I hate the guy." Keegan sighed and pinched the bridge of his nose. "I've hated him since we were kids, because he's a douche and he's always been a douche. But there's a line between being a douche and drowning his husband, and I don't think I've ever seen him get violent against someone, you know?"

Tracy shrugged. "I only know what the records say, and what the scouts reported back to me. Tyler, you knew him best. Do you think he's capable of violence?"

"Anyone is capable of it, but he never raised a hand to me, no." Ty unconsciously wrapped a hand around his neck and rubbed, just a little. "He could be... he could be really insistent about some things, I guess. I mean he felt pretty strongly. He likes to get his way. When I declined his invitation to dinner a few weeks ago, he stood up, got in my face and started shouting."

"Excuse me?" Carter crossed his arms over his chest.

"I was alone in the office, and I didn't want to piss him off more. So I went along with him to a more public place and texted Keegan to meet us there. Keegan ran him off as only Keegan can." He grinned at his brother with an exasperated smile. "But he was always like that, you know? He wants what he wants, and he's going to get it one way or another." He shrugged. "I hadn't dated an alpha who wasn't like that, until I married Carter."

Carter took his hand. "That doesn't say good things about the guys you've met." He squeezed. "But hey, I'm here now. That's over and done with. We're going to keep you safe from Sebastian, okay? Whether it's him or people who got pissed off at him, we're going to keep you safe."

"Damn straight." Keegan's mouth tightened, and he met Carter's eyes. It was more serious than Carter had ever seen him.

Chapter Nine

Ty counted on his fingers. If he was pregnant now, probably about a month in, he'd gotten pregnant sometime around opening day. If he'd gotten pregnant sometime around opening day, he was most likely due sometime around late December or early January. He could certainly live with that, assuming he could find a way to get to the hospital in time. He hadn't quite ironed out how he was going to manage that one yet. Maybe a rideshare driver would let him into the car, but he wouldn't count on it.

He closed his eyes and blew out a long, slow breath. It would all be okay. He didn't need to have it all figured out right now. He had time before he got to the due date before he had to have a plan, and babies tended to throw all but the most basic of plans out the window anyway. He should focus on work and on the fun things about the baby - things like decorating, or clothes.

He could deal with the more anxiety-producing aspects later.

He pulled up a home decor site and started looking through it. He could just go through a decorator like he had for the rest of the house, but he wanted this to be more personal. He didn't know if he was having a boy or a girl yet and it was far too soon to tell - only June, at this point, and he wouldn't know until September at the earliest. As he scrolled through beautiful images of girls' rooms, and rough-and-tumble images of boys' rooms, he had to wrinkle his nose just a little.

Okay, sure, the girls' rooms were lovely. And the boys' rooms had a certain adorable quality to them. Maybe they could wait to encourage destructive tendencies in a son until they knew he had them? And maybe a baby girl didn't need quite so many ruffles in her life? They'd just collect dust, and babies didn't need dust.

Carter walked into the apartment then, and Ty's heart leaped. He'd rather look at Carter than pictures of expertly-decorated baby bedrooms that hadn't yet made contact with a single soiled diaper or upset stomach.

Carter smiled at him and came to sit on the couch beside him. He had to dislodge Isis to do so, and she batted at his hand, but she kept her claws in so she probably didn't mean it. "What's with the cranky lawyer face? Who are you taking down now?"

Ty soothed Isis back into a good mood by scratching the underside of her chin, just the way she liked. "I'm thinking about suing the baby decor industry, actually. And I'll do it pro bono. Look at all this stuff. They've got people trying to force weird ideas about gender onto their kids before they've even developed limbs, for crying out loud. And trapping dust in their daughters' rooms, just to reinforce some bizarre notions of femininity that didn't even make sense when people basically wore ruffled curtains on the daily —"

Carter laughed and wrapped his arm around Ty. Ty ducked his head and relaxed. He didn't want to put all of the logistical planning on Carter's shoulders, but maybe Carter had some suggestions about how to get from the apartment to the hospital. "I know you didn't sign on for this part," he said, in a soft voice. "I just - I'm a little worried about how I'm going to get from here to the hospital. No Lyft driver's going to want someone in labor in their car. That's messy, you know?"

Carter frowned. "Do you want me to be part of the birth?"

Ty blushed. He couldn't help it. His family wasn't big on talking about wants or feelings. "That's not what matters, Carter. What matters is that it's not what you agreed to."

Carter leaned back, just a little. His mouth had a couple of little lines on the side. "Ty, I thought we'd talked about this.

We love each other, contract or no contract. *We're* going to be fathers. We like to make each other happy. Now come on, out with it. What is it that you want?"

Ty swallowed. "I'm sorry."

Carter lifted his chin, making Ty meet his eyes. "Don't be sorry. I saw your dads. I know how you were taught." He grinned. It looked a little forced to Ty, but he tried to remember to give Carter the benefit of the doubt. "What is it that you, Tyler Cunningham, want here?"

"In an ideal situation, I'd want my husband to be as involved with the birth as possible." He took a deep breath. "That said, I know you don't necessarily want kids, not yet, and birth is kind of a gross process. So I completely understand if you don't want to be part of it. I know you think it's just the way I was raised, the whole submissive omega thing, but it's also a matter of being raised to be one selfish son of a bitch. We both were, me and Keegan. It's really easy for me to throw money around and say, *Well, I paid for it, so I get what I want and screw everyone else.* I have to make a conscious choice to not be that guy, so this is me. Making that choice. I want you to be happy too. I've gotten what I wanted most, and I've got a husband I adore to boot."

Carter stroked Ty's face then, and Ty rested his head on his shoulder again. Isis let out a little mewl, reminding him that his primary responsibility was giving attention to her, and he petted her. Carter joined in, scratching her on her head, and she purred.

"Before we got to know each other, objectively speaking, you're right. I wanted to spend my baseball years focusing on the team, and on baseball. I wouldn't have had much interest in a kid, although I'd have done my duty because I'm not an asshole. But I'm excited about this, Ty. I'm excited because it's you. I'm excited because it's our baby. I'm excited because we're doing this together. We're starting a family and this baby is going to be the start of something amazing. Is it earlier than I'd planned when I was down in the minors? Sure. Life sometimes throws you curveballs and that's okay. I wouldn't trade any of this." Carter kissed the side of his head.

"Really?" Ty's heart swelled so much he couldn't catch his breath.

"Really. Even getting Madoffed, because I probably wouldn't have had a chance to meet you otherwise." Carter turned bright red. "That's a stupid thing to mention but here we are. Now - let's take a look at these rooms."

Ty moved his laptop over so Carter could see too. "Is it awful to admit I don't want to find out if we're having a boy or a girl until the day they're born?" He bit his lip. "I get finding out makes it easier for a lot of people, you know, picking out clothes and all that, but we've got the next eighteen years to load the poor thing up with our gender expectations. When it's born, it's not going to get a lot out of clothing besides 'I'm warm,' or 'I'm not warm.' It's not going to care about pink or blue, ruffled or not."

"Right?" Carter snickered. "And all of this construction stuff in this room - yeah, a lot of boys get fixated on construction equipment. So do a lot of girls, I guess. I don't know. We live in freaking New York. There's always construction equipment somewhere nearby. Maybe let them show an interest - or decide the noise is too much - before we fill their room with it? Jesus." He shook his head and scrolled away from one themed bedroom. "There has to be a place that doesn't design nurseries based on gender." He opened up a new tab and started a search.

Ty could feel his body relaxing. His jaw unclenched and his heart rate dialed back to a normal pace. "God. What would I do without you?"

Finding furniture places that sold gender-neutral nurseries was harder than it sounded, but between the two of them they managed to find a few choices they liked. “The big question is where are we going to put the nursery?” Carter turned to Ty and licked his lips. “Do we want to continue living apart, or do we want to get a place, you know, together?”

Ty stared at Carter. He couldn’t believe what he’d just heard. Living together, buying a place together, made everything so much more real. Sure, he had strong feelings for this amazing man who’d gone so far to make him so happy. He loved him. He liked the idea of living together, even if Carter would be traveling for a good part of the year.

But Ty’s apartment was *his*. He’d bought it, himself. He’d chosen the decor. It was steps from the office. He knew the restaurants. He didn’t need a car to get anywhere, he was happy with it.

He would be happy anywhere with Carter, wouldn’t he?

“Are you sure that’s something you want to do?” He looked up into his husband’s eyes. “It’s a huge step.”

Carter laughed. “We really are going about this whole thing backwards, aren’t we? Yeah. I do want to do this. I want to be your husband. I want to be the father of your baby. I want to come home to you. I want your cats to be our cats. I want to have the same mailing address. It’s fast, it’s sudden, and it’s a little unusual, but if we’re going to raise our kid together we should probably at least try to live together.”

Ty sat in stunned silence. Then, almost like it was an alien creature, a smile bubbled up from deep inside of him and spread across his face. “This is amazing.” He laughed and leaned back against the cushions. “I never thought I could be this kind of happy. I have to be dreaming. I have to be. It doesn’t make sense.”

Carter gave him an odd look and grabbed Ty's hands in his. This drew a disgruntled sound from Isis, who jumped down in a huff and trotted off toward the bedroom. "Ty. We can do this. We can have this. We can be happy together, I promise."

"Where do you want to live?" Ty hunched over the keyboard and found a real estate website.

"I'm not hugely picky," Carter said after a moment. "I'm okay with staying in the city, I'm okay with leaving it. It should be safe, have decent plumbing, and I should be able to get back and forth to the Stadium easily."

"And to the Hellion Club," Ty pointed out.

Carter hummed. "I mostly only go to the Hellion Club in other cities. Before we got married, I went to the New York one a lot, but now I only go there to meet up with specific people." He took Ty's hand again. "In other cities, I go because I want to get out around other people like me. It's a social thing. You can't just walk up to people in a bar and say, 'Hey, are you an alpha too?' It would be weird."

"Probably get you punched," Ty agreed. He had to chuckle at the thought.

"Right. So I go to a Hellion Club, because sometimes you just want to let your hair down and be yourself. I'm not flirting with the house omegas, I'm not getting into any wild and crazy shenanigans. It's just to get out and not be alone for a little while."

Ty blushed at himself. "I'm not really all that jealous," he said after a moment. "I'm just - well, that place always made me uncomfortable."

"I can see why it would make omegas uncomfortable. There are aspects of it that I find a little, er, unsavory, I guess. But it's a place that serves a purpose, and I can't complain about it.

The reason I was willing to take drastic measures to stay with the club, though, was because of the social outlet it gives me when I'm on the road. And now I'm doubly glad I did it because I wouldn't have met you without it."

"True." Ty laughed. "On the other hand, you wouldn't have to put up with Cunningham drama if it weren't for the Hellion Club, so there's that."

Carter laughed. "Okay, top of our list for the new place - no Cunningham drama. In fact, we can keep your relatives out altogether."

"Even Keegan?"

Carter frowned. "Well, probably not Keegan. I like Keegan."

"Sure, everyone likes Keegan until he replaces their shaving cream with whipped cream. How does he even manage to do that? I don't know, but he did." He pretended to pout, but he had to admit Keegan had come through for him more than once this year. "Fine, he can visit, but I'm not responsible for what happens to his wretched clothes."

"No. No one is responsible for what happens to his wretched clothes. They're wretched. Hence the catchy name." Carter laughed and stood up, offering his hand to Ty. "Let's hit the sack. We've got a day game tomorrow."

"I know. I've got a ticket." Ty beamed. "I've been talking to Ruiz's wife. She's actually pretty nice. Young, but nice."

"Yeah, they're a young couple. I like them, I think they'll go far." Carter led him back to the bedroom. "We'll stay away from the Upper West side, because that's where your parents are. Sound good?"

"Perfect." Ty beamed. He didn't want to live anywhere near his parents.

He was going to have a home with his husband. They were going to live together, and they were going to raise their child together. Who knew, maybe there would be more children down the road?

Ty shook himself out of it. He wasn't going to get greedy. His life was already pretty good. He would be happy with what he already had, and not grasp for more. He laid down beside Carter and went to sleep in his arms. Someday, he would be able to do this every night.

He couldn't wait.

***

Carter walked up to the plate. The team was down by two runs. The bases were loaded. A double would tie it up. He'd be content with a double. Hell, a double would be awesome right now. He'd been on the road for three weeks now, and he was sore. The other team's pitching had limited him to two bloop singles all night, and had kept the rest of the team hitless until now. A double would be fan-frigging-tastic, and nigh impossible to boot.

The pitcher, who was working on his third complete game of the season, stared him down. Carter hated this guy. Harrington was a homophobe of the old school, but he had the chops to avoid ever having to pay consequences for his bigotry. He'd won every pitching award there was, multiple times. He was built like a tank, too, so charging the mound was never going to go well.

The first pitch sailed past Carter before he could see it. The ump, one of those guys who thought he needed to put on a huge show for the audience, flailed around to give the sign. "STEE-rike-UH!" he yelled, loud enough for the TV cameras to pick it up.

Carter rolled his eyes. Umps who needed that kind of attention weren't usually good umps, but saying so didn't do a guy any favors. All he could do was dig in and wait for the next pitch.

He got a piece of it, but the ball went sailing off into the left field stands. "STEE-rike-UH!" the ump declared.

"Jesus, Bowman, Harrington's really getting to you guys tonight." Garcia, the other team's catcher, took the ball the ump offered him and threw it back to Harrington. "I mean usually he owns you, but tonight it's just pathetic. What's wrong? Don't tell me you're getting old already? Or maybe it's getting married that made you suck so bad."

Carter ground his teeth. All catchers talked trash. It was part of the game. Garcia used to play for New York, so he knew how to trash Carter better than a lot of other catchers, but it wasn't really all that different. Still, something about Garcia mentioning Ty pissed Carter off. Ty was watching at home, damn it. He couldn't let Ty see him lose. When the next pitch came in, Carter fouled it off toward right instead. The next pitch got fouled into the home team's dugout and nearly took off the coach's head.

Carter was warming up. His gut felt more solid. The ache in his shoulders disappeared.

He saw Harrington's jaw twitch. This time, when the ball came in, it sailed right down the middle of the strike zone. Carter was ready for it.

He knew it was out as soon as he heard it connect. He didn't gloat or showboat. He jogged around the bases the way he was supposed to and pretended he didn't hear his team cheering, or the crowd rising to watch his ball sail out of the stadium and into the players' lot. He hoped it hit Harrington's car and left a giant dent. Or maybe Garcia's. Garcia was a nice enough guy, but he should leave Ty's name out of his mouth.

His team high fived him when he got back into the dugout, and he watched as Harrington hit the next batter. He got thrown out of the game for that one, ruining his streak of complete games. Carter beamed to himself as he hit the showers a short time later. He was more than happy to make Harrington's day a little worse any way he could. Harrington making his own day worse because of Carter's success was even better.

He showered and changed into street clothes, not that the team allowed "street" clothes after games. What they did on their own time was their business, but if they were representing the team they had to meet dress code. He didn't mind, not really. It might be a little degrading to have someone telling him how to dress, but he got why they did it. They wanted team members to remember they were on the clock, they were representing the team, and they had to behave like professionals.

Tracy grabbed him once he was dressed. "Reporters are here. They want to talk to you."

Carter made a face. He'd hit the game-winning run, and reporters usually wanted to talk to the guy who'd done that. It was their job and he understood that. He'd just done an awful lot of talking to the press when news broke about how he'd been caught up in that stupid scam, and now he had a pit in his stomach about the whole thing. "All right." He rubbed at his face. "Let's just get it over with, shall we?"

He let Tracy lead him out to another room in the visitors' locker room, one that got used for press conferences. If the general public had any idea just how big and warren-like these clubhouses and locker rooms were, they'd demand they double as emergency shelters. Carter could remember sheltering in a minor league facility during a tornado back in Nebraska when he was a kid and thinking it was huge, but he hadn't seen anything yet.

The reporters were all there, a good mix of New York and national press. That was the thing with being on a New York team. Any time you did anything, good or bad, it got national coverage. He took his place at the table beside Tracy and plastered a smile onto his face.

The first question named from Donna Howell, a New York sports reporter. "Carter, thanks for joining us. Did it feel good to hit the game-winning run?"

Carter huffed out a laugh. "I'd be lying if I said it didn't, Donna. Harrington was a tough opponent all night, the other team played really well and kept us pinned down. It was super frustrating. Any time you can step in and help your team out like that feels good, definitely."

Bill Duncan, who wrote for one of the national publications, came next. "It's interesting to hear you praising Harrington. You and Harrington have had some conflicts over the years, haven't you?"

Carter winced. What was with this guy, anyway? What made a person sit there and think they had the right to just bring that crap up? Harrington was a headhunter. He wouldn't take it out on Duncan. No, he'd start throwing at Carter's head. Oh well, the question was out there. "Well, you know, Harrington and I have some important philosophical differences. That doesn't have any effect on my respect for his talent and dedication as a pitcher. He may be a bigot, but he's a bigot who does get his job done on the field. We saw that here tonight when he kept our team more or less hitless until the eighth inning."

Andrew Harris, who had a show on a major news network, stood up. "Hey, Carter, you've been having a pretty fantastic season so far and you've been on fire this road trip. Does this have anything to do with some off the field changes you've made? Like, say, tying the knot this winter?"

Carter blushed. He didn't like to make his private life public, but the question was out there. "You know what? It probably does. I always used to say I was married to baseball, and I didn't want to think about getting married or settling down until I was done playing. Then I met Ty. I've got to say, marrying him was the single best decision I have ever made in my life. I'm playing better. I'm concentrating better than I was before. I love my team, and I've always wanted to support my team and have them succeed. Now it feels like... I don't know. I *know* he's watching the games at home. I know he's up in the stands during home games, or at least the night games. And I want to make him proud." He ducked his head a little bit. "I want to make all of our fans proud, of course. With Ty it's just... I don't know. It's more personal."

Carter didn't have to answer any more questions, so he was allowed to leave. Tracy followed soon after and caught up to him. "So. That was exciting." He fluttered his eyelashes at Carter. "Oh, getting married to my amazing husband has made me a better player."

Carter laughed and nudged Tracy with his shoulder. "Oh my God would you shut up? You're making it weird."

"It was already pretty weird."

"Maybe. You're making it weirder." They headed out to the team bus. "I guess with a question like that there isn't a way for it to not get weird, but still."

"Right?" They climbed onto the bus and sat together for the drive back to the hotel. "Some of the questions they ask these days are pretty weird. It's like they want to make baseball into a soap opera for dudes. Why do you want to know about personal issues between my guy and Harrington? Harrington flunked out of third grade and doesn't know science. There's your story. Does it really need to be more complicated than that?"

Carter laughed. "Nope. I think you're right, though. They really do want to sell the drama behind it all. Maybe we should let them bring cameras into the locker room. They can see the drama right there up close and personal. You've got a twenty-five man roster and twenty-five individual weird superstitions and rituals. There's your drama."

"It's not a superstition," Ruiz challenged. "It's science. If you move my glove and change its orientation, all of the mojo will drain out the bottom and I'll start to suck. I'll have to go play ice hockey or something like that."

Tracy scoffed. "Do you even know how to play ice hockey?"

"No! Why do you think I'm so uptight about how I set my glove on the stairs, coach?"

Everyone on the bus laughed. Ruiz wasn't picky about the orientation of his glove. They all knew guys who were, though. They'd played with them, or against them. Maybe they'd worked with them in winter ball or something. Some guys refused to wash their cap all season, or had to fidget with their batting gloves in a certain set pattern before each at bat. All baseball players had a ritual or superstitious practice they engaged in before they played.

"Maybe Ty is your superstitious practice," Tracy suggested.

"Gross." Hoffman made gagging sounds from the seat behind him. "Now that is something that needs to be kept out of the clubhouse. I got a lot of vices, but I'm no voyeur."

Carter threw a wadded up piece of paper at him. "Dude. You couldn't handle the awesome."

They ribbed each other for the whole drive back to the hotel, and Carter lost a little bit of the tension in his shoulders by the time they arrived. Tracy followed him up.

"Are you still getting pestered by that Sebastian Britton jerk?"

"I haven't personally heard from him. Ty said he gets occasional voice mails, but deletes them without listening to them. Seems reasonable to me, but you know. Details, right?"

Tracy nodded slowly. "It definitely looks like the police over there wanted to charge him. If they can find enough evidence they might ask for an extradition. And they're actively looking for that evidence right now."

Carter shuddered. "Ty dodged a bullet when he said no to Sebastian. He's a smart guy."

"He is." Tracy took a deep breath. "Why do you think his parents are so keen for him to marry that jerk anyway? Don't get me wrong, I don't like the whole thing with him and you, but that doesn't mean I can't see the fact that his ex is a monster."

"Meh. They're friends of the family, they want their grandchildren to be raised with people who are like them. It's understandable. I'm a stranger. They have no idea who I am and they don't know what my values are. They just want their way of life to continue."

"Okay, but their way of life is weird." Tracy made a face. "I don't know. I shouldn't judge, but it seems to me that if Tyler has already said no it's not going to do any good to sit there and try to ram something through, you know? More to the point, this guy already dumped Ty once. And is under suspicion of murdering his last husband."

"They don't know that. I'm not sure they'd care, though. All they seem to know is that the guy they always wanted to marry Ty is suddenly single again. That's what matters to them."

"I see." Tracy stroked his beard. "Well, I don't pretend to understand, but it doesn't matter if I do or don't I guess. You don't think they'd hurt him, do you?"

"No. Not at all. I think they'd see it as vulgar." Carter took a deep breath. "And as for Sebastian, I think he'd only hurt Ty if he got something out of it. Right now, he's getting something out of stringing his parents along. I'm not sure what yet."

"So if we can figure out what he got out of hurting his ex, we can figure out what he's hiding." Tracy grinned and snapped his fingers.

Carter tilted his head to the side. "Tracy, I appreciate you helping out with this. I do. But we're baseball players. We're not detectives. We don't know for sure that he did hurt his ex, never mind killed him. We should leave this to the professionals and focus on keeping Ty safe."

"It's all bound up together, Carter. Can't you see that? There's no part of me that doesn't think Britton killed his husband. And my guess is that it involved whatever shady crap he got up to with his old job." Tracy bit the inside of his cheek. "And we need to figure out what exactly Britton gets from Ty now, since he's sniffing around."

Carter stretched his neck out. "Yeah. Yeah, I know. I want to say he'd get to be with the most amazing guy in the world, but we already know he doesn't see it that way. And we know it's not going to happen because I'm not letting him anywhere near Ty, so..."

"Right." Tracy huffed out a little laugh. "I wonder if he's sniffing around just to try to get a decent lawyer on the cheap? Because his husband would definitely defend him for free, right?"

"Probably not. Lawyers aren't supposed to defend family. Something about conflict of interest." He scratched his stubbly chin. “But that doesn’t mean Sebastian understands that, or accepts that. He’s definitely got an issue with entitlement.”

“It’s totally feasible.” Tracy licked his lips. “I know a guy or two. I’ll have them look into some stuff. I’ll tell you what I find out, okay?”

“Yeah. Yeah, thanks, Tracy.” Carter didn’t know if he should be grateful or terrified. He’d settle for both until he knew more.

Chapter Ten

Ty sat at his desk and tapped his pen against his jaw. His client was fighting for custody of his three children, which his alpha ex-husband currently held. Custody law wasn't his strong suit, but he had a junior associate to handle the intricacies there. He needed to focus on presentation, and how he wanted the judge to view the facts in the case.

He was no stranger to overbearing alphas. He was no stranger to alphas who threw their money around and expected their partners to be grateful for it. He was new at thinking it was unusual behavior, or that it was wrong. Would that hurt him, going into the custody hearing?

He was looking at this all wrong. What was it that the ex wanted? According to reports from both partners and from the children, the alpha preferred to have a nanny taking care of them. That wasn't unusual and it wasn't neglectful. Ty himself was going to have to bring on a nanny, when his baby was born. Nannies constituted appropriate care. Of course, the alpha had gone through four nannies in the space of a year.

He sent an email to one of the paralegals, asking her to reach out to each of the nannies for a deposition. A loving father would want stability for the children. He couldn't be held responsible if a nanny suddenly had a family emergency, or if she got ill, or if she decided his kids were too awful to deal with and had to leave. But four in one year? That was just too much.

He made a face at himself. Something else was going on here, he just didn't know what it might be.

Darren, from the mailroom, knocked on his door. "I've got a package for you, Mr. Cunningham."

Ty looked up and smiled, then he frowned. The package had telltale stripes on the edge of the envelope to signify that it was an air mail package. He'd studied international law, but he didn't have any clients at the moment with overseas entanglements. "Thanks, Darren. How's law school going?"

Darren blushed. "It's going, sir. It's going as well as can be expected. I love the work, and I love studying, but it is a grind."

"Yes, it is." Ty chuckled and shook his head. He could remember those days, and he hadn't even needed to have a job to support himself. "Just wait until your first law job. Hope you like coffee."

"Things to look forward to." Darren grinned and headed out again.

Ty picked up the package. Okay, he didn't have any current clients with international entanglements, and he didn't have any international criminal clients at all. It made no sense at all for Scotland Yard to send him a package filled with what felt like documents, of any sort.

He grabbed a letter opener and slit the top of the thick envelope. Yes, those were definitely documents, A4 paper all bound or stapled or paper clipped together. He racked his brain to try to find any clients who might have gotten into legal trouble in Great Britain, but couldn't think of any.

He laughed at himself. It had to be pregnancy brain. He wasn't showing yet, but his pants were already a little tight. He'd have to get around to getting some paternity suits soon. He could sit here and try to figure out which of his clients these documents pertained to, or he could pull the papers out and look at them.

He did exactly that, still shaking his head at himself. Just as he'd expected, he found a cover letter. According to said cover letter, D. I. Jamal Blackwell was sending the enclosed to Ty as a courtesy to Sebastian Britton's attorney. The documents related to the matter of the murder of Britton's husband, Niall Griffin-Britton, and had already been sent to the Home Office for review...

Ty dropped the cover letter onto his desk, like it was radioactive. He wasn't Seb's lawyer. He would never be Seb's lawyer. As a partner he wouldn't be assigned to a case without being told, and his firm was far too upright and stodgy to risk their reputation on such a strong conflict of interest. He scowled and fired off a message to the managing partners, informing them of the situation.

He was gratified, although embarrassed, when Madison Clarke himself walked into his office ten minutes later. Clarke was probably seventy-five years old, and the third Madison Clark to be a managing partner with the firm. He had a full head of snowy white hair, a scowl to beat the band, and a law library locked up inside of his head that Ty could only dream of. "What's all this, then?" he thundered.

Ty used to be intimidated by Clarke's bluster. Now he knew it was just the old man's way. He repeated the information he'd given by email. "It would be a gross conflict of interest for me to represent him, obviously," he said, taking a deep breath. "I was his fiancé and he's been pestering my parents ever since he got back to the States. But more than that, this whole thing where he decides we're representing him without even reaching out to us is a little... sleazy, don't you think?"

"Frankly it offends me." Clarke put one spotted hand onto the stack of documents. "It offends me on a deep level, that he would even think about trying to put one of my colleagues into this position. I will deal with this personally, Mr. Cunningham. Your time is too valuable to waste on this nonsense. That said, should you happen to encounter him again, please tell him in no uncertain terms that one does not engage an attorney by telling the police that someone is their attorney and presenting it as a *fait accomplit*." He sniffed, picked up the package, and strode out of the room. His back was as stiff as a rod, and he walked faster than Ty had ever seen him.

Ty slid down in his seat. Thank God for Clarke. He would have to deal with the fallout, of course, but for now he'd successfully offloaded it onto someone else and he could be grateful. He had no idea what Seb had been thinking, listing Ty as his lawyer.

He looked at the phone. The baseball season had chugged into the All-Star break, but that didn't mean Carter was home. Of course it didn't. No, Carter had been an All-Star for years, and he was having the best year of his career. He'd have been an All-Star no matter what. Ty would have felt a lot safer if Carter was here.

He bit down on the inside of his cheek and put his head down. He had an amazing husband, who he loved and who loved him. Probably. That didn't mean he had suddenly turned into some kind of delicate flower who couldn't take care of himself. It was nice to have someone who wanted to defend him, but he'd done just fine for the past seven years by himself. He didn't need to go running to an alpha just because his ex did something dumb.

That said, Seb had done something weird and foolish. Keegan, Carter, and Carter's coach were trying to figure out whatever it was that Seb was up to. They should know about this little shenanigan. He picked up the phone and texted Keegan. *You'll never believe what Seb did.*

Keegan texted him back two minutes later. *Flowers? Dead flowers? A jar full of dead roaches?*

Ty stared at his screen for a moment, trying to figure out where in Hell that had come from. *No. And gross. I just got a package from Scotland Yard. He told them I was his lawyer.*

OMG. WTF. Then, *Do you still have it?*

Ty chuckled. *No. Our managing partner was NOT HAPPY about it. He took the whole package and went to go deal with the problem.*

Keegan didn't text back. He called, which was odd for him. "Hey. So he seriously tried to set you up as his lawyer? Like, for free?"

"I don't know. It must be, because we never had the talk about fees. Or retainers. Or me acting as his attorney. The answer would have been no on all counts, of course." Ty scanned his laptop screen as he spoke to his brother. He needed to figure out what it was that the alpha with all of the nannies was hiding. He would try to depose the kids, too, but he'd need something to go in with beyond the fact that they were chewing up nannies and spitting them out.

"Well, duh. Lawyers don't work for free."

"Sometimes we do, actually. I wrapped up a pro bono case last week for a guy who's been in Riker's for two years without ever being charged with a crime. But we only work pro bono on cases that are in the public interest, or for indigent clients. We don't do pro bono for investment bankers who come from rich families." He sat up a little straighter. "Why does he need a lawyer with Scotland Yard?"

"The husband is always a suspect, Ty. Come on, you're a freaking lawyer. It's criminal law 101. Even I know that." Keegan snorted.

"Okay, but they wouldn't have let him leave England if he was enough of a suspect to need a lawyer." Ty tapped his pen on the desk. "Maybe it wasn't ruled a homicide at that point."

"You could be right." Keegan went quiet for a second. "Let's get together tonight. I want to talk to Tracy about this. Maybe we can watch the game."

"Yeah, let's do that." Ty forced himself to calm down. "We'll meet at my place at seven thirty, maybe? I'll get take-out."

"Sounds good."

Ty got back to work. He filed a request to subpoena the alpha's financial records. If the nannies had signed non-disclosure agreements, any payments to emergency rooms would show up in the financial documents. Payouts to the nannies would show up there too.

He made sure he had enough takeout to feed Tracy, and he wasn't surprised when Carter's coach showed up at the apartment. "Good to see you, Tracy," he lied. He didn't exactly hate Tracy, but he knew Tracy didn't like him. Welcoming the guy into the house wasn't exactly easy, but he did it anyway, for Carter's sake.

Tracy faked a little smile. "How's it going?" He edged into the apartment. "I hear you got a package today. Some interesting information from Scotland Yard."

Ty led them into the kitchen. He'd laid the food out on the counter, so the cats were less likely to make a move on it. He figured the guys could help themselves. "I didn't really look it over," he told them. "I figure that's confidential information, governed by attorney-client privilege."

Tracy scowled at him. "But aren't you his attorney?"

"No. As a matter of fact I'm not." Ty smiled brightly at Tracy and dished himself out some vegetables. "He would have to engage me, and pay me, and I would have to agree to it. None of these things have happened, nor would they, so here we are. What I did see is that Scotland Yard is sending his lawyer, or the person they believe to be his lawyer, information about his husband's murder 'as a courtesy.' That's... disturbing."

“They think he did it.” Keegan loaded up a plate with as much food as would fit and grabbed a beer from the fridge.

“I think he did it.” Tracy was more selective in choosing food, but he also grabbed a beer.

“Do either of you have any evidence?” Ty looked back and forth between them.

Tracy squirmed. “So some of the people I’ve been talking to have been, ah, making some inquiries. They obviously haven’t been getting in Scotland Yard’s way, but they’ve been keeping up with the investigation and letting me know what’s going on. If you’d bothered to read the packet Scotland Yard was good enough to send you, you’d know that.”

“It’s not my business,” Ty reminded him, clenching his jaw. “If I’d done that, he might be able to sue me.”

“How can he sue you if he’s the reason you got the stuff in the first place.” Tracy scoffed at him. “Anyway, what they found out is that the Brittons had a volatile marriage. Apparently the police showed up to their flat several times for domestics. That doesn’t happen over there, not for rich people.”

Keegan winced. “If the husband was the kind of guy I’d imagine good ol’ Seb would have married, he’d have been mortified.”

“I can only imagine.” Ty would be mortified if the neighbors called the police for a domestic disturbance in his home. He couldn’t think of what it would be like for some upper-crust Englishman, where they took class distinctions even more seriously. “Is there any more evidence or just ‘they argued a lot?’”

“I thought it wasn’t your business?” Tracy rolled his eyes. “Some inquiries into Britton’s financial dealings showed he was having some challenges. He’d made some bad investments, and he wound up getting fined because of the scandal back here in the States. I thought he'd gotten away with it, and since he got promoted and still has a job I guess he did. He didn't go to jail or anything, so from that perspective he got off light."

Ty nodded slowly. "But if he got hit with a substantial fine, and he had some other money trouble, it would have still been a pretty big issue." He sighed. "I guess I can see the motive. I'm not sure how they'd prove the husband was murdered, but that's not my job."

"No. Your job, little brother, is to stay alive." Keegan stuffed his mouth full of pasta and swallowed. "This explains why he came back to the States and immediately came to sniff around your door, bro. He knew you were loaded, and he probably figured you'd be so besotted with him still that you wouldn't think twice about defending him from murder charges. For free even."

Ty made a face. "You're not wrong. It's a little ego-shattering, but you're not wrong. I wasn't good enough for him seven years ago, I'm certainly not going to be good enough for him now." He cackled with delight. "It must absolutely burn him to be the one being rejected, especially since he literally can't compete with Carter."

Ty sat up straighter as the realization slammed into him. "Carter."

Tracy scowled at him. "Yeah. Your husband, father of your child, All-Star second baseman, too good for you by an order of magnitude?"

"That's the guy," Ty replied as Keegan growled. "If Seb will kill to get at his ex's money, what would he do to get at mine?"

Keegan stopped growling and turned pale. "Crap. We've got to warn Carter, man."

Tracy rubbed at his face. “Hopefully he won’t go there.”

“I still don’t see him as a murderer. But the motivation fits. If he’d kill his husband, what else would he do?” Ty put his plate down and pushed it away. He couldn’t even think about food anymore.

***

Carter slept on the plane from San Francisco to New York. He didn’t usually sleep on planes, but the All-Star game had taken a lot out of him. He’d played hard and played to win, and the coach hadn’t taken him out of the game at all. *Sorry, Bowman, but a lot of these fans paid specifically to see you. So as long as you’re good to go, we’re going to keep you out there.*

Carter got it, he really did. He also got that the coach of the AL team at the All-Star game was a division rival who was not above taking an opportunity to bust up a team that was giving him trouble in the standings. Fortunately, Carter had been in good condition going into the game. He’d have a few days off to rest, maybe look at a few houses, and then he’d be as good as new.

Screw Al King, anyway.

When the plane landed, the flight attendant woke him up and he deplaned with the rest of the first class passengers. He got into the car Ty had sent for him and relaxed on the way home.

Home. He hadn’t been back to his own apartment in how long now? He needed to get around to putting the place on the market. Ty’s place wasn’t big enough to store all of Carter’s crap, but Carter just didn’t want to keep going back there anymore. He didn’t want to be apart from Ty when he didn’t have to be. They were in the same city, they loved each other, they should be together.

Ty was home when he got there. It was early for him, but it turned out there was good reason for it. "I took a half day at work today. I had an appointment with the obstetrician." His hazel eyes almost glowed as he pulled out a strip of printed photos.

The thing in the photos didn't look human. It looked like an alien. Still, Carter could make out a distinct head, and limbs, and a cord. "Is that your sonogram?" He found he was whispering, like he could somehow disturb the baby with a loud voice.

Ty nodded, a huge smile creasing his handsome face. "It was the first one. I can't... it's... there aren't words. I heard the baby's heart. It was magic. It was absolute magic. The baby is in there, and it has a heart that's beating." He threw his arms around Carter and squeezed. "Thank you, Carter. Thank you for giving this to me."

Carter put his bag down and held Ty close. He loved the way his husband smelled, the scent of his shampoo and the way his body heat warmed Carter's skin. "Can we nap?" he asked, running his hand through Ty's hair. "I want to be in the bed. I want to hold you close, and celebrate, but I'm too tired for anything more energetic."

Ty kissed him. "Of course."

They retreated to the bedroom. The cats eyed them suspiciously when they disrobed, but when they made no move to get frisky the cats calmed down. Amun seemed particularly happy to see Carter, curling up on Carter's side as Carter wrapped himself around Ty. "I have missed you so much," Carter told Ty. He put a hand over Ty's still-flat stomach. "I wish I could have been there with you and heard its heartbeat for myself."

"I understand why you couldn't," Ty told him. Both Isis and Ra had found sleeping places for themselves pressed up against

Ty, and he looked blissfully happy. "I do. It would have been great to have you there, but I understand why you had to be at the All-Star game. " He yawned. "We watched it, you know."

"Who's we?" Carter refused to indulge in the imaginative part of his brain that immediately sprang to Seb Britton.

"Me, Keegan, and Tracy."

Carter had been about to close his eyes, but there was no way he'd be able to sleep after that. "Wait, Tracy came over here without me?"

"Yeah. He, ah, Seb kind of told Scotland Yard that I was his lawyer. It was this whole thing." Ty squirmed, and Carter's dick made a valiant effort to convince him he wasn't as tired as he thought he was. "We're a little worried."

"You should be worried. The guy's a psycho."

"About you."

Carter chuckled, and Amun dug his claws into his skin as a warning. "It's not my sweet flesh he's after, sweetheart."

Ty snorted. "It's not mine either. We think we've figured out his motive in chasing around after me, and it's not my good looks and charming personality." He made a face, and then he grinned. "You know, a few years ago I wouldn't have looked a gift horse in the mouth. Now I'm all, 'What kind of guy knows a guy is married and still chases after him?' That's weird. It is weird, right?"

"Well, I wouldn't do it." Carter relaxed. "For all that's appealing about erasing the other guy from someone's memory - and don't get me wrong, I'm totally gloating about that right now - there's something just icky about chasing a dude when you know he's happy with someone else. Of course,

Sebastian is completely devoid of human decency, so I'm not surprised or anything, but still."

Ty laughed quietly. "Apparently. But, um, evidently Scotland Yard thinks he's a suspect in his husband's murder. It looks like the motive is financial, which explains why he's suddenly interested in the guy he couldn't even tolerate seven years ago. It's my bank account he wants, not me. And there's one thing, in his mind, standing between him and my money."

"Your actual inclinations?"

Ty's laugh had a tinge of bitterness to it that Carter didn't like at all. "No. Those don't seem to have ever mattered to him. It's you. So we're all kind of worried about him taking things into his own hands with you. You know... safety wise."

Carter's skin ran with goose bumps. He couldn't deny that it was a possibility. He couldn't be surprised at the idea of Seb killing his husband. "Seb can try to take me out, babe, but I'm not some undersized overbred English aristocrat. I'm a good old-fashioned corn-fed American athlete who carries a club for a living, okay?" He kissed the back of Ty's head. "Sleep now, then houses."

They had a good nap. Carter woke up later than Ty did, but that was okay. When he did wake up, Ty had dinner on the table, and a message from a realtor named Larson who wanted to take them to look at houses on Saturday. Carter had the day off, it still being the All-Star Break, so he agreed on the condition that he got to sleep in.

The next day was Friday. Ty headed in to work. Carter went to see Tracy.

Tracy, as it turned out, was actually pretty upset with Ty. "The guy knows we're in the middle of looking into his ex's crap and he can't read the gift Scotland Yard drops into his lap? He's useless. He's worse than useless."

Carter closed his eyes and tried to remember that Tracy was one of his best friends. "I'm sure he had his reasons. He is a lawyer. He went to school for a long time to know how these things work. You know he took on Garcia's brother-in-law's case pro bono, right?"

"I hadn't heard that, actually. Really?"

"Yeah. Already the guy's out of jail on his own recognizance, so that's something. If Ty says he couldn't look at the file, then he couldn't look at the file. Anyhow. He says he thinks Seb's going to go after me?"

Tracy massaged his temples. His kids were playing in the pool just outside the window, and it looked like fun. Carter wondered if he could get away with jumping in with them, clothes and all. "It makes sense, given his motivations. The guy's trash, Carter. He's just in it for the money, and he's having a lot of financial problems. Desperate people do desperate things, and if the insurance payout from the husband is already running out..."

"Dude gets paid how much for being an investment banker and he's got to kill his husband for money?" Carter shook his head in disgust. "Look, I know I'm clueless when it comes to finance and investing. That's how I got into this position. I went with Chambers in the first place, because I needed guidance. But this guy, he had the gall to give me crap for getting taken for a ride when he was part of a massive fraud and he's so desperate for money he's killing people and chasing after a married man he dumped years ago?"

"Preaching to the choir, buddy. I get it. Dude is trash," Tracy repeated, and kicked the trash can beside him for emphasis. "That said, I have to agree with Mr. Buys-a-husband. You're what stands between him and his goal, at least in his brain. I don't know if Tyler would go to him if you weren't around. He didn't want to believe Britton was capable of doing something like this, but in the end he had the evidence in front of him.

"And as much as I don't like the guy, I have to say, the idea of something happening to you was what shook him into action. He wasn't okay with that by any stretch of the imagination. I think he really does care for you, and love you." Tracy made a face.

Carter laughed at him. "You'll find yourself liking him in spite of yourself, Tracy. Just you wait and see. He's a good guy, and he makes me feel good. That's the important thing, right?"

"I guess. I just - there's got to be something wrong with a dude who has to buy a husband, damn it."

"Oh, there is. There is, Tracy. But it's all... it's all stuff that Sebastian put there, and that his parents put there. I'm telling you, this guy is as good as gold. I love him, and that's good enough for me." He grinned and changed the subject, and before he knew what was happening the day had passed. It was time for him to go home to Ty.

The next day, he and Ty slept in a bit before heading out for a long day of house hunting. Their realtor, a youngish guy by the name of Larson, had a plan. "I'm going to stick with Manhattan today, if that's okay with you guys," he told them. "You guys both seem content here, and you work here. If you don't see anything you like we can start looking a little further out, but neither of you strikes me as the 'six acres of property' type."

Carter laughed and put his arm around Ty. "I grew up on a farm, but I don't need to try to recreate it. I'm okay with public parks, thanks."

Ty nodded. "I think we're both okay with that."

The first place they visited was a tall glass structure with a distinctly modern vibe. Carter didn't mind it, and it had a courtyard and a private play space for residents' children. That had a lot of appeal, but when they asked Larson to double check the building bylaws it turned out the place had a strict no pets policy. Ty would sooner cut off his hands than give up the cats, so they moved on.

"You like pre-war buildings anyway, don't you?" Carter pointed out, hoping to ease the sting a little.

"I mean yeah, I like them aesthetically." Ty shrugged. "I also like plumbing and electricity that work, so there's sometimes a tradeoff."

Larson pulled out his tablet. "That's not a problem, actually. I've got, ah, five places on here that are fully renovated pre-war buildings, four of them allow pets. Let me see, you guys want to avoid the Upper West Side for some reason, which is a total bummer but it's your choice. This one here over 76th should be right up your alley. It's quiet, it's got great skyline views, and you'll have an easy commute."

Carter looked over at Ty, who shrugged. "We'll take a look, sure."

The building had an elegant lobby, the kind that made Carter think of elegant hotels from the twenties and not anyplace people actually lived. He couldn't imagine a kid toddling across the black marble floors, so shiny he could see his face in it. "Do people with children actually live here?"

Larson huffed out a little laugh. "More than you'd think, although their kids do tend to wear shoes with extra traction. Come on, I'll show you the unit."

Carter had thought the elevator in Ty's building was pretentious. This one was positively gilded, although it didn't have an actual human being employed to run the thing so he guessed he'd take what he could get. The fourteenth floor was as silent as a mausoleum when they emerged onto it, and Carter recoiled. This wasn't a home, it was a tomb.

Then they walked into the unit Larson was trying to sell. It was beautiful. His breath caught in his chest as he looked out over the city. The kitchen was beautiful, and not excessive at all. Every bedroom had a view, and the whole apartment had a homelike warmth that made him smile. He reached out to take Ty's hand in his as they explored the four bedrooms and five bathrooms of this palatial home.

It cost a fortune, because of course it did. It was a mammoth apartment with more bathrooms than bedrooms in Manhattan, near Central Park and the museums. Carter almost felt like it was a bargain, but he also knew Ty was going to be contributing more to the purchase than he was.

He took Ty aside, away from Larson. "What do you think?"

Ty looked up at him. "What do you think? I can live almost anywhere, Carter. You're the one who makes a living with his body. Physical comfort is more important to you." He huffed out a little laugh. "Not that it's trivial to me, but it actually has a measurable effect on you and your job. Do you think you can live here and be happy?"

Carter took a deep breath. "I hated it until we saw the apartment itself. But up here - it feels good. It feels pretty amazing, actually."

"Awesome. We'll buy it, then." He walked in and had a conversation with Larson.

Ty made an offer for half a million less than the sellers wanted. Larson wasn't optimistic about their chances of getting the house, but the sellers agreed immediately and they had an appointment to close on Thursday. Carter should have figured

Ty would manage that. He was a lawyer, of course he was a master negotiator.
And that was that. All that remained was to buy furniture. Ty turned to Carter, eyes shining. “Welcome home, Carter.”

Carter wondered if a grin had ever broken someone’s face. His felt big enough to do exactly that. “Welcome home, Ty.”

Chapter Eleven

Ty had always liked August in New York. He liked the bustle. He liked the fuss. He liked the energy, and he even liked the smell of hot asphalt. He'd never been pregnant in New York in the summer, and he kind of hoped he could avoid it in the future. Not that pregnancy was a thing that could be timed, of course.

He wasn't even heavily pregnant. He was barely far enough along to allow for his new favorite hobby, Resting Things On The Baby Bump. He was still pregnant enough to sweat through his clothes. He was still pregnant enough to feel like he was fighting his way through a sauna every time he stepped out of the air conditioning.

The doctor said it was hormones. So did the middle-aged office manager at work. He didn't care what was causing it, he just wanted it over. He'd waited a long time to get pregnant, and he was still happy to be pregnant, but he would have been lying if he tried to pretend this part didn't suck.

Right now, Carter was away on a West Coast road trip. It was a long one. He'd been away for two weeks already and he wasn't due back for a good while yet. On the one hand, Ty hated sleeping alone in the new place they'd bought together. It felt too huge for one person. On the other hand, if Carter was off in Oakland or Seattle or Houston or Colorado, he wasn't in Seb's path. Ty would rather have Carter alive and on the road than in New York and in harm's way.

Or was he just being paranoid? He'd read pregnancy could do that to a guy.

He stood up and stretched, and then he headed over to the courthouse. Today he had closing arguments in the case of the omega trying to get custody of his children from their alpha father. He wasn't sure what to expect. He thought he had all of his ducks in a row. The alpha was definitely using his kids to get back at the omega for having the temerity to leave him. He also seemed to be lashing out at his children as his business dealings went south. None of the nannies would talk, but Ty was pretty sure the financial records did the work for him.

He got a car service to the courthouse. Everything was running on time, so he didn't have to wait long. His client sat beside him, chewing on the end of a pen and fidgeting. "Chew all you want," Ty whispered to the red-haired omega. "That's fine. But you have got to sit still. You're still making a final impression on the judge, and you don't want him to think you're on something."

The omega glared, but he slumped his shoulders. "Seriously?"

Ty put a hand on his client's back. "I know. It's hard. Believe me, it took a long time for me to train myself out of that kind of thing. Once we get that verdict you can express yourself as much as you want."

The judge walked in, and everyone stood.

Ty went first, since his client was suing for custody. He stood before the court. There was no jury here, and no observers. This was Family Court, and the privacy of children was supposed to be the primary concern. Ty still treated the room like he had a full audience. It wouldn't do to get sloppy.

"Your Honor, my client has come here before you to ask for custody of his children. When the divorce was first finalized, custody was given to the alpha father. While my client was disappointed, he accepted the decision. He wanted his children to have stability, and he didn't want to subject them to a long court fight.

"As the year progressed, however, he noticed changes in those children. He noticed behavioral changes. He noticed bruises.

Those changes have also been noticed by the children's teachers, as we heard in their testimony and saw in the evidence. The children have visited the emergency room on multiple occasions during the year, going to a different ER on each occasion and never going to the ER near their home. They've burned through four caregivers in one year. The defendant's financial records will show significant losses in his business that coincide with each spate of injuries.

"My client," Ty continued, not looking at the omega in question, "is a good man. He wants what's best for his children. When the courts deemed that going with their alpha father was what was best for them, my client acquiesced. When my client saw that the alpha father was not living up to his end of the bargain, he reached out to the courts yet again. He was willing to trust the courts to do what is best for the children. We ask the courts to validate his trust in them by proving that they do, indeed, have the children's best interests at heart."

Ty sat down. His opponent tried to rebut his argument with talk of "family matters." The children's trips to the ER were "family matters," and it was absurd for a man to have to document his reasons for choosing a specific ER every time he needed to take his kids to the doctor. Surely it would be better to get treatment for the children? And surely it was better for the alpha father, as the moneyed spouse, to have custody over the children since he was better able to provide for them? To send the children to the omega parent would be to attack the very cornerstone of family law - keeping families together.

Ty expected the judge to dismiss them, to retire and go to his chambers to consider the case. He did not. Instead he favored both parties with a stern glance. "Don't go anywhere yet, gentlemen. I've reached my ruling. You could probably have been spared the effort of closing arguments, but I knew you'd both worked hard on them and I'd hate to deprive the court of your oratory." His grin was cold, almost cruel. "I'll be the first to admit that I'm a little concerned that the omega father didn't go to DSS or the police with his concerns about abuse to the children. That said, I find more than ample cause to begin an investigation. Custody is awarded to the omega father with the caveat that he check in periodically to ensure the children's safety." He trained the full weight of his steely gaze onto the omega parent.

Ty's client didn't shrink. He just nodded his head, and Ty spoke for him. "My client doesn't have a problem with that, your Honor."

"Mine does, your Honor. We resent the implication that my client would harm his children in any way." Ty's opponent spoke calmly, almost like he was bored. His client, however, had gone so red in the face he was almost purple.

"Resent away, Counselor. You just make sure your client pays his annual child support, and make sure he gets anger management counseling as well. He can have supervised visitation every other week, which we can revisit in a year. If he's gotten his temper under control, we'll see if he can have unsupervised visits. Defendant is to pay all court costs incurred by the plaintiff. Until then, court is adjourned." He banged his gavel.

Ty shook his client's hand. "Congratulations. I'm very happy for you."

The red-haired omega sagged with relief. "Thank you. I couldn't have done it without you."

"That's my job." Ty grinned at him and headed out. He was, after all, getting paid for this.

He intended to go back to the office, but strong fingers wrapped themselves around his wrist and pulled him off to the side. Ty broke free of their grasp and turned to face his assailant, only to come face to face Seb Britton. "Seb." He didn't smile. He didn't want to encourage his ex in any way at all. "What are you doing here?"

"I came to see why you told Scotland Yard that you're not my lawyer." Seb's gaze fell and froze on Ty's baby bump. "You're pregnant."

"Yes. Yes, as a matter of fact I am pregnant. I'm not your lawyer. Mr. Clarke called and spoke to you about that. At great length, if his notes are anything to go by."

Seb curled his lip at Ty's belly. "Some old windbag called and babbled at me for a while. I muted him. Look, maybe we should talk about this someplace. Your house, maybe?"

"Like Hell." Ty snorted.

"Fine. There's a coffee shop around the corner. It's the middle of the work day so that brother of yours shouldn't be able to come and pester us." He grabbed Ty's arm again. "I absolutely insist."

Ty considered fighting. He decided not to, only because he couldn't afford a scene here. Seb knew that, of course. That was why he did it.

What had Ty ever seen in him?

Ty let himself be led to a coffee shop near the courthouse. It was a small, independently owned place that charged an arm and a leg for coffee. They could afford to around here. Ty got a decaf mocha and sat down to text the office while he waited for Seb. *Got dragged to Garibaldi's Coffee by Seb Britton. Tell Clarke.*

Seb sat down across from Ty with his own coffee. "So," he said, in an artificially casual voice. "You're actually pregnant."

"Yep. Actually pregnant." Ty didn't give him more information than that. Seb didn't need it, or deserve it. Besides, who knew what he would do with the knowledge? Would he go after Carter?

"I suppose you're going to tell me that idiot with the club is the father."

"I hadn't planned to tell you anything, Seb."

Seb slapped his hand down on the table loudly enough to draw the attention of several nearby patrons. "I have a right to know. You're my omega, and my lawyer."

"I'm neither, Seb. I'm married, to someone else. You left me years ago, and that turns out to have been the absolute best thing you could have done for me. And I'm sure as hell not your lawyer."

"You are if I say you are." Seb waved a hand dismissively.

"That's not actually how it works."

"That's exactly how it works!" Seb yelled. A nearby woman flinched. "You'll do as you're told."

Ty sighed. "Do you want to get kicked out of here, Seb? Because the owner just came out of the office, and he's looking right at you."

"People like us don't get kicked out of places." Seb returned his voice to normal. "You've been spending too much time with your jumped-up trailer trash to realize it. Look. I could overlook it when you married that guy in a fit of desperation. I can get it. You're over thirty, and it's shameful for an omega to get that old and still be single."

Ty pinched the bridge of his nose. "Maybe you'd be ashamed, but I had a good and fulfilling career. Which is what I wanted, if you'll recall."

"Whatever. I can understand why you'd take any offer that came along, just for appearances' sake, but you let him... touch you." Seb screwed up his face with distaste. "I mean that is how you got pregnant."

"That is how pregnancies generally happen, yeah. But Seb, I didn't just let it happen. I loved every minute of it. And so did he."

"That's ridiculous. You're awful in bed, Ty."

"Maybe I was just awful when I didn't have anything to inspire me to feats of greatness, Seb." Ty beamed. "That's not the point. The point is yes, our marriage is real, and yes, I'm pregnant. No, it's not any of your business, and yes, you need to go away now." He ticked off each point on his fingers as he spoke, feeling the weight of Seb's eye on his hands as he did.

"On the contrary. This guy is taking you for a ride. It's obvious to anyone with a brain that you need someone to take care of you. You need someone to help you make these decisions, because you're doing crap on your own. This guy, this Carter Bowman? He doesn't love you, Tyler. He's using you for your money."

Ty rolled his eyes so hard they hurt. "We've been through this. He's not."

"He is. What exactly is it that you think you have to offer him, Ty? He's famous. You're not. He's hot. You're a six at best. He's got an exciting life in a different city every week, while the highlight of your week is a hairball on the carpet. You're not capable of thinking critically of these things. Your head is all romance and love, and you just think everything is sweetness and light. You're just not capable of thinking long term and that's leaving you vulnerable."

Ty scoffed. "I was more than capable of thinking clearly and critically when I refused to go to England with you, wasn't I?"

"If you had, you wouldn't be in this situation right now." Seb's teeth were clenched, and a vein stood out on the side of his face.

"Or I'd be at the bottom of the Thames myself." He met his ex's eye.

"Wow." Seb sat back and made a pissy face. "You'd throw my dead husband in my face?"

"Give it a rest, Seb. We both know you're not exactly mourning. The thing is, when you go around telling people someone's your lawyer, and a law enforcement organization has something to say to you, they send it to that attorney." Ty held Seb's gaze as his words sunk in.

"I chose you for my attorney because I trusted you," Seb hissed.

Ty smirked. "More fool you. I don't trust you, Seb. And I wouldn't have taken the job on anyway, because of the conflict of interest. I honestly think you should get a British criminal defense attorney, one who can look at your case with a neutral eye —"

"No!" Seb spat the words out with a spray of mocha and whipped cream. "You are my attorney!"

"I'm not going around and around with you, Seb. The answer is no. The answer will always be no."

"Did your precious alpha tell you not to?" Seb sneered at him. "You know he's off with some younger, prettier omega right now, right?"

"Basic ethics told me to say no, Seb. And what Carter does is between me and Carter. It has nothing to do with you. You're not my alpha. You're not my friend. You're just some guy. " He stood up. "I'm going back to work now. You should do the same thing, if you don't want to get canned."

He headed out into the hot August sun and hailed a cab before Seb could chase after him. Seb seemed to really be losing it. Was there anything Ty could do to keep Carter safe?

***

Carter heard about Ty's meeting with the eternally charming Sebastian the day it happened, although Ty waited until he was in the middle of the game to text him anything. He knew Carter didn't check his messages until after the game. According to Ty, he didn't want Carter to worry. He probably just didn't want Carter getting on a plane and rushing back to New York. Carter had an overwhelming urge to do exactly that anyway, but he held off.

If he had to see Sebastian face to face, though, all bets were off.

The team was in Seattle when the whole thing happened. Carter had Ty write the incident up and email it to him and Tracy. He wasn't sure if anything would come of it, but he wanted the whole thing documented if it did.

The team was finishing up week two of a three week road trip. They headed to Colorado from Seattle for a four game series, which didn't exactly fill Carter with joy but what could he do? He would get through it, the same as he always did, and at the end of it they'd have a couple of days off in New York to rest up. He was definitely looking forward to that. All of his things were still in boxes, for crying out loud.

They got in to Denver late on Sunday night and played their first game on Monday afternoon. They took the loss. Carter didn't even mind. He felt like a zombie out there, between his personal exhaustion and the time changes. The elevation out here was a killer, too, and he hadn't had a chance to get used to it yet. The team rode the bus back to the hotel in silence. Most of the guys headed up to their rooms, ready to call it a night or maybe order room service. Carter was ready to join them, but a bulky man with silver hair and an outlandish mustache blocked his way.

"Ed Cunningham." Carter tried to muster a smile for his father-in-law. All he could come up with was a grimace. He decided it would have to be good enough. "Are you in Denver on business?" He felt Tracy pause beside him and thanked the universe for sending him such a supportive coach.

Ed curled his lip, just a little bit. "Actually no. I came out here specifically to see you." He flicked his gaze over to Tracy. "Privately, if at all possible."

Carter narrowed his eyes. He didn't know Ed well. Ed hadn't had much to say during their brunch meeting, and he hadn't had anything at all to say since then. He did know that, given the way things stood between the two couples, there was no way he was meeting with Ed without witnesses. "Well, I'd already planned to grab dinner with my coach, Tracy Belmonte. Tracy, this is my father-in-law, Ed. Maybe we could all grab dinner together in the hotel restaurant or bar? Trust me, no halfway decent major leaguer has many secrets from his coach." He slung his arm around Ed's shoulders and guided him toward the hotel bar.

Tracy glared at him and muttered to him in Spanish. *"You're so going to owe me for this one, Bowman."*

"*Oh, I know it.*" Carter switched back to English. "When did you get in? Are you staying here?"

"Actually I am. I got here today. I'm planning to leave tomorrow morning and I hope I'll have what I came for with me when I go." Ed had clenched his jaw good and tight as he walked alongside the two ball players.

They got a seat toward the back of the dining area, where they weren't likely to be easily spotted or pestered. They ordered drinks and meals, and they waited until both had been delivered to get down to business. Ed sat back and held his glass in his hand, staring at Carter for a long moment. "I feel a little odd, having this conversation in front of an outsider," he began. "Then again, I suppose I should feel odd. You did say you had no secrets from him." He sipped his drink and gave Carter a hard look.

"I've spoken with Seb Britton. He tells me you went and got my son pregnant."

Carter shrugged. "As far as I know, Keegan's an alpha. He can't get pregnant."

Tracy elbowed him. "Be nice, Carter."

Carter huffed out a little laugh. "Okay. Yes, Ty is pregnant. I am the father, in case you had any doubts. He's due in late December or early January. Congratulations on the impending arrival of your first grandchild, Ed. I'm sure you and Beau must be very excited."

Ed curled his lip. "I'm not sure 'excited' is the word I'd use. If it were legal, and if I wouldn't be the first suspect, I'd take you out and shoot you right now."

"Tell me how you really feel, Ed." Carter rolled his eyes.

Tracy wasn't feeling quite so sanguine about Ed's comment. "Excuse me, did you just threaten one of my players in front of me? Because I'm pretty sure that's what I just heard."

"I said I would, if there weren't strong arguments against it. Don't be vulgar, Belmonte." Ed scoffed.

"If you want to see vulgar, I'll give you vulgar." Tracy put his fork down and moved to push his chair back.

Carter put a hand on his coach's arm. "We're all a little run down, I guess. Tracy, let's hear what Ed has to say. That's why we came out here tonight, isn't it?" He emphasized the plural, hoping Tracy got the hint.

Tracy did. "Fine."

Ed harrumphed. "This is exactly what I'm talking about, Bowman. You have no idea what you're doing around people like us. You don't belong. Ty should never have married you, and I'm pretty sure he wouldn't have if he'd been in his right mind. You're uncouth. You lack anything resembling refinement. Seb Britton is rich, he grew up with Tyler, he knows exactly what Tyler expects and needs in his alpha. He's a better match."

Carter snickered. He didn't bother to hide it. Tracy grinned openly too. "Buddy, I don't know where you're getting your information from, but your boy Seb has got plenty of issues of his own. He's shady. He's dishonest. One of the things he's being dishonest about is his money and another is how his last husband died. Now you may not care how he treats his husbands. I don't care much for your parenting style, but you know. To each his own." Tracy pointed a finger at Ed and moved it in a circle.

"What in the hell gives you the right to sit there and criticize someone else's parenting?" Ed's face flushed tomato red. "You're gone for three quarters of the year."

"And yet look at me sitting here not trying to force my kid to marry a murderer. See how easy it is? You're setting a low bar, there, Eddie." Tracy patted Ed on the shoulder and went back to eating his dinner.

Carter smirked. He hadn't intended for Tracy to say everything that was on Carter's mind, but hey - he wasn't going to say no, either. "Look. You can go on thinking that someone else would be a better fit, and I'll go right on thinking I'm just fine for Ty, but at the end of the day Ty will do what Ty wants to do."

Ed waved a hand. "Ty is going to do what Ty is told to do. He might dig in his heels, but he'll cave in eventually. He understands that he doesn't have the temperament to make these kinds of decisions for himself, especially not when they affect so many more people than just him.

"It's not like you care, anyway. You're not really married."

Carter snorted. "There's plenty of documentation that says otherwise, sport."

"I mean not for real. You're using him for his money. You're not really interested in him. If someone - anyone - was going to be interested in him it would have happened years ago. Now he's well beyond anything of the sort." Ed leaned forward, knife and fork in his hand. Carter had a moment of horror wondering if his father-in-law would cut right into his arm and try to eat him.

"And yet you're sitting here trying to force him to marry someone who apparently wants to marry him over his own loud objections. Fascinating." He made himself keep eating calmly, even though Ed was making his skin crawl.

"Sebastian is a good man. He's willing to take him back. He knows Tyler's been pining for him."

"He certainly doesn't seem to have been pining when we conceived our child." Carter smiled and took a bite of his salad. "In fact, I'm pretty sure Sebastian's name didn't come up once."

Tracy almost choked on his drink when Carter said that. "TMI, Carter."

"You've deluded him into thinking you care. Soon he'll realize you don't and he'll come running back to us. Only we won't have anything left to offer him. Sebastian will be long gone, and he'll be all alone. Is that what you want? You want to deny him the husband his parents know is right for him? Are you really that selfish?"

"I'm not leaving him. I'm not leaving him now. I'm not leaving him ever. He's my husband. I think it's kind of gross, really, the way all of you treat him. He's a brilliant lawyer, a handsome man, and he's got a good soul. You all treat him like a bunny with a head injury. It's disgusting. At this point I wouldn't let you near the baby with a ten foot pole. I can't let them see anyone treat their dad that way, and I don't want them to know they come from that kind of family." He signaled the waitress. "I'm not leaving Ty. We're having a baby, we're in love, and we're getting our happily ever after. Is that clear enough for you?"

"You'll never be accepted by the family! You're tearing him away from the people who care for him most. Is that what you want?"

"If tying him to a murderer is how you 'care' for him, then yeah. Yeah, I kind of do. Have a great night, Ed." He stood up and sought out their server. Tracy hastened to follow.

They explained they'd had a bit of a disagreement with the gentleman with whom they'd had dinner, and they were going to head up to their rooms, but Carter wanted to make sure she got paid. He charged their meals and their drinks up to that point to his room, left a generous tip, and headed upstairs. Anything else that Ed might want, he'd pay for himself.

He and Tracy retired to his room. "Well, that was exciting," Carter said, flopping down on the couch in his room when they arrived. "I kind of feel like I could have lived the rest of my life without another encounter with any Cunningham over forty, but you know. Everything happens for a reason."

"Christ." Tracy shook his head and took the chair. "You know, when I met those two, I thought they were just another couple of boring rich kids who came from too much money. Now I can't even begin to guess how they turned out so well. Even Keegan."

"Right?" Carter huffed out a little laugh. "I never thought boarding school was a good idea before I met Ed and Beau." He sighed. "I mean you saw that, right? You saw me telling Ed that Seb's a killer, and he just ignored it."

"I don't get that. Either he doesn't get it, doesn't believe it, or he doesn't care. And I'm not sure which is worse."

Carter shuddered. He didn't know either. "The sooner we can put this Sebastian thing to bed, the sooner we can be safer. The Terrible Twosome might not want to have contact with us anymore, but I think we can probably live with that."

"They're your husband's parents, man." Tracy stood up. "Don't forget about that. Most guys, until a major break happens, they're going to want to keep up good relations with them."

"Well, sure. But Ty's not going to want to hang around with people who want him to leave someone he loves to hook up with a killer." Carter couldn't quite shake the discomfort, deep inside of him, that Ty might give in. He had to ignore it. He had to be bigger than it. "He knows better than that now," he said, rubbing at his arm. "He's learned. He said so, you know? He said he had no idea alphas weren't supposed to act like

Sebastian until he spent time with me." He sighed. "I mean yeah I know I'm not what he grew up with, but I think he's okay with that."

Tracy glared at the door, since no one named Cunningham was within range. "He'd better. He'd damn well better." He patted Carter on the shoulder. "I'll see you in the morning, okay?"

"You bet. God, I can't wait to get back to New York."

"Your lips to God's ears." Tracy managed half a smile and left the room.

Carter crawled into bed. He could only hope the night brought him some peace.

Chapter Twelve

Ty was thirty-one years old and September still felt like back to school time for him. He'd been out of law school for years now, finished with education entirely, and every year at the same time he still had the pressing urge to run out and buy new clothes and shoes. Of course, this year he had a perfectly good reason to do that.

He rested his hand on his baby bump. It wasn't "barely there" anymore. He hadn't reached the uncomfortable, big-as-a-house stage, but no one could doubt that he was very much pregnant. He could feel his child moving around in there sometimes, making fluttering kicks in his belly. The logical side of him knew they were just random firings of the fetal brain, which hadn't really developed yet. The paternal side of him imagined the kicks were responses to specific stimuli, like the sound of Carter's voice or one of the cats sitting on his baby bump and purring.

Right now Ty was at work, pressing a yarn shop's lawsuit against a multinational conglomerate for copyright infringement. Part of him felt like he had this case in the bag. The conglomerate hadn't even been subtle about what they were doing and they'd tried to intimidate the yarn shop into yielding to them... in writing... multiple times. They'd trusted their size and the fact that the yarn shop was run by women to get them what they wanted.

Ty couldn't afford to be complacent. He knew the law was on his side, and he knew his client was morally right as well. That didn't necessarily translate to "winning." He had to focus and put every bit as much energy into this case as he would into a more complex lawsuit if he wanted to win.

His phone rang, making him jump. When he glanced at the screen, he groaned. He hadn't heard from Beau since that disastrous brunch. He hadn't missed his father either. He'd once gone for two years without speaking to either of his fathers, and that was without having had a big blowout fight. Was it too much to ask to be given the same amount of peace at a minimum after a fight?

He sighed and answered. Beau would just keep calling, or worse - he'd come to the office. If it was important enough to have Beau pick up the phone and call him, it was probably important enough for him to answer. Maybe Ty had gotten lucky and Sebastian had dropped dead.

"Hello?"

"Tyler? This is your father."

Ty pinched the bridge of his nose. He knew Beau wasn't stupid. He knew Beau was perfectly capable of using his phone successfully. Why then could he not understand basic concepts like Caller ID. "I know, Dad. How can I help you today?"

"I've heard from your fiancé. I understand you're expecting."

Ty slumped and banged his head on the table. "I don't have a fiancé, dad. I have a husband, but I somehow doubt the two of you chat socially." He sighed and picked his head up. "Yes, I'm pregnant."

"Don't be vulgar, Tyler." Beau softened his tone. "I know we've had some tense moments over the past few months, but I'd like for us to get together and talk. Maybe for dinner."

Ty bit his tongue. "Dad, I don't think that's the best idea. I'm super busy, and I'm not going to go off and not have my baby because you don't like the father."

Beau gasped. "I would never!" He sniffed and choked back a sob. "I just thought - well, this is my first grandchild. At least it's the first one I know about. And I know you think you're

Mr. Independent, but you must want to talk about things with someone who's been through all of this before. I know you, Tyler. I changed your diapers. I nursed you at my own breast. I know you have questions, and I'm the logical one to answer them for you. Can't we pretend to be a proper family, just for the baby's sake?"

Ty put a hand over his baby bump. The baby didn't seem to have an opinion on the subject either way. Ty's discomfort came entirely from his own disgust. He'd been in enough courtrooms to recognize crocodile tears when he heard them, and Beau was notorious for his "attacks of the vapors" when he didn't get his way.

And yet, Ty knew he'd go. Beau had pushed all the right buttons. Ty knew Beau hadn't nursed him, or changed any diapers at all. They'd had a nanny for all of that. With a new baby on the way, Ty did want to ask questions of someone, another omega if possible. He wanted to talk to someone about this amazing thing he was going through, and there wasn't anyone around. Carter did what he could, but he wasn't all that interested in children and he wasn't in town at the moment. He was currently up in Boston, in the middle of a losing series. Keegan was useless, and he didn't have any omega friends.

"Fine," he finally said. "But we meet someplace public, and it's just us. I don't want any ambushes or crap like that."

"I'm offended, Tyler. I'll meet you at Gotham in an hour."

Ty slumped in his chair. Leave it to Beau to pick someplace inconvenient and expensive. Not that he couldn't afford it, but Ty just didn't feel compelled to spend that kind of money these days. He knew it bugged Carter, that kind of ostentatious display. Oh well - Carter wasn't here, and it would get this meet-up out of the way.

He texted Keegan to let him know what was happening. Beau had insisted on a private, omegas-only meet up, but he had no faith in his father. He wanted to make sure he was safe. Keegan's response consisted entirely of a gif of a cheesy, 1960s robot bouncing up and down saying, "Danger, Will Robinson, Danger."

He didn't understand the reference, and Ty didn't need to have bad special effects tell him this was a bad idea. He still didn't feel like he had much of a choice. He got up from his desk, got his things ready, and headed out.

It occurred to him, once he was in the car, to text Carter too. He usually tried not to bother Carter before a game, but something in him warned him that this wasn't going to go his way.

He got to the restaurant his dad had suggested and got a seat. He wanted to be in a position to welcome Beau, not the other way around. Maybe it was petty, and he'd learned over the years that most families didn't play these stupid games with each other, but he wasn't going to change Beau or Ed. Not at this late date. He might as well just accept who they were and try to limit contact.

He saw Keegan arrive. That was more than Ty had expected. His brother got a seat at the bar, in an out of the way location. Ty almost didn't recognize him. He'd dressed to blend in, almost, with only his bright pink dress shirt being offensive. Keegan texted him once he'd gotten settled. *I've got your back, li'l bro.*

Ty grinned as his baby kicked in delight. *Thanks, Keegan.*

We'll call it even for the time I tricked you into going out on a blind date with Kris Cordioli.

Ty shuddered. He'd almost forgotten about that. Maybe it was less organic forgetfulness and more of a deliberate mental block. *That was so not cool.*

Everything I do is cool, bro.

She's still in therapy! Ty hid a laugh behind his hand.

Beau showed up fifteen minutes late, because that was just who he was. He gave Ty a fake kiss on each cheek. "Tyler, son! You're looking well. The baby bump suits you. It's too bad it's taken you so long to get around to it."

Ty forced a little smile onto his face. Beau probably didn't even mean anything cruel by his comment. He would, later, but right now he probably legitimately meant his words as a complement. "Dad. How've you been?"

They made small talk and caught up on gossip while they put in their dinner orders. Beau ordered a cocktail, of course. Ty couldn't remember a time when Beau hadn't had a drink with dinner. "I went down to visit my family in Georgia," Beau told him. "I thought you might like to know that your cousins asked about you. They were shocked to hear that you'd gone off and married some athlete."

"I'm sure they'll get over it." He looked up and didn't have to fake his relief when their food was delivered. "Oh good. Here comes dinner." Beau couldn't deliver little barbs if he was eating.

But Beau was looking somewhere else. The food didn't interest him. The arrival of someone new did. "Why, would you look at that? I wasn't expecting Sebastian to show up tonight." He brightened up and waved at Seb, like some kind of drunken monkey. "Well this is a pleasant surprise, let's make some room for him."

"There's plenty of room for him at another restaurant." Ty pushed his plate away. He didn't believe for a minute that Beau hadn't set this up beforehand. He knew Beau wouldn't ever admit it, though.

He pulled out his phone and texted Keegan. *I'm shocked. Shocked, I tell you.*

Keegan replied with a picture of *The Scream.*

Beau stomped on Ty's foot under the table. "Don't be rude, Tyler. We have a guest." He beamed as Seb walked up to them and pretended to be surprised to find them there. "Sebastian, how lovely to see you. Do sit down and join us, won't you?"

Ty was stuck. He couldn't leave, not without paying. He didn't want to risk a scene, either. "You could, you know, not do that, too. Don't let us pressure you or anything."

"Oh, that Tyler. Always thinking of his alpha's comfort." Beau shot him a vicious glare.

"Well, yeah. I'm pretty sure my husband wouldn't be thrilled about you setting me up to meet with Seb, so I guess it does relate back to his comfort too. But really it's all about me right now." Ty gave a thin, humorless grin. He didn't feel compelled to play nice. He didn't want them to be able to misconstrue anything.

Seb kissed Ty's cheek before sitting down. "Droll as ever, Ty. And it should be all about you. After all, your supposed husband went off and left you all alone in your condition. Someone has to think about your needs, even if he won't."

"He's fine in that regard, thanks. What about Niall? He must have had times when you left him alone too, for work and such." Ty tried to look innocent.

Keegan strode up to the table then and straddled the chair beside Beau, across from Seb. Ty managed to relax a little then, although it wasn't easy. At least Keegan was there to help him push back. "Hey there, Dad." He stared Seb down. "Seb."

Beau glared at Keegan. "Keegan, darling, I'm sure you can understand that this is supposed to be an omegas-only get together."

Keegan widened his eyes to a comically large degree, like in a cartoon. "Holy crap, Seb, did they finally get that uterus transplant thing right?" He raised his voice just enough to carry, not so much that it constituted shouting. Not enough to get him kicked out by management. Ty had never quite appreciated his brother's genius enough. "Congratulations, man. I know you've been working hard to make it happen. It's been a long road, but I knew you'd get there eventually. Gimme a hug."

Seb flushed dark red. "Keegan, your japes are not appreciated right now. This is a very important discussion between your father, me, and Tyler."

Keegan put his hands on the side of his face. "Oh, so it's not bonding time between omegas? Oh, I'm disappointed. But since I'm not intruding on omega bonding time, I'm going to hang out right here and spend some quality time with my family." He smiled wide and bright, showing all of his teeth.

Ty fought to hide his laughter.

Beau ground his teeth. Ty could see his eyes darkening, but he would never be so vulgar as to give full voice to his emotions in public. "If you must," he snapped at last. He reached down into his bag and pulled out a dark brown legal file. "These are your divorce papers, Tyler. Sign them right now and I'll deliver them to the lawyer myself." He passed them over to Ty, along with a turned wooden pen that had probably cost a small fortune.

Ty looked the papers over. They seemed legit, or at least as legit as divorce papers drawn up for two parties that hadn't sought a divorce could be. "You're on drugs." He snapped a picture of the papers and passed them over to Keegan. "He's on drugs."

Beau made a grab for the papers. "Tyler, you will stop being a stubborn ass this instant. Sebastian is willing to have you, despite this absurd stunt you've pulled with your farmer. Despite the fact that you let that Neanderthal touch you, and make you pregnant. Which I still find repulsive, by the way. You have no idea who his family is, or what might run in his family —"

Ty held up a hand. "That's enough. I'm not going to sit here and listen while you insult my husband and the father of my child. Honestly, did you really think drawing up divorce papers would do something? Seriously?"

"I will sign them myself." Beau stuck his chin out. "You are my son, and I will do whatever I have to do to save you from your own idiocy."

Seb grabbed Ty's hand. "Listen to your father, Ty. I know the way we parted wasn't good. Your priorities weren't in the right place, but I'm willing to give you another chance. All you have to do is listen to your father."

"Seb, if you ever think of putting your hand on me again I will make sure that hand is useless." Now Ty did stand up. Screw making a scene. "Do not contact me, either of you. I'm getting a restraining order as soon as the courthouse opens up in the morning. Do you understand this? Beau, you're trying to force me to marry someone who is under suspicion of murdering his last husband. Does that not matter to you, or are you just that determined to get rid of me?" He shook his head. "Don't answer that. Feel free to wrap that up, I haven't touched it." He left the restaurant, followed closely by Keegan.

His brother waited for his Lyft with him, and even headed back to the new apartment with him. "That was disturbing," he said once they were safely inside. "I don't mind telling you that. It was creepy. The divorce thing? The fake papers? I don't know what they were thinking that would accomplish."

Ty sighed. "They're real enough papers. I'm filing a complaint with the bar association about lawyers who write up divorce papers for couples who don't come to them looking for a divorce, but that's not here nor there. I don't understand what they get by trying to force this."

"I don't get it either. I get what Seb thinks he gets, but our dads don't make any sense here." Keegan glared at the door. "I'm staying here until Carter gets home. I just don't trust them."

Tyler wrapped his arms around his baby bump. "I hate to put you out like that. But I'm glad you'll be here."

***

Carter got texts from Ty and from Keegan that night, and he had no idea what he was going to do about them. The stunt with the divorce papers was just bizarre. He could wrap his head around Ed coming to try to shake him down or something, even if flying to Denver to do it seemed a bit outside the realm of normal. He could understand sitting Ty down and trying to talk to him, even if it seemed like beating a dead horse. That was what parents were for, wasn't it?

But divorce papers? Did they think Ty was so fickle that he'd up and divorce his husband of only a few months, so soon after getting pregnant and buying a new home together? It didn't make sense. Carter would be the first to admit he didn't know Ty all that well, but he knew him better than that.

He shared what he knew with Tracy, who recoiled. "Man, I'll believe you love this guy. And I'll even believe that he loves you, although how that's possible under the circumstances I cannot understand for the life of me. But he is not worth all this drama, son. His parents are nuts. His ex is nuts. And his brother dresses like a psychedelic peacock in Las Vegas."

"You're not exactly wrong. About any of it, except Ty not being worth it. Those people are all... I don't even know, Tracy. I can't understand what they're thinking of." He rubbed his temples. "You know what? This was a crappy game, my head hurts, and I really feel like I just need to get out among friends right now. I'm going to the local Hellions."

Tracy shook his head. "It's not a good idea for you to go anywhere without witnesses right now, Bowman. Witnesses you can trust. Me, or Ruiz."

Carter clenched his hands into fists. "I can't live my life like that, Tracy. I need independence. I need to be free. I'm faithful, and I know I'm faithful. Ty knows I'm faithful too." Well, Carter wasn't sure that was true. Ty didn't seem to need Carter to be faithful, since he hadn't been raised to expect alphas to be faithful. But Carter had been raised that way, and he was going to act right by his husband. "I just need to go somewhere where I can relax a little. If I was in New York I'd put my feet up in my own home, and play with the cats. I can't do that here. I just need to not be alone in my own head, or else I'll wind up obsessing over this, you know?"

Tracy threw his hands up into the air. "It's your funeral, bro. Don't say I didn't warn you."

Carter grinned and headed back out. The Boston Hellion Club was located not in a hotel, but in two elegant old brownstones on Newbury Street. It wasn't as large or as grand as the New York Hellion Club, or as modern or lavish as the Los Angeles Hellion Club, but it worked for the locals.

It worked for Carter, too. Sure it was nice to have some attractive, willing omegas around when he'd been single. They were here in the Boston facility, but they weren't quite so in your face. They didn't have a stage here. The omegas walked between tables in the bar, providing table service instead. They flirted gently, and Carter responded politely but restricted himself to a drink and a little conversation.

One of the omegas turned out to be a baseball player, in the single-As. He had some questions for Carter that had nothing to do with sex or flirtation. Carter almost fell off his chair in relief at that. The kid, whose name was Ron, said he was a catcher but he sometimes played second. Carter wasted no time encouraging him to switch positions. "Catcher is an awesome job, don't get me wrong. The only thing about it is it'll mess up your knees big time. You won't last long there, not if you want to be productive. What's your batting average?"

Ron told him, and Carter almost choked on his drink.

"You'll be moving up soon, Ron. Trust me on that. When you do, take every chance you can get to prove yourself at second."

"Will you be doing winter ball this year?" Ron asked eagerly.

"No. Actually I won't. Usually I'm game for it, but my husband's going to be delivering our first child that time of year and I just can't leave him alone." He ducked his head and grinned. "I figured I'd wait until I was done with baseball to have kids, but Ty wanted to get on with it, and now I'm at least as eager to see that baby come into the world as he is. Funny how that kind of thing works."

Ron grinned. It was a pretty grin, one that probably got him plenty of tips. "That's good to hear. I don't want to sound like I'm denigrating any of the guys who are here, because I like what I do and I'm grateful for the opportunity..."

Carter smirked. "But the guys you meet in this job aren't exactly showing their 'family side' to advantage? I get it. Most guys come here to be distracted from whatever's troubling them. And nothing troubles people more than family, sadly. My husband's awesome, but his family's a little nuts.

Sometimes it's good to get out and be somewhere with friendlier faces."

Ron nodded. "Can I get you anything? Another drink, something to eat?"

"No thanks, Ron. I'm really just here to get away for a moment or two. But when we all get to spring training, make sure you give me a call. We'll get together and work out. I know my coach would love to have a guy who could fill in at catcher if he had to." Ron's eyes shone. The kid couldn't be more than nineteen, and he likely had plenty of polishing to do in the minors before he could even think about coming up to the bigs. With an average like he'd claimed, though, he'd probably be a huge asset to any team.

And if he was going to be the first omega major league athlete in any sport, he'd do well to have a coach like Tracy Belmonte having his back. And a team like the one Carter played for. No one would tolerate any harassment in the clubhouse for one thing, and he could talk to Tracy about anything without getting a line of bullshit.

Carter already felt better, just from having spoken to Ron. He finished his drink, got ready to leave, and left a generous tip. He couldn't afford to stay too late anyway. He had a day-night doubleheader tomorrow, and here in Boston if he was anything less than on his toes the fans would eat him alive. They might eat him alive anyway, who knew?

Just as he was getting ready to head out the door, though, someone he didn't recognize barreled through the crowd and threw himself into Carter's lap. Carter didn't recognize the omega sitting on him. His booty shorts didn't leave much to the imagination. His abs could have been picked out of an anatomy textbook, and his soft lips would have made Carter's knees weak only a year ago.

“Well, hi there, sailor,” the omega said, and slung an arm over the back of Carter’s neck. “Fancy meeting a guy like you in a place like this.”

God, he even had a tongue ring. When Carter had been single, that alone would have been enough for him to go rent one of the available private rooms. He hadn’t thought about body jewelry, or any other purely physical turn-ons, since he and Ty had gotten to know one another.

He pulled his head out of the stranger’s grasp. “Do I know you?”

“Not yet.” The unknown omega simpered at him, eyes sparkling. “We can fix that in private, sweetheart. My name’s Steve.”

Carter sighed and stood up. He placed Steve, or whatever his real name might be, on the ground very carefully. “I’m sure you’re a great guy, Steve, but I’m a married man.” He enunciated carefully, so anyone around could hear him. “I’m not going to risk my marriage that way, but you have a good day now.”

He walked toward the exit. He’d always liked omegas who knew what they wanted and who weren’t afraid to ask for it, but this seemed like something else. This went beyond anything he’d seen at any Hellion Club before. Other members were staring. Some were laughing, some curled their lips.

And some had their phones out, recording.

That was strictly against Club rules. Those members risked losing their membership for life if they were caught, and indeed Carter could see black-clad security men moving through the crowd with scowls on their faces. The damage would have been done, though. At least some of those members would have already uploaded their footage to whatever social media platform they preferred.

And Steve, of course, Steve wasn't done. His eyes widened in panic, and he reached out to grab Carter's hand. "No? Maybe you'll think again." He tried to slip Carter's hand under his waistband and into his booty shorts.

Carter had only had one drink, and he made a living from his reflexes. He broke away from Steve's hold and snatched his hand back. "Steve! That isn't okay! It wouldn't be okay for me to do to you, so it's not okay for you to do to me." Since he was being filmed and all, he might as well use the opportunity for good. "I said no, I meant no. Now you have a good night."

"Your husband is divorcing you!" Steve called as Carter walked away from the club.

Carter ignored him, even though the words were like a splash of cold water down his back. He hailed a cab and got it to take him back to his hotel, all the while staring at his phone. His social media notifications were already blowing up, and it had only been a few seconds.

Christ. This was going to be a nightmare.

Tracy was waiting for him when he got back to his room. How Tracy had gotten a key to his room would remain a mystery, but that wasn't important right now. "One of these days, Bowman, you're going to learn to listen to me. Have you seen some of these posts? 'Carter Bowman Grope Caught On Film.' 'New York Second Baseman Gets To Second Base In Public Sex Act.' It doesn't get better."

"Almost as if it was planned." Carter flopped down on his bed. Then he grabbed his phone and sent a text, to both Ty and Keegan at the same time. *It was a setup.*

Ty's response brought tears to Carter's eyes. It came back immediately and it said only, *I know.*

"Who plans for you to go groping strangers in a bar?" Tracy threw his hands into the air.

"I don't know, but I have some ideas. One of them involves people who decided to have divorce papers drawn up for my husband. The omega involved yelled out that Ty was divorcing me as I left." Carter grabbed a pillow and held it over his face as he screamed his frustration into it. "What good does it do them to try to trash my reputation?"

"It's not you they're trying to trash. You being a sleaze doesn't hurt you at all. Baseball players are kind of expected to screw around when they're on the road." Tracy shrugged. "We don't, not all of us, but it's a stereotype, right?" He sat down beside Carter. "But Ty couldn't just go out and get pregnant. He had to be married, right?"

"The firm he works for is pretty conservative." Realization hit Carter like a meteor. "Damn it. They're trying to get him fired."

"For having a husband who doesn't match up with the firm's morals." Tracy shook his head. "You did all the right things, except going in without a witness. And you couldn't go in with a witness, because your friends are all betas."

Carter sat up and punched the pillow. "I'm going to find that son of a bitch and I'm going to throw him in the East River."

"No, you're not. Then you'd go to jail, which doesn't help Ty at all. You're going to sit back and let team PR handle this. And much as it pains me to have to tell you this, you're going to be a good little boy and stay in your hotel room when you're not in New York. Any time you leave, you're going to have at least one teammate with you."

Carter grabbed two fists of hair and pulled. He understood what his friend was saying, but that didn't mean it hurt any less. "I didn't do anything wrong!"

"I know that. I know." Tracy gently disengaged Carter's hands from his hair. "But man, these bastards are gunning for you. They're using you to get at Ty. Do you want that? Do you want to be a tool like that?"

Carter shook his head. "No, no, of course not. I just don't want to be a prisoner either."

"Then we need to figure out a way to deal with Sebastian Britton for good. I heard from Scotland Yard."

"Now you're hearing directly from them?" Carter whistled. "Tracy Belmonte, champion coach and international man of mystery."

"And don't you forget it. I heard from them. They asked if he'd found a new attorney. They said they weren't quite ready to bring charges yet, but they'll get there soon. We've got to have faith."

Carter slumped. Faith was getting harder and harder to come by. What choice did he have, though? This crap would keep happening until he agreed to leave Ty, and he couldn't make himself break Ty's heart like that.

Tracy patted his shoulder. "Keep your chin up. We'll get to the bottom of all of this."

Tracy left the room, and Keegan called maybe ten minutes later.

"I'm going to assume you were telling the truth about the weird omega being a setup. Because bro, he was just your type."

Carter sighed and bowed his head. "He was before I got to know Ty, okay? I just wanted to get him a shirt and get him off of me, not in that order. Look, you don't have to believe me. As I was leaving, he mentioned the divorce."

Keegan breathed out, long and slow. "The one my dad is trying to push on Ty?"

"That's the one."

"Son of a bitch."

"That's mostly what I said." Carter managed a weak laugh. "I'm telling you, this was a new low."

"He'll get lower. Don't worry, I'm staying here with Ty until you get home. I don't trust the little turd as far as I can throw him."

"Thank you, Keegan. I appreciate it."

"That's what family's for, bro. I'll let you know if anything changes. I told him to delete his social media accounts for the time being, for his own mental health."

Carter grimaced. "Yeah, that's probably for the best."

Chapter Thirteen

October rolled around, crisp and clear and beautiful. Carter's team had made it into the playoffs. Ty didn't understand exactly how those were supposed to work. It was supposed to be the best of the best, except for two teams who were kind of the best of the rest and had to slug it out in the end. Whatever, it wasn't something he was going to worry too much about. He was just going to wait patiently for it all to be over.

He would never go so far as to hope Carter's team got knocked out of the playoffs early so he could spend more time with his husband. That would be wrong.

Carter's head was full of "postseason." He tried to participate in discussions about nannies, but inevitably the word "clutch" would come into play and given that they lived in the middle of Manhattan Ty didn't think his husband was talking about the gear shift. Ty figured he should be upset about it, but if he were in the middle of a big case he wouldn't be any better. He just made sure he kept Carter in the loop and moved along.

He worked to keep Carter in the loop with the whole issue of the divorce papers as well. Dealing with it was Ty's responsibility. It was his family that had taken that extra, insane step, and his ex who was pushing for it all. Besides, Ty was here in New York full time, and Ty was the one who had the knowledge to deal with it.

If Ty were an alpha, he would go out and break some heads. He might rant and storm and shout a bit. Ty was not an alpha. He wasn't an athlete either. He didn't have a club to wield. He had one thing available to him, and that was the law. So he turned to the law, and he made it work for him.

The first thing he did was to file a complaint with the Bar Association. The lawyer who'd drawn up those stupid divorce papers should have known better than to make papers for a couple if at least one of the pair wasn't right in front of him. The Bar Association would take their sweet time to investigate Ty's complaint, but there would be a record of his action that would affect his ability to close deals.

Ty knew exactly how to send a message. He knew what would carry, and what would not. He needed to hit the bad guys in the wallet.

His next act was to file a lawsuit for professional malpractice, again against the lawyer. If Ty were the one being sued he'd settle as soon as possible. It was less about the money involved than about the negative publicity. Beau's lawyer might have different feelings on the subject, but Ty was willing to bet the guy was more interested in bringing in new and paying business than defending himself in a case for which he wasn't being paid.

He approached Mr. Clarke before taking on the next step of his plan. Filing complaints against a specific attorney was one thing. What he had in mind threatened to go against everything the firm held dear.

He sat across from the managing partner and explained his situation. He spoke about Seb, and about Carter. He made it clear that he had zero interest in reuniting with his ex. He was committed to Carter, and he thought it was unreasonable for his family to assume that his marriage was finished.

"I'm okay with them not liking my husband. And I'm okay with them not approving. They have a right to their opinion. What they don't have a right to do is to try to force those opinions on me and on Carter. Considering that the omega who tried to force himself on Carter at that club in Boston referenced the divorce papers, I suspect he was set up by my family or by Seb. And Seb is the one who tried to get us to work for him for free."

Clarke shuddered at the four-letter word. "Dreadful business, that. What is it that you want to do?"

"I want to file a lawsuit. It isn't about the money, not exactly. It's about forcing my family to stay out of my marriage. I understand that we're a family values firm and we want to continue in that vein. Believe me, no one can want that more than I do. But trying to break up a marriage and force one to someone else? That's not consistent with family values either." Ty held his breath as he waited for his boss to reply.

"It most certainly is not." Clark wrinkled his nose in distaste. "Honestly, the whole thing is vulgar. You shouldn't be forced to go to court to defend your marriage, for crying out loud. It's yours." He sighed and looked out the window. "We will ask for an order of no contact to be given to your family, by the judge, to last for a period of three years. At that time, we'll re-evaluate the situation. Hopefully your family will have seen the light and come to recognize that you're not about to yield.

"As for this other young man, I think it's important that he be prevented from contacting you entirely. Some people might consider his attentions romantic, but that just makes me shudder to think what their ideas of romance must be. Honestly these people frighten me. I consider myself to be a fairly conservative man, Tyler, but that doesn't mean I condone this kind of aggressive, proprietary behavior. The firm will back you every step of the way."

"Thank you, sir." Ty relaxed and smiled. "I knew I'd found a home here."

"Of course you did. Now tell me about the Watson case. Do we have any movement on that?"

"No, sir. The plaintiffs are still filing motions to extend their discovery period. I've filed a motion to dismiss the charges based on lack of evidence, and I'm more or less confident that the judge will see things my way. I think she's probably as sick of the case clogging up the docket as I am."

"Excellent. Keep me posted on any new developments."

Ty went ahead and filed his new lawsuits. Carter winced at both of them. "I've got to say, I can't think of another solution but I'm super uncomfortable with filing a lawsuit against your parents."

Ty bowed his head for a moment. "Me too." Then he picked it up. "But like you said, I can't think of a better solution. The only way they're going to learn is if it costs them something to keep going through the same old patterns. And I'm the only one who can really get away with suing. If you bring the suit, you're a cranky and jealous alpha and they're innocent victims."

"That's such horseshit." Carter crossed his arms over his chest. "I mean really."

Ty shrugged. "You won't get an argument from me, but here we are. But since it's me, it has more impact to the court. It could still backfire of course. We could still wind up with a judge or jury that takes their side, but I doubt it." He slouched back against the pillows in their big bed. "I'm a pregnant omega who's being harassed by multiple sides."

"True." Carter climbed into bed beside him and spread one of his big hands over Ty's burgeoning belly. "The baby's feeling feisty today."

Ty snickered. "No, that's just me. I told you I was uncomfortable with this whole thing." He pressed himself up against his husband's side. "I'm not okay with the way they're treating us. And I'm not okay with the way they're treating either of us. I don't know if that makes sense to you."

"It does," Carter said, laughing a little. "It might not make a lot of sense to you, college boy, but it makes sense to me. If you think this is the best solution, I guess we have to go for it."

"I guess we do."

Carter's team won their series in the fewest number of games possible, so they had more time off than they'd expected. That meant Carter was around for a long weekend. Ty was beside himself with joy. They went shopping for baby supplies and they spent some time just enjoying the quiet of their apartment.

The quiet was broken, of course, by Keegan. It was his single best talent. He showed up at Ty's place on Saturday night dressed entirely in shades of lime green. "You look like a margarita," Ty told him when Keegan walked in the door.

"Wrong. I look like a Midori Sour. A margarita would be more yellow, and I don't have jaundice. Yet." Keegan waved a finger at him. "If you keep suing our parents and driving me to drink, liver damage will come soon enough."

Ty winced, and Carter had to turn his head away. "So I take it you spoke with our dads," Ty surmised, squirming.

"More like was spoken at. They're pissed, dude. And they're looking into their options. They've talked about having you involuntarily committed. They've talked about having you investigated for child abuse." Keegan lifted his eyebrows. "I'm not sure how that's supposed to work, since your kid hasn't been born yet, but these are also people who think you should marry a dude who killed his husband so here we are."

Now it was Ty's turn to look away. "I get that it's exactly like that, but can we not talk about it like that? It's a little uncomfortable for me."

"It's more uncomfortable for Niall Griffin-Britton or whomever it was." Keegan headed into the kitchen and helped himself to some whiskey. Ty opened his mouth to object, but stopped himself. It was all Keegan's whiskey for the time being. Ty and Carter were both avoiding liquor right now.

"I didn't mean that kind of uncomfortable. I meant it's uncomfortable to think of my parents as being willing to just hand me over to a guy who would do that - or do they still not want to believe it?" Ty made a face at his brother.

"They can believe it or not, but the police showed up to our folks' place during brunch to arrest him for it. The UK authorities put in an extradition request. He's fighting extradition, because he's that guy, so it could take a while. As many as two years, or more. Fun times." Keegan took a swig straight from the bottle. Then he burped.

"So he's in jail?" Carter perked up.

Keegan gave him a pitying look. "I keep forgetting just how young you are. No. Beau and Ed followed him down to the precinct, waited there, and posted bail for him. I'm not kidding. Charming, right?"

Ty rubbed his baby bump, frowning. "Wait a minute. Where are Seb's parents in all of this?" He licked his lips. "Why is it that he's always with our dads, why are Beau and Ed shelling out for his bail money? I get that they've always been super into him, but why can't the Brittons pay for their own son to get out of jail?"

Carter stood up, face contorted with disgust. "Let's be real. If he was your son, would you shell out for his bail money? He's already been fined for one crime, he treats omegas like crap, he's accused of murder..."

"I'd like to think I'd stand by my kid. I wouldn't support him in murder, but I'd like to pretend I'd be able to keep him from going around killing people if he doesn't get his way." Ty ran a hand through his dark hair. "But there are a lot of factors that go into it and I shouldn't be judgmental."

"Dude. He drowned his husband. Judge away." Keegan saluted Ty with his whiskey bottle. "Come on. You do have a point. I should look into that."

"It's not like you have anything better to do with your day." Ty sighed. "It's my mess, I should be the one to dig us out of it."

"Hey. My work is flexible, little bro. I can go be as nosy as I want. All day if I so choose." Keegan's smile had a nasty edge to it that kind of appealed to Ty right now. "And as for it being 'your mess,' no. That's not how it works. Family isn't supposed to abandon family to deal with assholes. We support each other, and we help each other."

"Where'd you learn that?" Ty chuckled.

"Boarding school." Keegan burped again. "Come on. If they'll do it to you, they'll do it to me. And honestly, I don't want my name associated with their kind of snobbery. So it's not a hundred percent altruistic. Just ninety percent." He winked. "I'll look into where his parents are, and you'll focus on the legal side of things, and Carter will swing a bat really hard and hit a small fast-moving object with it."

Carter laughed. His laugh had a touch of hysteria to it. "That's a real meaningful contribution right there."

"Hey." Ty caught Carter's hand and pulled him back down beside him. "Hey. It actually is. You're having a career year here. Success is the best way to stick it to your enemies." He smirked. "Trust me on this one. Nothing burns Beau and Ed more than seeing me fill my bank account without them, okay? Plus, you make me happy. While I fight them in court, you give me something to fight for."

Carter kissed him, long enough that Keegan started to make gagging sounds. "Isn't that kind of the inverse of the traditional alpha-omega relationship?" he asked when they came up for air.

"So?" Ty looked into Carter's eyes. "If we're happy, who cares? Beau and Ed have the traditional relationship and it's not like either of them can even spell joy, much less understand it."

"Point," Carter said.

"Game, set, and match," Keegan added, with a grimace. "I'll leave you two lovebirds alone. I've got a hot date tonight anyway. Who knows, maybe even I'll settle down someday?" He shuddered. "Never thought I'd hear those words in my own voice. You two are contagious. And gross. I'll see you later."

Carter and Ty laughed as they watched Keegan leave. Somehow it felt like they might actually get the upper hand this time.

***

Carter was shocked when the lawyer who had drawn up the stupid divorce papers offered to settle the case for a million dollars. In return, Ty had to drop his lawsuit and accept that the attorney in question had taken the job "without malice aforethought." Ty didn't have a problem doing that. When Carter expressed his disbelief, Ty just snorted.

"I don't know this guy, but I definitely believe he didn't have any bad intentions going in. I think he got a job, smelled easy money and said 'sign me right up.' Accepting that he did what he did without intentional malice is basically an admission that he knows his clients did have plenty of malice in their hearts. Whether or not he knew it at the time is debatable, but he's not the one I really want to go after right now."

Ty looked so at ease when he spoke about this, so natural, it kind of disturbed Carter. He knew his husband was a lawyer, but he'd never seen that big beautiful brain at work on something like this before. It was a completely different side of Ty. When Carter had first seen Ty's picture, he'd thought of him as attractive but intense. This was that intensity coming out to play.

Fortunately, Carter didn't have to face his husband in court. Gentle Ty, who made him feel like he'd hung the moon, would probably eat him alive.

Ty took the lawyer's plea deal and moved on. He donated most of the money to a local domestic violence shelter, and the rest to a cat sanctuary because it was Ty. It hadn't been about the money. It had really been about sending a message.

"And," Ty admitted, when Carter called him on it after a game one night, "about establishing a precedent. We can now enter this settlement into evidence during the trial against my parents. Their conversations with one another are protected by attorney-client privilege, but the lawyer admits it was wrong and he can't take it back now."

Carter blushed and kissed his husband. "My God, you're smart."

"It's a problem," Ty laughed. He seemed to be trying to push the praise off, but it wasn't hard to see that Ty was glowing under the praise.

Carter did have a job to do, and it was a pretty big one. Playing baseball during the offseason was different than baseball during the regular season. Baseball during the regular season was a grind. A guy had to know how to pace himself, or else he'd blow something out and injure himself before they were two months in. A hundred and sixty-two games was a lot of baseball.

The postseason was something else. Every game you played could be your last. Okay, maybe it wasn't quite that bad, but the goal was usually to win as many games as they could, as fast as they could. It didn't make for the best TV revenues, but it did minimize the possibility of getting hurt while making sure they could have as much time to rest as possible.

The guys were beat up by the time October rolled around. Almost all of them were playing with some kind of injury. Carter had escaped serious injury this year, thankfully, but there was still time between the playoffs and the end of the World Series. If they lost a game, that was one more day the team had to trot out there and throw their all out into the universe, and hope they were rewarded with some kind of momentum.

They'd already won their division. That hadn't been a problem. The team had blown away the competition like it was nothing. Their next opponent would be harder. Carter and the others watched with bated breath to see who would win the other half of the division series. Both options were great teams, but New York tended to play better against one than the other.

So of course, that was the team they had to play against.

They had home field advantage, so they waited for the enemy to come to them. They watched hours of tape, which they still called tape even though it was all digital recordings now. They practiced fielding drills against the worst that the other team had to offer. They practiced batting drills to counter the other team's deadly shift.

And then they played. They won their first game. Carter couldn't have explained how. He had his suspicions. There might have been a miracle or two involved. Rumors of ghosts in the stadium had circulated for years, but Carter didn't take them seriously. Not until he saw a ball he was sure was a home run sail out toward the bleachers, reverse course, and land in the center fielder's glove.

He'd take all the help they could get. They won by the skin of their teeth that night, with Carter himself driving in the game-winning run in the bottom of the ninth on a bloop single toward third. With all of the home runs he'd hit in the regular season, and all of the homers and extra base hits he'd racked up in the division series, he couldn't believe they'd won the game on a blooper. A win was a win, though, and he celebrated with the rest of them.

There was no ghost, no blooper to help them out the next night, though. They lost in a blowout, six to one. The mood in the clubhouse was somber, and silent. Finding a copy of the fake divorce papers in his locker after the game didn't help.

Carter punched the locker next to his, much to the consternation of the reliever who owned it. Fortunately Elder hadn't pitched tonight. He didn't have his "game face" on and he wasn't ready to fight. He just held up his hands and told Carter it hadn't been him who put the papers there. Meanwhile, Ruiz went to get Tracy.

Tracy cussed up a mean streak, in English and in Spanish and even in Japanese. Carter hadn't realized Tracy spoke Japanese, never mind well enough to cuss in it, but here they were. Then Tracy called stadium security and took pictures of the papers in the locker.

Security showed up, and they said they'd review camera footage. They'd involve police, too. It was absolutely an issue if someone was getting into the locker room during a game. Who knew what else could have been done? Hidden cameras was the first danger that sprang to mind, but planted PEDs and bombs was another possibility.

And of course by the time Carter got home, news had hit social media. Carter found Ty sitting up in bed, biting his nails. "Are you okay?" He jumped up out of the bed, which was really comical considering how far along he was in his pregnancy by this point, and waddled over to Carter. "I heard about the break-in. I don't like that at all."

Carter wrapped his arms around Ty and helped him back to bed. "It's okay, Ty. No one was hurt. Yet, I mean, because when I get my hands on those bastards, I'm going to wring their necks." He kissed Ty's cheek. "Don't worry. We're flying off to Chicago tomorrow, so they'll have some time to beef up security around the stadium."

Ty let Carter tuck him in. "I know, I know, I have to trust them. I just - you know how screwed up this is, right?"

"Yeah. Yeah, I do. But we'll be okay soon." He stroked Ty's soft brown hair. "How much longer can they go without extraditing this son of a bitch?"

Ty sighed. "I don't know. Hopefully this will be enough to nail him, although I'm sure he'll have been smart enough to not have left traces. I don't know." He massaged his temples. "Maybe you will be safer in Chicago."

"I'm not the one he wants, babe." Carter kissed Ty's forehead. He got ready for bed and lay down beside him, ready to sleep.

The incident with the break-in threw a pall over the team's play for game three, which they lost two to one. Carter blamed himself. His personal drama couldn't be allowed to bring the rest of the team down, damn it. He forced a smile onto his face. "Well, at least we narrowed the margin, right?"

Ruiz blinked at him. "Huh?"

"Last time they beat us six to one. This time we lost two to one. Tomorrow, we come back here, how much do you want to bet we can make it a two to one victory?"

Elder picked up on what Carter was getting at. "Ah, come on, Bowman. I want to see us winning by a bigger margin than that. Make it three to one!"

"Four!" yelled Keppler, from the back.

Other guys jumped in with even more grandiose scores, and soon the clubhouse was as loose and carefree as it had ever been. And the next night, they went out and won game four by a score of five to nothing. They took game five by a score of four to two, and then they were flying back to New York with the lead in the series.

Carter held his breath going into the stadium, but he noticed more cameras when he walked into the locker room. He saw more stadium personnel around the doors, too. The head of security asked to speak with him when he arrived.

He headed into the security office, along with Tracy. He didn't go anywhere alone anymore. The change no longer really chafed. "Hi." He gave the head of security a broad smile and shook his hand. "How are you today?"

"I've had better weeks, Mr. Bowman. But I've spoken with your lawyers —"

"He's got lawyers?" Tracy turned to Carter. "Is this true or is this more crap your in-laws are pulling?"

"They work for your husband's firm?" The security chief hesitated, his hand over his file. "I spoke with your husband, too, if that's any help. In person, so I know it was really him, along with a guy dressed like an actual jack-o-lantern."

"My brother-in-law. I never thought predictability would be so useful. Anyway, please, go on." Carter tried to keep a straight face as he visualized what Keegan might have been wearing.

"NYPD compared the fingerprints on the fake divorce papers against the ones we know belong to Mr. Britton and they are a match. This has been submitted to the judge presiding at his extradition hearing, but I don't know how long it's going to take for it to have an effect. He's been ordered to stay away from the stadium, from the team, from anything to do with you or Tyler Cunningham. The advantage we have is that the Stadium is technically private property and we can have him arrested if he shows up. I just wanted to let you know what the status was."

Carter smiled past the disappointment in his mouth, as bitter as bile. "Thank you. I appreciate the update. I know you're doing all you can."

The team took game six, seven to three. They were going to the World Series.

Ty was happy for them, although he admitted he was more than ready to be able to see more of Carter. "It's been a long season," he said. "I've missed you. But I'll still be here when you win."

The team celebrated quietly in the clubhouse after their victory. They only cheered a little bit, and shared decorous glasses of champagne. A reporter asked about their apparently subdued celebration, and since someone had apparently decided that Carter was the face of the franchise he got the joyful task of responding.

He stood up straight and put on his most reassuring and professional smile as he spoke into the reporter's microphone. "Look, we're not trying to take away from other teams that do enjoy a big party for the conference series win. It's a big occasion, you know? You're going to the world championships. It's a huge accomplishment.

"We get that. No one knows what the future holds for any of these guys. Any one of us could get hurt out there, our careers could be over. We could get traded, or we could have a string of bad luck and just never make it back to the postseason. We hope that's not the case, but it's important to be able to enjoy the moments. That's why we are celebrating tonight.

"But we also don't want to let ourselves get caught in the trap of thinking, 'Oh, it's over, we've done it.' For us, for any New York team I think, the job isn't done until you've taken home that championship trophy. It doesn't matter what the sport is, you can't truly let your hair down and celebrate until you've finished the whole job. So while we're going to enjoy the moment, we're still gearing up for the next fight. Tennessee is a tough team, They're going to have two extra days of rest, and they play a very different style of baseball. We need every advantage we can get over them, and one of them is not getting complacent." He lifted his glass to the camera. "Cheers."

He got two more nights with Ty before the final series began. Because New York had the better record, they retained home field advantage. The sound of the fans as they took the field for game one was deafening. Carter would never forget it as long as he lived. Fifty thousand people chanted in perfect unison with one another as they waited for the game to start, and every time they thought an umpire blew a call.

Blown calls and all, New York won the game two to one. They won game two three to nothing.

Carter could feel victory in his jaws. As he boarded the plane for Memphis, every beat of his heart recirculated one word, over and over again. *Champion.* It wasn't a declaration, not yet. It was a promise to himself. He didn't taste the food he ate. He didn't feel the sheets under him as he slept in his hotel room. Every molecule of his being was completely focused on the game.

They took game three seven to two.

Game four loomed. Everyone on the team would have preferred to win at home, but they couldn't lose now. Carter couldn't have stopped himself if he'd tried. He was running faster, throwing harder, hitting the ball farther than he ever had before. He even felt like he was seeing the ball better. He didn't strike out once during the entire series.

It wasn't that this level of competition sharpened his skills that much more, although it could have had something to do with it. No, every step closer to victory was a step closer to Ty. If he caught this fly ball, or made this double play, he was that much closer to keeping Ty safe from the bad people in their lives.

When Tennessee squandered their final out, he headed into the dugout with the rest of his team. Only there did he let himself go and fully recognize what had just happened. They'd won the championship. The season was over.

Carter Bowman was a world champion, and he was going home to his husband.

Chapter Fourteen

Ty hadn't ever given much thought to Thanksgiving before, or at least not since leaving grade school. It was the kind of holiday when everyone else had something to do, so he could spend time catching up on work without fear of being disturbed. Sometimes, if he wasn't terribly backed up, he went to the cat shelter and volunteered to help out.

This year was different. This year he would be of limited use at the shelter, because his pregnancy excluded him from being able to clean litter boxes and his increasing size made other tasks difficult. Plus, he had Carter. Carter didn't want to make a big deal out of the holiday, but he wanted to do *something*. "I'd usually go home and spend the holiday with my folks, but the airlines won't let you fly right now. And I'm pretty sure if you got off the plane in Nebraska or set foot on a farm you'd explode," he said, face serious.

"I've been on a farm!" Ty put his hands on his hips. "I even took care of cows once!"

"You're joking." Carter's lips twitched. He seemed to be having trouble keeping a straight face.

"Nope. It was a summer job, between junior and senior year of high school, and I did it specifically so I wouldn't have to go down to Georgia with Beau." Ty shuddered. "It's not that Georgia is a bad place. I've been there a few times since then, and there are good things about it. But these are the people who raised Beau."

Carter nodded once. "Yeah, I've got a vision of a giant old plantation where they haven't quite figured out it isn't 1855."

"You're not far off. So yeah - I took a job for the summer on a farm upstate, as a farm hand. I don't think I've ever appreciated indoor plumbing and showers more in my life, because that was hard and messy work. Cows are filthy animals, man."

"I've noticed you tend to avoid dairy. I figured you were lactose intolerant."

"No. I can digest it. I just don't want people to keep cows. Miserable, nasty, filthy creatures." Ty made a face. "But you're not wrong about the airlines letting me fly. And at least cows are interactive. Corn just kind of stands there and corns at you. It's malevolent. Things hide in the corn, waiting for you."

Carter burst out laughing, doubling over. "You do understand that it will be late November. The corn will be dead. There won't be anyplace for the corn critters to hide. Just acres and acres of empty dead corn fields, waiting."

Ty pulled the blanket up to his chin. "You make it so appealing, Carter. Seriously, though. It's not like your family would want me there anyway."

Carter blinked at him. "Of course they would. You're my husband. You're pregnant with their third grandchild."

"Third?" Ty did a double take at that. "What do you mean third?"

"My older sister has two kids. Twins, both boys. They're five years old and they're unholy terrors. One reason I try to avoid going back to Nebraska is so I don't have them trying to climb me and eat my eyeballs or whatever." Carter pulled Ty into his arms, or at least he tried to. Ty's baby bump got in the way a little bit. "Anyway, there's plenty of time to worry about that later on. How about if we worry about it next year, and focus on something that's just us this year? We'll invite Keegan, if you want."

"I don't. I'm afraid of what he'll do. One year at my dads' place he used the turkey as a marionette and made it do a little Rockette routine. I still can't quite figure out how he pulled that one off." Ty took a deep breath. "But he's been an absolute godsend through this whole thing, so maybe we should invite him. Chances are he'll say no anyway."

Keegan, much to Ty's shock, did not say no. He accepted, with enthusiasm. Ty now had the unmitigated joy of having to figure out a way to make Thanksgiving dinner for three when he'd never done anything like that in his life.

Fortunately for him, *Bronx Bar and Grill* did an episode about how to do exactly that. Well, they expected there to be a few more people, and they expected the kitchen to be a little bit smaller than the one Ty was using, but it was close enough for jazz. And miracle of miracles, he was able to follow the recipes on the show's website.

It felt good to see someone pregnant up there on the screen, moving around gracefully and being comparatively normal. Ty knew the episode had been filmed a while ago, that Alex was wearing a ton of makeup and that if he had to take a break because of dizziness or fatigue they'd just edit it out. Ty also knew he probably wasn't as much of a clumsy balloon as he felt like he was. Seeing someone like him on a screen, confident and unashamed, made him feel a thousand times better about himself.

He made a plan and stuck with it, just like Alex counseled. On the TV, Alex turned to his friend and co-host. "Okay, Buddy. I'm going to share something with the audience at home, something you told me when I was still a young kid."

Buddy gave him an old-fashioned look. "I will give you twenty dollars if anything I told you when you were a kid stuck."

"Get your wallet out and prepare to kiss them bills goodbye, Buddy. The trick to getting ready for a big event, like

Thanksgiving, is doing as much ahead of time as you can. Can you roast the turkey ahead of time? No, don't be stupid. Can you get the pie ready ahead of time and finish it in the oven day-of? Hell yeah you can, and you look like a rock star when you do it. No one needs green bean casserole anyway, it's an abomination, but if you absolutely must have it you can fix it *months* ahead of time, reheat it, and no one will know the difference. Seriously. Roll out of bed, throw that turkey in the oven, make yourselves pretty, and watch your in-laws puke with envy."

Ty nodded as he leaned toward the TV. He could do that. It didn't take much extra energy to fix a side dish while he was making dinner, and he could freeze it and reheat it. Thanksgiving dinner was looking less and less like a sweat-inducing source of misery and more like a chance for fun.

Thanksgiving Day rolled around. Ty eased his way out of bed, feeling like a beached whale as he struggled, and got dressed. He preheated the oven, fed the cats, made the coffee, and got to work.

Carter milled around cleaning, not that the place needed much of it. They both liked a clean house, but Carter bordered on obsessive. Ty was more than happy to let him take care of the things that mattered to him, especially while Ty himself concentrated on his own strengths. Keegan showed up at the house at two, by which point two things were clear.

The house was so clean it sparkled, even with three cats running amok and shedding everywhere, and...

Ty might have a problem when it came to preparing in advance. He tried not to look at the table as he set out his dishes. Maybe the table wasn't as big as he'd thought it was?

Keegan admired the state of their apartment, remarking particularly on how it hadn't been at all dirty before. "I kind of missed the cat hair, little bro. I wore vinyl specifically so the cat hair wouldn't stick to me. But you thwarted me."

"I do live to thwart my big brother," Ty told him with a straight face. "But I can't take the credit. Carter's got a gift for cleaning. I'm good, but he's the best."

"You're not kidding." Keegan laughed and ambled into the dining room, where he stopped short. "Er, Ty?"

Ty bit his lip. "Is there not enough? I think Fairway is still open. I can run out quickly."

Carter peered around Keegan's shoulder and gaped. "Um, Ty?"

"Yeah?"

"Who exactly is going to be eating all of this stuff?"

Ty looked at the spread. "Maybe three dishes per person was a little excessive." He ducked his head, blushing. "I've never done Thanksgiving before. I'm sorry. I've never even been to Thanksgiving since I was a little kid, you know?"

To his credit, Keegan managed to hide his laughter behind his hands. "Oh, I know," he said when it had subsided. He sat down, face as red as a beet. "I know you always managed to avoid coming home whenever you could. But seriously, dude. Did you just lose track?"

Carter ushered Ty to his seat and kissed his cheek. "It's okay, babe. We'll just eat leftovers for a while. And if you decide to cook between now and the time we're done, we'll freeze it for when the baby is born." He dropped his hand and caressed Ty's baby bump briefly, and then he took his seat beside Ty.

"There's dessert too," Ty whispered.

"You don't even have a sweet tooth!" Keegan chortled. "It's okay, little bro. It's okay. We can deal with it. I'm sure it's all tasty."

Ty squirmed. At least it was all healthy - okay, except for the pie, and the cake. And the pudding. But the rest of it was healthy.

Ty managed to relax a little bit as they got into the meal. His brother and husband had no problems snickering every time they asked for another dish to be passed, so they clearly had no tension to worry about, but soon even Ty was able to join them. Eventually he'd learn to relax, and not to overdo it. Like Carter had said, they could eat the leftovers, and send some home with Keegan. It meant less takeout for them, which could only be good for the baby.

His phone buzzed with an incoming message just as Keegan was clearing the dinner dishes away in preparation for dessert. Carter's phone buzzed at the same time, and so did Keegan's. Ty frowned as he pulled his phone out. Carter and Keegan were both members of the Hellion Club, and so they had some intersecting social circles, but Ty didn't have any friends in common with the two of them. It would be one hell of a coincidence for them to be getting messages at the same time, unless there was an emergency alert or something.

Of course, given that it was New York, and a major holiday that drew a huge crowd of tourists every year, an emergency alert wasn't exactly out of the question.

When Ty checked his phone, though, he didn't have an emergency alert demanding his attention. Instead, he had a text message from an unknown number, one that had a link to an article on a major sports news network.

"Baseball MVP Carter Bowman Caught in Gay Sex Scandal," Keegan read aloud, as Carter paled.

Ty's stomach lurched. He barely had time to run to the nearest bathroom before everything he'd eaten at the Thanksgiving meal came rushing up. He heaved until he was empty, and then he heaved some more.

He hadn't thought it would matter if Carter was unfaithful. He'd even worked it into their contract. He knew alphas weren't usually very good at sticking with one omega. It was just the way they were wired. But somehow now, faced with a major national news organization having caught Carter with his pants down so to speak, he couldn't cope. How could he have been so blind? How could he have trusted Carter?

Light footsteps padded into the bathroom. Ty recognized Carter without having to lift his head, or needing to turn his head and look. "You know it's not true, Ty."

Ty heaved again. Nothing came up, but his body didn't seem to care. "They wouldn't have run the article without fact checking."

"You're kidding, right?" Carter gave a bitter little laugh. "Have you read the article? The pictures are all a bad Photoshop job." He rubbed little circles into Ty's back.

Ty leaned into the touch in spite of himself. He wanted to believe, so badly. He lifted his head and tried to ignore the sour taste in his mouth. When he took the phone Carter passed him, and looked at the pictures from the article, he could see exactly what Carter meant. He could see the bad edits even through his tears.

"What's going on here?" He looked up at Carter. "I don't understand this. I just don't get it."

"There's only one possible culprit. It's Sebastian, with our dads." Keegan leaned against the door frame. He hadn't made a sound as he approached, which was surprising considering how much vinyl he wore.

Carter's phone rang. He looked down at the screen, only to see Tracy's name and picture pop up. "It's your coach," he said, and passed it over.

"Awesome." Carter pinched the bridge of his nose and stepped away. "I'd better take this. He's going to be pissed."

Carter headed off into the bedroom for privacy. Ty was alone with Keegan. "Why would they do something like this? I don't get it." Ty struggled to get up onto his feet, but he wound up needing Keegan's help. Once he made it, he rinsed his mouth out and continued. "I honestly don't understand. Seb is getting extradited, and I'm not getting back together with him no matter what Beau and Ed do. He doesn't even really want me. He wants my money, and he wants a good lawyer."

"Something about it doesn't make sense," Keegan agreed. "I don't know either. I get why Seb's doing it. He's broke and desperate. As for our dads, well, that's another story. I'm going to have to sit down and have a good long talk with them. And as for why they'd need to ruin Carter over it..."

Ty waved a hand. "That, I get. And I'm ninety percent sure it all came from Beau." He blinked back tears. Beau should have been Ty's biggest cheerleader. Instead, Beau was the one hurting him the most. "You know how Beau's family has always been. They've got those ideas about who 'belongs,' who's 'pure.'" He felt his stomach lurching again when he spoke those poisoned words. "Carter didn't stay in his place. He didn't listen to his betters, he dared to touch me. They gave him the opportunity to back away and he refused. If Dad were behind it, he'd do something violent. But Beau - he's vicious, and sneaky, and underhanded."

"And you're a lawyer. That's kind of a pot calling the kettle black."

Ty straightened his back. "You know what? You're right. And it's high time everyone remembered that. I'm a goddamn shark, and Beau is a rabid dolphin with a cheap grill. I've been going too easy on them."

His phone rang. He didn't look at the screen before he answered it. "Hi, Mr. Clarke."

"Have you seen this article?" Clarke asked, his voice shaking with outrage. "It's the worst photo editing I've ever seen in my life."

"Isn't it, though?" Ty swallowed the pang he felt when he remembered that he'd briefly believed the accusation. "And with your permission, I have every intention of going after the publication."

"You can't sue journalists, Ty. We have a constitution in this country."

"This is open slander, sir. But that's not why I want to sue them. I have a pretty good idea of who sent these doctored photos to the website."

"And you want to be able to prove it. Do it." Clarke's voice took on a steely note of glee. "Make them pay."

***

Tracy didn't say much. He told Carter to get his ass up to the Stadium, that ownership wanted to meet with him as soon as possible. And that the union would be sending a rep as well. That wasn't good.

He told Ty and Keegan where he was going, and he drove himself up to the Stadium. On Thanksgiving Day, driving wasn't such a misery in New York City and Carter needed the alone time. He needed to think. It was obvious that Tracy and ownership believed the accusations. Hell, Ty had believed the story.

Ty had only believed it before he'd opened the article up. And he'd only believed it because he was the single most insecure hotshot lawyer Carter had ever met. Carter had pointed out the issues, and he'd talked him around, but it had taken some doing. Carter had earned a lot of money for the team's owners, but they didn't love him. He couldn't trust them to give him the benefit of the doubt.

The union rep on site turned out to be a player for one of the other teams in town, a guy named Nestor who was getting on toward the end of his career. He wasn't thrilled to be dragged away from his family on Thanksgiving. Carter got it. He wasn't thrilled about it either.

Tracy's face was stone, and he sat at the conference table with his arms crossed. Great. Carter had figured he'd be able to count on at least one person. He was completely on his own here. Well, Ty had been on his own for years. If he could do it and come out as one of the best lawyers in New York, Carter could hold it together long enough to fight for his career.

His phone buzzed with an incoming message. It came from Ty, because of course it did. *The firm is behind you. I'm drawing up the lawsuit against the website now.*

Carter grinned. Sure, Ty hadn't believed at first. Ty loved him. If he had Ty, and Ty had his back, the team could do whatever it wanted. They'd take on the world, chew it up, and spit it out. Hell, Ty might wind up owning the team before it was all over.

The senior managing partner, Mr. Lenox, narrowed his eyes at Carter. "I'm sure you know why you're here."

"Yes, Mr. Lenox." Carter relaxed his shoulders. "I'm here because a previously reputable sports news publication decided they needed to slander my good name and publish libel, complete with photo edits my five year old nephews could see through." He held his head up.

Lenox scoffed. "What, you think there's some sort of grand conspiracy against you? Get real, Bowman. Don't blame reporters - who, up until now, have always been pretty sweet on you - because you couldn't keep it in your pants.

"We took an awful big chance on you, Bowman. The jury is still out on a lot of people on whether or not that alpha gene counts as an unfair advantage for athletes. Now none of us has ever cared what you do with your dick, so long as it's just your business. This right here?" He thumped his phone, which just went to prove he'd gotten the message at dinner as well. "This makes it not your business anymore."

Nestor rolled his eyes. "So you've already decided he's guilty."

"I don't give a crap if he's guilty." Lenox sucked his cheeks in. "I care about this team, and its reputation. We're a clean team, a clean-cut team. We make our athletes dress up for every interaction with the public and we don't even allow facial hair. Our brand is built on this team being made up of the kind of men you can trust to expose your children to. If your kids are looking at pictures of our second baseman with his hands down some scantily-clad omega's pants in a seedy club, how are we different from Boston?"

Carter scoffed and shook his head. This was one hell of a railroad job. "Are you kidding me right now? Tracy, I told you about what happened there when it freaking happened. Are you going to just sit there and keep your mouth shut like someone sewed it, or is that what you're being paid for?"

Tracy glowered at him. "That's not fair, Carter. I told you not to go to that place, I told you not to go out alone, and you completely disregarded me. You brought this down on yourself."

"Way to victim blame." Nestor gave Tracy a dirty look, and then he turned back to Carter. "Since Coach of the Year here isn't choosing to speak up, you want to share with the rest of us?"

"I went to the Hellion Club up in Boston to get out for a hot minute. I had exactly one drink. I was chatting with one of the servers about baseball - he's in A ball. Just as I was getting ready to leave, this other omega comes up and throws himself into my lap. When I won't give him what he wants, he grabs my hand and sticks it into his pants. It was gross, I told him no, and I left. Unfortunately, plenty of people were recording. Club security bounced 'em, but obviously the damage was done." Carter crossed his arms, and then he let them fall. He refused to give off defensive body language, even if he did feel like he was under attack.

"An omega in the minors? Pull the other one." Lenox scoffed.

Tracy shifted and grimaced. "It's true. His name is Ron Steele, and he's a catcher in the Pittsburgh organization. He can hit like there's no tomorrow. Carter mentioned him to me after this incident, and I did some digging. I sent a file on him to our scouting manager. We could use some better hitting in our farm system, and if we can bring up some young talent that can double as a backup catcher - well, I won't complain." He shook his head. "That's not the point."

"The *point*," Carter said, stabbing one finger into the mahogany tabletop, "is that Ron was there and saw the whole thing. And he would have heard this other guy, Steve, refer to a specific incident that happened when security at the clubhouse was breached."

"Jesus." Nestor whistled. "There really is a conspiracy, isn't there?"

"You have no idea, brother." Carter gritted his teeth.

Lenox waved a hand. “You think someone conspired to try to make you look like a cheating scoundrel? Get real.”

Tracy rubbed the back of his neck. “His husband’s ex has been trying to get back together with him. I can’t understand why, but he is. He even went so far as to have divorce papers drawn up by a lawyer, break into the clubhouse, and leave them in Bowman’s locker.”

Lenox blinked, jaw slack. “That doesn’t happen. No lawyer would do that.”

“Which is the point of the lawsuit my husband filed in court, which the guy in question settled. And which is the point of the ethics complaint Ty filed with the bar association too.” Carter lounged back in his chair. “Did I mention Ty’s a lawyer? And a good one, too? Tyler Cunningham. I don’t know if you’re familiar with the name.”

Lenox blanched. “I am. He basically beat me up and stole my lunch money a couple of years ago.” He tugged at his collar. “Legally speaking, anyway.”

Nestor snickered. “Even I’ve heard the name. And I wouldn’t piss him off.”

“Oh, he’s already pissed. The only reason he hasn’t already filed suits about this is because the courthouse is closed on Thanksgiving. But let me tell you, he’s sitting in front of his computer right now, drawing up documents. He’ll be at that courthouse tomorrow morning. He is brilliant, he is savage, and he is patient. He’s happy to tie everyone involved up in court until the sun goes out.” Carter smiled the kind of broad, cold smile he’d seen Keegan deploy.

Lenox sighed. “The thing is, Carter, these pictures are already pretty damning. And the team has already been brought into disrepute because of it. We can’t let that stand.”

Nestor laughed. "You're joking, right? A guy gets convicted of beating the crap out of his wife and all you can say is that it's 'a private family matter and doesn't relate to baseball,' but a guy gets deliberately slandered with the intention of damaging his reputation and you want to throw him to the wolves. That's some crap right there.

"The way I see it, you've got two choices," Nestor continued. "You can either stand up and say, 'Look, these pictures are so fake Russian bots retweeted them, we're standing by this guy who's done a lot for us,' or you can be craven cowards who want to feed into a bizarre conspiracy of people who want to end this man's marriage for reasons I don't understand. Either way, after this meeting, the next time someone tries to call this the best organization in all of baseball to work for, I'm going to puke on their shoe."

"Colorful," Carter murmured.

"I try. I've got an eight year old. They've got a lot of descriptive skills."

Lenox took a deep breath and looked at his fellow owners. "You've got a week to make this go away," he said after a moment. "Maybe it's a double standard, but here we are. I have a bottom line to consider. This year our clean-cut newlywed put butts in seats. A liar and a cheat isn't going to bring in nearly as many fans."

"I ain't worried," Carter lied. He somehow doubted that a major corporate news source would roll over and make a proper retraction in one week, during the holiday season. Well, if they didn't, he could always sue.

This whole being married to a lawyer thing was getting to be handier by the day.

"We'll meet again in a week, then." Nestor glowered at the owners, and then he glowered at Tracy. "And we *will* be ready for that meeting. You want to talk contracts? We'll talk contracts."

Carter could barely contain a smirk as they walked away. Nestor all but had smoke coming out of his ears as they moved out into the reception area. "Thanks for your help, Nestor. Our union rep would never have gotten here in time. He's still off in the DR."

"Meh. I know Jose. He's kind of useless anyway." Nestor waved a hand. "I was kind of pissed until I found out what was going on. Man, I don't know what's going on with your family, but it sounds seriously screwed up. Good luck getting it all sorted out. I don't envy you, bro."

Tracy appeared on the scene. Carter turned on him. "Wow. That was something else, *Coach*."

Tracy held up a hand. "You aren't the only player on this team, Carter. I have to think of everyone. We can't have someone whose off the field issues become a distraction for the whole team."

"Funny how they didn't seem to be a problem for the team this year." Carter pursed his lips. "It's not like we won the World Series or anything."

Nestor shook his head. "Right? I don't get this."

"Look." Tracy rubbed at his face. "I don't want to lose you either, Carter. And I want to help you get to the bottom of all of this. Who is it, exactly, that's been working to help you get to the bottom of all of this crap with that Britton guy? Huh? Who is it who's been working with Scotland Yard this whole time?"

Nestor snapped his head around. "Wait, what? Scotland Yard?"

Carter rolled his eyes. "Dude killed his husband. Or at least it looks that way. They're trying to extradite him to England, it's taking a while."

"That's messed up." Nestor stepped back. "And now he's after you?"

"Long story," Tracy said. "I'm not sure I get all of it myself. I think you have to have been born a New York blue blood to understand it. But yeah, that's it in a nutshell. Anyway, Carter, the article looked legit. I know that reporter. He's not going to publish something he hasn't researched. And while you've never been the kind of guy to cheat much, we both know this isn't much of a marriage."

Carter growled. He balled his hands into fists. He wanted to smash Tracy's head into a wall, but he got control of his temper. Maybe once upon a time those alpha instincts had been helpful to someone, but those days were long gone. "Maybe we didn't go about meeting each other, or courting each other, in a way you approve of. But Ty and I are married. We love each other. We're going to be together forever, and that's just all there is to it. And hey, both of us have only been married once. You're on what, spouse four? Maybe instead of assuming an article about me cheating is true just because there are some badly altered pictures, you should think about not assuming everyone does the things you do."

Tracy turned bright red. Some of it was rage. Most of it was shame. "How do you think I know how tempting it can be when you're out on the road? Especially when there isn't any love there?"

"If your marriages have been loveless that's on you, Tracy. Get some therapy. Ty and I didn't expect to fall in love, but we did. I think that says something about us, and who we are. We're good, honest guys. We went into it with an open mind and we were willing to love each other. Try not expecting it to fail, I guess?" Carter shook himself. "I'm rambling. The point is, most of us are loyal. If you can't make yourself believe other people can be, you should look at yourself and not punish other people."

Tracy took a deep breath. "Look, Carter, I'm sorry. I just can't see why you'd want to be with someone who had to do what he did." He glanced over at Nestor.

"Because he's amazing. We're going to get to the bottom of all of this stuff, and we're going to make it stop. I'm grateful that you've been so helpful with that so far. I'd like your help going forward, but if you can't do that then I have to ask you to stay out of the way." Carter turned on his heel and headed for the exit. "Happy Thanksgiving."

Chapter Fifteen

Ty woke up to a hideous, tearing pain between his legs. He hadn't been able to move very quickly in weeks, but pain jolted him into speed and action. He rushed into the master bathroom and dropped his pajama bottoms, just in time to see water tinged with blood gushing out.

Panic rose in him. That wasn't normal. He wasn't supposed to be bleeding down there, for crying out loud. Then he forced himself to breathe normally. The blood was perfectly normal under the circumstances, and so was the pain. His body had just torn itself a brand-new, temporary orifice. Skin bled when it was torn, for crying out loud.

His baby was on its way.

"Carter!"

Carter didn't respond, at least not verbally. His only response was a muffled grunt and snore.

"Carter!" Ty barked out the name, as loud and as sharply as he could.

This time Carter did respond. "What is it, babe?"

"Get me to the hospital, please." As soon as the words came out of his mouth he had to wonder what he was thinking. He wasn't wearing any pants. How could he go to the hospital without pants? "And, ah, a clean pair of pants?"

"Mrrph?" something hit the ground as Carter got out of bed. A few seconds later, Carter shuffled into the half-lit bathroom. "Why is the floor wet? Do we have a leak?"

Ty understood now why so many sitcoms had so many jokes about incompetent men faced with childbirth. "Yes, Carter," he said, in as patient a voice as he could. A contraction racked his body. "The leak is coming from me, and it consists of amniotic fluid. From inside of me. Because it needs to come out before the baby can."

"Baby." Carter blinked, and then his eyes widened comically. "Baby!"

Oh thank God. Hopefully the hospital would have some coffee, because Carter was woefully useless without it. "Can you bring me some pants and get me to the hospital, please?"

Carter flailed for a moment and ran back into the bedroom. Ty wrapped a towel around his lower parts and hoped that would take care of everything. By the time he was done, Carter had a pair of pants, and Ty's go bag over his shoulder. He was dressed, too, and ready to go.

Getting to the hospital didn't take long, especially at this hour. Getting through check-in, on the other hand, felt like it was taking forever. He felt like he was sitting in a warm, uncomfortable pool and no one seemed to notice. He tried to stay focused and keep his outward appearance normal as each contraction tore through him, but it got harder and harder every time he had to move. First he had to sit with one check-in person, and then he moved to another. Each time, he had to answer the same questions over and over. Carter looked irritated, but he didn't say anything. It must be normal, then. It wasn't like Ty went to the hospital all that often, what did he know?

Finally, Ty's midwife showed up. Neal was a certified nurse practitioner, and all he did was deliver babies for omegas all day long. He stuck his head around the corner and saw Ty hunched over at yet another desk, and he walked right out. "Excuse me," he said, putting a hand on Ty's back. "This man called me at four o'clock this morning to tell me his water broke. He's been in labor this whole time, and I'm sure he's been uncomfortable. Look, there's a mess all around his chair.

Can we maybe deal with paperwork later, or do you want the baby born in his chair?"

The poor clerk blushed bright red. "Oh my God, no one said anything. I'm so sorry. We didn't realize. Here, let me get you a chair."

"Never mind, Cynthia. I'm sure it just got lost in translation." Neal gestured to someone Ty couldn't see with his eyes on the ground as they were. A moment later, someone popped out with a gurney, and Cynthia was wrapping bracelets around his and Carter's arms. "We'll finish the paperwork later."

Neal stayed by Ty's right side and Carter by his left. "We're going to bring you up to Labor and Delivery, and we're going to check you out to see how far along you are. Okay?"

Ty nodded. He just wanted to stare up at the ceiling. Everyone could see what a mess he'd made. "I'm sorry," he whispered. "I didn't mean to be so gross."

"Hey. It's not gross. It's part of the process, and that's why we're here. And it's their fault for leaving you to deal with it." Neal patted his hand.

Ty had been excited to be pregnant. He was still excited to have his baby - their baby, his and Carter's. Even with all of this crap swirling around them thanks to Ty's dads and Seb, this new little life coming into the world would be a source of unalloyed joy. The process of getting from point A to point B, though, was ten times more humiliating than he'd expected.

It only got worse when he got up to labor and delivery. He had to get undressed, which he could only do with Carter's help. His hands shook too badly. Carter didn't laugh at him or joke about it, though. He just held Ty gently and helped him with his clothes. Then he got back onto a bed, and covered himself with a sheet. That was the only cover he was allowed, because Neal had to be able to see and access everything.

Carter had to hold his phone, which started buzzing at seven thirty. “Oh crap.” Ty tried to sit up as yet another contraction made him bite down on his lip. “I’ve got to make arrangements.”

“You’ve got to sit back and have a baby, Ty.” Neal gave him an amused look. “You realize you’re almost completely dilated here?”

“Is that good?”

“It’s unusual to open up this quickly. Just sit back and let your body do its thing. I’ll tell you when it’s time to push. This isn’t time to think about the office.”

Ty shook his head. “You don’t understand, no one’s going to know I won’t be in today. Someone has to show up in court.” He took the phone out of Carter’s hands.

Carter just snickered. “He’s got like six lawsuits pending right now, Doc. He’s not kidding about needing to make arrangements.”

Neal hadn’t known what Ty did for a living. He paled. He didn’t bother correcting Carter on his title, but just said, “Lawsuits?”

“It’s ten,” Ty gasped. He didn’t want to scream and humiliate himself further. “Also, the next person who says this doesn’t hurt but just feels like pressure is getting sued. And punched.”

Neal frowned and took a look at Ty’s nether regions. “I’d send your messages quickly if I were you. You’re bleeding an awful lot, and I’m concerned. Hopefully we can get your little one out quickly.”

Doctors didn’t say things like “concerned” unless things were bad. Ty grabbed his phone and messaged three different people at the firm. Then he handed his phone back to Carter. If the worst was to happen, at least he'd know he'd tried.

And he'd know he'd been loved. That made all the difference. When he'd signed the contract with Carter, he'd wanted a baby for himself. He wanted someone to exist who cared for him, who had some kind of connection with him and who would notice when he died. Now that same baby would be a living testament to the fact that Ty had lived, and someone had loved him. Even if Ty didn't make it out of this alive, his child would go on and prove to the world that Ty was worthy of love.

"It's coming out now. One good push should do it," Neal told him, with an encouraging little smile.

Carter took his hand. Ty had been preparing for this for months - years, really. He'd read all of the instructions. He'd come in with a birth plan, printed out in triplicate. The room was already spinning, and he'd cheerfully stab someone for a drink of water. He couldn't remember a single word of the advice or instructions he'd studied as carefully as any criminal law or tort text. He bore down out of instinct, not knowledge, and hoped for the best.

"Got her!" Neal said, in the satisfied tone of a man who'd done the job he'd come there to do.

"Her?" Carter's sweaty face shone as he stared at whatever it was Neal held in his hands. "The baby's a girl?"

Ty groaned in pain as he felt someone doing something he couldn't see down in the underside of his body. "We've got to get the bleeding under control," Neal said, as a nurse added something to his IV. "It's not uncommon to have some hemorrhaging when a birth goes as quickly as yours did. It's something we have experience with and it's something we can get the better of, don't you worry." He handed the baby off to someone else, and they took his daughter off into a corner to be cleaned and weighed and tested.

“Is she okay?” he asked, trying to lift his head up.

“She’s perfect,” Carter told him, kissing his forehead. “She’s perfect in every possible way.”

The pain abated suddenly as whatever drug they’d given him kicked in. Now he just felt drowsy. Maybe that was just the blood loss, though, or the dehydration. He reached out toward his daughter. He needed to touch her, to feel her, to see for himself that she was okay and as perfect as she could be.

They brought her over after five minutes. “Apgar is perfect,” reported a doctor, who Ty had to assume was the pediatrician. She passed the baby over to him. “She’s seven and a half pounds, twenty-three inches, and all of her fingers and toes are exactly where they should be.” Their daughter had been wrapped in a hospital receiving blanket and crowned with a little pink cotton cap. “Do you gentlemen have a name for her yet, or are you still working on that part?”

Ty looked up at Carter. Carter smiled down at him. They’d talked about names a few times, and they’d settled on one. That had been before they met their daughter, but Ty still felt they’d made the right choice. He looked down into his baby girl’s unfocused blue eyes while Carter replied to the doctor.

“Emily.” Carter reached out and stroked Emily’s little cheek with his hand. “Emily Sophia.”

“Fantastic. We’ll take care of filing the birth certificate for you. All you need to worry about is enjoying your daughter and recovering.” She smiled brightly at them both.

This hospital gave private rooms to all of their newly parturient patients. That had been part of the reason Ty chose it. He found himself transferred to a clean gurney and wheeled to the omega ward only a few moments later, with Carter by his side as always.

They had a clear plastic bassinet for Emily, and a fold-out chair for Carter. Apparently they weren't supposed to share a bed. While Ty wasn't feeling great about being separated from his husband right now, he could see why Carter might prefer to be in the chair. Ty was a mess, he had a catheter, he smelled, and he was bleeding heavily. Ty wouldn't sleep next to himself if he could avoid it.

Emily didn't seem to mind any of that, though. She stared up at Ty like he was her whole world. She didn't know any different. She'd learn soon enough. "Hi, beautiful." Ty blinked back tears. He didn't know if the tears were because he was upset over his current state or because he was overjoyed by Emily's arrival. He didn't think it mattered which - he chalked it up to hormones and a combination of the two. "I'm your dad. Over here is also your dad. We've been waiting for you for a long time. I think you were in a bit of a rush yourself, since you basically clawed your way out."

Carter laughed at that. He bent down to drop a kiss onto Emily's little forehead. "She's a fighter, just like her dads." He met Emily's eyes. "I can't wait to get to know you better. Your dad Ty, he's had you under his heart for nine months. He already knows you pretty well. I've got a lot of catching up to do. And I cannot wait to get started."

Ty choked on a laugh that was at least part sob. "My God. These hormones don't give you half a second to breathe, do they? She's your kid too, and I want you to play with her and enjoy her. I want us all to be a family and enjoy that. But when you said that about catching up and all, I just got hit with the worst wave of jealousy."

Carter stroked Ty's hair. "Thanks for telling me that. A lot of guys wouldn't, you know? They'd fake it, and let it build up. That's part of what happened with Tracy and his second spouse, his husband. He couldn't admit what was going on and they split up." He kissed Ty's head too. "You know what else?

You've got the presence of mind to admit it's a hormonal thing. You know yourself well enough to understand that. It feels real, but you know what you actually want." He grinned. "I'm proud of you."

Ty blinked back tears. "How did I get this lucky?"

"We'll send Keegan a fruit basket." Carter chuckled. "I have to say, I've done a lot of growing up over the past few months. You inspired it. You've made me the happiest guy in the world. Whatever happens going forward, with all the BS from those outside forces, I want you to know that you've made me happier than anyone has a right to be. Thank you."

"Thank you," Ty said, and kissed him.

Emily had no interest in the kiss. She rubbed her little face against Ty's chest and fell asleep.

Carter pulled out his phone. "Is it all right if I tell Keegan? With everything happening so fast I never got the chance."

Ty grimaced. "Yeah, that's probably a good idea. If you pass me my phone, I'll tell Mr. Clarke. Keegan's not allowed to buy her clothes, though."

"No," Carter agreed. "I'll text from your phone. You don't need to try to text and cuddle at the same time. You're on paternity leave."

Ty smiled. He might be filthy, and stinky, and bloody and gross, but he might also be glowing. He'd waited for so long to hear those words. "I am on paternity leave, aren't I? I might just forget every piece of tort law I ever knew for the next three months. And it's going to be amazing."

***

Emily was the most perfect baby in the history of time. Everyone said so, or at least everyone who Carter and Ty decided to share the good news with. Considering that the team made a formal announcement the day after Carter told them, that number turned out to be fairly high. Carter let his agent filter his social media accounts for him, so he only saw the positive responses to this one. Most of the time he didn't mind getting negative feedback from fans - sometimes he had crappy outings, and he needed to know it. And some people in the world just needed to get some stuff off their chest. His skin was thick enough to deal with it.

This was different. This was Carter's family. This was a newborn baby. He wasn't about to put up with any negativity toward his little girl.

Ty had a hard time letting go of Emily, even when the nurses wanted to give her a bath or give her a checkup. It was kind of funny, really. Ty was the most independent guy Carter had ever met, but he held onto their daughter like she provided him with oxygen or something. The nurses told him that was perfectly normal and natural, especially in guys who'd been trying for a while. He'd get over it eventually.

In the meantime, he still had to get over his hemorrhage issue. When they'd planned for Emily's birth, they'd expected to spend a night in the hospital. When Ty's bleeding wouldn't stop, or even slow down, doctors had to take steps. Carter got to stay with Emily while Ty had to go in for some intense exams, which was where doctors found their worst-case scenario. Emily's rapid birth had caused a lot of tearing, not just to Ty's birth canal but to his uterus. The damage was too severe to be repaired. He would need a hysterectomy.

It was an unusual birth injury, although by no means one for the record books. According to their surgeon, Dr. Wayne, it happened more often in omegas than in women. "We aren't sure why, and part of the reason we aren't sure why is that we lost out on a lot of time. For centuries we weren't able to study omegas as well, and omegas still aren't exactly common in the general population. But it does happen. It's one of the risks, and we need to fix it."

Ty cried a little. It was a bitter pill for him to swallow, but he was the kind of guy who could take these things in stride. He kissed Emily before handing her off to Carter. "At least I've gotten to have this one," he said, as they got ready to bring him in for his surgery.

"Hey." Carter grabbed his hand. "We can always adopt, when it comes right down to it. Okay? This doesn't stop anything but the bleeding."

"God, I love you." Ty squeezed his hand and they wheeled him away.

Carter was left to sit in their room, alone with Emily. He texted Keegan to ask him to take care of the cats for a few days, as Ty would have to stay longer than expected. Further details would be up to Ty to share. He cuddled Emily, who had already decided she had no use for her hats and figured out a way to wiggle out of them.

He read the good wishes of his fans out loud to Emily, who didn't care. She seemed to be content to hear his voice, or at least it didn't make her scream, but she didn't have a lot to say.

They'd been hanging out in the room for about an hour and a half when some of the footsteps that constantly passed by the little room paused. Carter couldn't hear any accompanying wheels, so he knew Ty hadn't come back yet. For a second, just a second, he got scared. All surgery came with risks, and Ty had already been bleeding pretty heavily...

But the people striding into the room like they owned the place weren't doctors, or nurses, or chaplains or social workers. Carter sighed when he saw Beau, Ed, and Sebastian. He stood up and pressed the nurses' call button. "You bastards don't take 'no' for an answer, do you?"

"Not from upstarts like you," Beau sniffed. "Give me the baby."

"Like hell." Carter cradled Emily a little closer to his chest. "Now get out."

"Do you really want to fight about this?" Sebastian walked closer, lip curled. "There's two of us alphas here, and we don't have one hand tied behind our back."

"So you guys saw the words 'restraining order' and you thought what, it just didn't apply to you?" Carter huffed out a laugh. Where were the nurses? Better yet, where was security? He tapped out an "SOS" in Morse code with the call button. "Look. Ty's been through a lot and the last thing he needs to see when he gets back here is your faces. Go away."

"We are his parents!" Beau hissed. "We have more of a right to be here than you do!"

"Actually you don't. It's that whole law thing. I may not be a lawyer, but I did marry one and he's pretty sure the restraining order means you have no right to be here, at all."

"The baby doesn't have a restraining order." Ed smirked at him. "Hand her over, you sack of hired muscle."

"No."

"I will make my son see reason." Beau stomped his foot on the linoleum floor. "He does not get to just cut us out and go rogue like this! He can have other babies, babies who have proper backgrounds."

Carter laughed. He couldn't help it. It was Ty's injury, and his story to tell, but Carter was so done with these awful people and their awful attitude he just wanted to get rid of them. "I notice you haven't shown a whole lot of interest in Ty's welfare. I shouldn't be surprised, all things considered. You never showed much interested in his well-being before, so why would you start now?"

Sebastian scoffed. "It's not for you to police how they interact with their son."

"Actually it is. I'm his alpha. It's my job to protect him. Ty's in surgery right now. I'm not going into why. The birth was very hard on him, and even if he was to give in and leave me for everyone's favorite homicidal maniac here —"

Sebastian snarled and took a swing at Carter. He wasn't much of a brawler. He telegraphed his moves bad enough for Carter to see what he had in mind from a mile away. Carter ducked under the punch and head-butted Sebastian in the nose. It was the only weapon he had, or at least the only one he could use if he wanted to keep Emily stable. "You're not doing a whole lot to prove your stability here," he pointed out, as Sebastian exhaled blood.

"You broke my nose!" Sebastian wailed. "You broke my nose!"

Three security guards rushed into the room. There wasn't a lot of space left. Hopefully no one else would feel compelled to get violent. "What seems to be the problem here?" the security guard near the front of the pack demanded with a scowl.

Beau pointed at Carter. "This man won't give my grand baby back to me. And he broke my son-in-law's nose."

Carter sputtered in outrage. How in hell could Beau say such a thing? But the security guard didn't seem inclined to believe him. "He has the bracelet that matches the baby's. None of you do, to include your son-in-law."

Some of the tension ebbed from Carter. He could speak again at least. "My husband and I have restraining orders against all three of these people. They're not allowed to be here. They need to be arrested." He met Sebastian's eyes. "The one with all the blood is violating his bail by breaking his restraining order, so this should be fun."

Sebastian rolled his eyes and scoffed. "We both know they're not sending me to prison. Rich people don't go to jail."

One of the other security guards was already on the phone. "They'll meet us downstairs at the security office," he said. "Do you want to come downstairs the nice way, or do you want us to get creative?"

"If you even think about putting a hand on us, we'll sue." Ed sniffed contemptuously. "My son is a lawyer."

"Ty is on paternity leave and he'd no more help you out than he would poke a sharp stick in his own eye." Carter couldn't help but snarl at his father-in-law.

"Creative it is." The head security guard grabbed Beau and hauled him out into the hallway. He wasn't gentle about it.

The other guards cuffed Ed and Sebastian and dragged them away too. Someone from Housekeeping showed up to mop up the blood from Sebastian's broken nose, and Carter sat back down to wait for Ty. He was probably in the recovery room, trying to purge himself of the anesthesia. Would he get back before Carter gave his statement? Carter hoped not. He didn't want Ty to know about this visit. He just wanted him to be happy and content.

Fortunately, two uniformed officers showed up ten minutes later to take Carter's statement. They'd found a record of the restraining orders pretty easily, so there wasn't much for Carter to say. He described the threats, and he spoke about the circumstances leading up to Sebastian's broken nose, which only made the cops laugh. He signed autographs for both officers and got selfies with them too. It was probably unprofessional of them, but he was beyond caring at this point. As long as he, Emily, and Ty were safe, he'd sign as many autographs as they wanted.

Then they went away again. Ty was brought in a couple of hours later, and Carter wasn't sure he shouldn't have stayed longer. He was groggy, and he slept a lot. Every once in a while he seemed to wake up, but when he spoke he spoke nonsense. Then he'd pass back out again.

He didn't truly wake up until the next day. Even now he was still exhausted, but he was more with-it and could hold a conversation. "You've been through a lot in the past couple of days. You really need to just rest and relax. Do you think you can do that for me?"

Ty made a face. "I'm bad at resting and relaxing. Can you pass Emily over here, please?"

Carter did. As a look of utter bliss came over Ty's face, Carter smiled. "Me and Miss Emily have been having a grand old time while you were off in surgery. We read fan mail out loud, and we had a discussion about hats and why they should stay on her head."

"Did she listen?"

"Not even a little bit."

Ty chuckled. "I didn't think she would." He nuzzled her cheek. "I missed you, little one."

Of course, Carter couldn't keep Ty in the dark forever. He would have loved to be able to keep him from ever finding out about the attack, but Ty wasn't exactly the sort of guy to run around with his head in the clouds. He got a text from Mr. Clarke the next day, after a notice about the arrests appeared in the paper.

Ty wasn't thrilled that Carter had tried to hide it from him. "Seriously, Carter? Why did you think this was something I didn't need to know?"

Carter bowed his head. He'd screwed up, and he knew it. "I just... you'd already had to deal with so much. Your body had been through the wringer, you were going to be all messed up from surgery and everything, and I just didn't want to ramp up any anxiety or anything by dumping their little wretched visit on you. I'm sorry. Maybe I should have said something, but honestly I just wanted you to go home with as many good memories as you could."

Ty made a face at him. "Here I was getting my dander up all good and fierce, and you come up with the best possible reasoning. Honestly, I'm not even sure how to reply to that." He closed his eyes and sighed. "Why can't they just leave us alone?"

"I don't know." Carter didn't point out that Ty knew them all better than he did. He didn't think that would be at all helpful. "Does it make you feel better to know that I broke Sebastian's nose?"

Ty gasped and laughed. His laugh was weak thanks to the surgery, but it was genuine. "That's awesome. I think his life - and mine - would have turned out a lot differently if someone had punched him in the face a little more often as a kid."

Carter blushed. "Well, I didn't so much punch him as head butt him. I didn't want to drop the baby," he protested when Ty gaped. "I mean you wouldn't want me to drop her either, would you?"

Ty just laughed. "I guess not, no I wouldn't. I guess all those bench-clearing brawls were good for something, huh?"

Carter pretended to be affronted. "Hey, that only happened against Boston!"

"And Detroit."

"One time!"

"Three."

"Fine. Three. But to be fair, their guys charged the mound every time."

"I didn't say they didn't." Ty was grinning now. Carter passed him a bottle, which Emily took with gusto. "You're amazing."

Ty's condition improved over the next few days. It would be a long recovery period, but not as long as it would have been if they'd done it through the abdomen. He was clearly frustrated by the delay, but he passed the time walking around the ward to build his muscle tone back up. He checked in with the office a few times, because someone like Ty couldn't separate himself from the office entirely, and he spent time with Emily.

Carter loved hanging out with Emily. He supposed all parents thought their kid was exceptional, but Emily clearly had something unique to her. She could lift her head after only a day or so. She could grip his finger with a strong, enthusiastic hand, and she made little sounds that could be imagined by a person with the right mindset to be enthusiasm.

The team reached out to him, gingerly after the whole thing with the fake photos and the article and all that. They wanted to set up a charity drive in Emily's name to celebrate her birth. It was a thing, they said. A lot of celebrities were doing that now, to cut down on extraneous and occasionally creepy gifts sent in by fans. No one needed seven million baby blankets, even the beautiful hand-knit ones, and everyone felt weird about giving them away. Did they have a particular charity they wanted to recommend?

Carter checked with Ty. Ty raised his eyebrows at the request from the team, but didn't say anything against them. He did ask what specific perks went along with the drive, like photos and the like, because he was smart like that. In the end, they selected a domestic violence charity and a charity to support families who couldn't afford emergency obstetric care like what Ty had endured.

They left the hospital a week after they went in. It would be a whole new world, but they were prepared to face it - as a family.

Chapter Sixteen

Ty didn't necessarily find it easy to settle back into life at home. Everything was different now, and while Emily was very much a wanted child, he couldn't help but feel that everything was somehow screwed up. In the hospital, there had been nurses around that he could call on if something went wrong. If he needed a new bottle for Emily, he could just press the button and call someone. If she got the hiccups and they lasted for twenty minutes, or thirty minutes, or an hour, he could call the nurse and she would just tell him not to worry.

At home, he didn't have that luxury. At home, it was just Ty, Carter, and three cats. Keegan offered to come by and help out, but Keegan wasn't someone Carter would generally allow around children or anyone else with a sensitive constitution. Carter's parents wanted to come up to New York and help out, but Ty hadn't even met them yet. He didn't want their first encounter to involve Ty flailing around like a chicken with its head cut off and being incredibly incompetent with their grandchild.

It did occur to Ty, once late at night when Emily wouldn't stop crying, that he could call Beau. Then he pushed that thought firmly out of his mind. Beau hadn't even helped when Ty had been as small as Emily. He'd made the nanny deal with it.

Together, he and Carter hunkered down and muddled through. Slowly, they figured things out. It wasn't as if they were stupid. They could do research on the Internet. They could call informational hotlines. Carter could call his coach, who had a bunch of children of his own. Ty could call Ruiz' wife Yolanda, who not only had kids but was still in New York.

Yolanda came over to the house. She brought her kids. She also brought a bunch of food. Apparently she'd been prepared for this, because she'd made the food ahead of time so they didn't have to rely on takeout. "I know you're probably used to takeout," she told him, "but your body will thank you. Trust me."

Yolanda helped them find a nanny, too. None of Ty's contacts otherwise would have thought to look in the Dominican community for a nanny, but Yolanda helped to find a nanny that made both Carter and Ty feel perfectly at home and comfortable right away. Isabella was older, in her fifties, and she came with impeccable references. She spoke English just fine, but Ty didn't mind if she spoke to Emily in Spanish. It was best for babies' neurological development to hear multiple languages.

Emily had been born between Christmas and New Year. By the time February rolled around, Ty was feeling more like a human again. His incisions were healed, and he'd passed his first checkup with flying colors. Isabella was already on duty, even with both fathers home, and everyone agreed that was best. They needed her maternal touch.

Carter would be going back to Spring Training soon. Ty knew he was being selfish when he said he didn't want Carter to go, but it was the truth. He wanted Carter at home with him, to cuddle and to play with Emily. There would be time enough for that to happen. Carter didn't technically *need* the money anymore, since their agreement ensured he'd be well taken care of even if Ty ran off with their entirely fictitious pool boy. His ego had taken a blow when the extent of the financial scam had become known, though, and he needed to recoup his money.

Besides, Carter loved baseball. Ty might want his husband by his side, but he would never try to keep him away from something he loved. When Valentine's Day rolled around, Ty left Emily alone with Isabella for the first time. He went out to dinner with Carter, and they came home and made love for the first time since Emily had been born.

The next day, Carter left for Florida. Ty pouted for a little while. Then he called Keegan and asked him to take care of the cats again.

He, Isabella, and Emily headed down to Florida at the end of February. It wasn't a pleasant flight. Emily didn't care for the pressure changes, but out of all of the children on the flight she was the best behaved. Ty considered kissing the ground when he landed, but decided it would be undignified. He got into the car he'd pre-arranged for, helped get Emily and Isabella settled, and the three of them headed off toward the hotel.

Going to the hotel was a risk. Ty trusted Carter. Rather, he accepted there was a given likelihood that Carter might cheat, and he accepted that as a done deal. He knew he didn't have much to offer, especially not with the baby weight that still lingered and the big bags that hung around under his eyes from lack of sleep. Carter said he was faithful, and Ty believed him, he just accepted that it wasn't necessarily likely. He wouldn't blame Carter if he did stray, especially at Spring Training when he was in an exclusively spouse-free environment.

The hotel Ty had picked was probably a little too indulgent. It was top of the line, a luxury facility that Ty knew Carter would scoff at under normal circumstances. But he wanted to surround himself with familiar things, just in case. It wasn't like they couldn't afford it.

He met Yolanda in the WAGs section the next afternoon at the Spring Training game. It was a split squad game versus Boston, but it was at home with most of their real players. The game was televised too, although due to scheduling weirdness it was being shown at five o'clock eastern even though it was being played at one. Ty didn't care. All he cared about was the man at second base.

Yolanda elbowed him. “You should bring Tracy in on this. He’ll send your man up, once he’s done playing for the day.”

Ty blushed and ducked his head. “Not me. Tracy doesn’t like me at all.”

Isabella scowled at that. She demanded Ty’s phone, and Ty handed it over without thinking about it. She sent a few texts, and a few moments later Isabella was handing the phone back. “Tracy will be sending your husband back to you,” she promised. “Sixth inning, look for him.”

Emily giggled. She’d become so much livelier over the past few weeks. Sometime around week six she’d learned to smile, and that had made a huge difference in everyone’s life. All she did was smile and giggle now, and all anyone else did was try to pull a smile and giggle out of her. Sometimes Ty hoped no one had a video camera. The rest of the time he hoped they did.

Tracy pulled Carter in the fifth. When the sixth inning started, Carter showed up in the stands. He wore street clothes, khakis and a team polo shirt, and he beamed over at Ty. “I can’t believe you flew all the way down here.”

“I had the time off. That’s not going to happen again.” Ty ducked his head and blushed. “I didn’t want to miss any more opportunities, not with you. You’re the love of my life and I’m proud of you. I want to support you.”

Carter grinned. “Okay, but Florida? Babies on a plane? Florida?”

Ty wasn’t given to public displays of affection, but now he pulled Carter in for a deep kiss. “Babies on a plane, Florida, a public baseball stadium, I don’t care. I honestly just want to show the world how proud I am that you’re my husband.”

Carter kissed him then. Ty would never have realized there was a camera on them until the whole stadium started chanting for them to kiss.

"Maybe we could go to the hotel?" Carter chuckled.

"That might be a good idea."

Oddly enough, Tracy didn't raise hell about them going back to the hotel. Ty knew that Carter was supposed to go to the dorm, and he asked about it. He didn't want to jam Carter up. Carter just shook his head and laughed. "Tracy thinks you're hiding under his bed waiting to sue him for breathing wrong. He's not going to make a fuss about where I sleep."

Ty wasn't going to look a gift horse in the mouth. He shuddered and let Isabella take Emily for the night, and he let his husband pound him into the mattress. It felt incredible. Carter had been solicitous. He'd been a little too solicitous, if Ty was being honest. He'd seemed like he thought Ty's pregnancy somehow turned his bones to the finest porcelain, when that hadn't been the case at all.

Ty would never have that issue again. The thought gave him a pang. He tried not to think about that as Carter drove into him, again and again. It was okay to love and to be loved. He didn't exist entirely to have babies. He had one, who was perfect, and now he could look at the rest of his life as a bonus.

He spent the weekend in Florida, and then he went back to New York. He would have spent the rest of his paternity leave there, but he missed the cats. Besides, he didn't want to pull Cater away from his team. Spring Training was about more than just mechanically preparing for the season. It was about team building, and Carter couldn't do that right if he was frolicking in a nice hotel with Ty the whole time.

Back in New York, he figured out pretty quickly that his enemies had been busy while he'd been away. Seb had shown up a day after he left for Florida. Keegan had dealt with him, in his usual flamboyant and messy fashion. That didn't change the fact that Seb had been able to get out of prison to try to pester him while he knew Carter was away. Keegan didn't say if their parents were involved, and after a moments' resentment Ty decided that it didn't matter.

Their parents had enabled Sebastian. The fact that he was there at all tied back to their parents. It was enough.

He sighed and reached out to the police, who started a manhunt. Sebastian had previously made bail, again thanks to Ty's parents, but now no one knew how to find him. Ty needed to address this once and for all. He filed a suit against the state department, to finally remove this nuisance man from his life. Sebastian should have been extradited a long time ago, and it was well past time for him to leave.

Ty's suit didn't get the job done. But it did get Seb taken into custody, and the judge finally refused him bail. It was a sad ending for a guy who had once shown so much promise, but then again he'd had plenty of opportunities to not end up where he did. For one thing, he could have not killed his husband.

Once Seb was safely locked up without the possibility of getting out, Ty knew he was safe. He could relax. Seb couldn't get to him. The season started, and Ty could cheer from the stands with Emily, knowing everything would finally be all right.

***

Carter had learned a lot in the past year. He'd learned a lot about himself. He'd learned a lot about families. He'd learned a lot about pregnancy, and about childbirth. He'd learned a lot about love, about falling in love, and about how happy he could be when his expectations were low.

This year, he learned a lot about the legal system. The first thing he learned was that the legal system was slow. He'd been spoiled when Ty got the sports website to retract their story about him so quickly. Apparently if people didn't cave to the mere threat of being sued, cases could drag on forever.

That meant Ty's parents were free to enjoy their palace on the Upper West Side as much as they chose, even though they'd burst in on Carter in the hospital and tried to take Emily from him. They told their side of the story to anyone who would listen, and since Carter was a celebrity in the sports world plenty of people were willing to hear them out. And Carter couldn't respond, since there was pending litigation and a pending criminal case against them.

It frustrated and infuriated him. He tried to take it out on the baseballs that came his way. Last year he'd been MVP. This year the talk of sports media was his home run count. A few outlets whispered about performance enhancing drugs, and that gave him an outlet. "That's cute," he said when the subject came up. "The only performance enhancer I've got is my anger. My husband and I have gone through a lot in the past year or so. His parents are saying a lot of things about us, and about me, and we can't respond. I'm trying to channel my anger into something productive and positive. I do get tested on the regular, because PEDs are a concern and baseball has had such a problem with them in the past. Seriously, though, it's just me trying to take something bad and make something good out of it."

Carter was still angry about Tracy's abandonment during his meeting with ownership, but they put their relationship back together one step at a time. They'd been through a lot together, and Carter couldn't make himself forget that. Besides, Tracy did have a job to do. He worked for ownership, not for Carter, and he'd told the truth when asked.

The first case to come to court was the criminal case against Sebastian, Ed, and Beau. It popped up on the docket in June, and Carter had to take time away from the team to testify. The media made something of a circus around the courthouse because of it, which only made Carter's mood worse. Still, he plastered a big smile onto his face and forced himself to be civil for the media. You never knew who was watching.

He had no idea how the defense would cross examine him. What was there really to say? Much to his surprise, they lied outright. Their attorney, a guy named Johnston, approached the stand. "Isn't it true that you invited them to the hospital room?"

"No, it is not." Carter did a double take. Had he just stepped into the twilight zone? "Ty didn't want any visitors after the birth, and certainly not those particular people."

"But you hadn't wanted children in the first place, had you?"

Now Carter understood. "I hadn't wanted children before my marriage. I was willing to have children because Ty wanted them, and then after Ty got pregnant I got more excited about our child." He smirked, because he knew what the lawyer was trying to imply, but he didn't say it out loud. He didn't want the jury to get ideas from such an absurd accusation.

"So you didn't invite them into the room to give them the child in the hopes of ridding yourself of an encumbrance you didn't want?"

Carter rolled his eyes. "No, no I did not. Given that my agent had already announced the birth, that would have been a self-defeating move, don't you think?"

Johnston scowled. "But you called them to the room."

"I did not."

"They say you did."

"Phone records say I did not."

"Why would they lie, Mr. Bowman?"

"I don't pretend I can see into the minds of people like your clients, Mr. Johnston. I love my family and I do my job. Maybe you should call a psychiatrist to the stand?"

The jury snickered. Johnston flounced back to his table and declared there to be no further questions.

Carter was allowed to rejoin his team on the road now that his testimony was complete, but Ty kept him updated as the trial wore on. "I kind of feel sorry for Johnston. He's an ass, but he was also handed a case he couldn't win."

"He should have told them to plead guilty then." Carter shrugged. He couldn't feel bad for a jerk like that.

In the end, all three defendants were found guilty. "Super guilty, your honor," were the foreman's exact words. The Cunninghams, who had never been in trouble before, were sentenced to house arrest. Since this meant they had to stay in their home with each other, Carter figured this was a pretty serious sentence.

Sebastian's sentence was for two to five years, but it was not to be served yet. "Mr. Britton, you're facing some serious charges in the United Kingdom. The court rules that you will begin serving your sentence for the attempted kidnapping after you've finished your trial there, and after you've served any sentence should you be found guilty."

That was not something Sebastian wanted to hear, and Ty told Carter he made a pretty big spectacle of himself when he tried to charge the bench. "Is it wrong to admit I kind of liked watching him get tased by the bailiffs?" he asked.

The next case to come before the court was the civil suit, and here was where it got interesting. The judge did find that all three defendants had engaged in a series of actions designed to harass Carter and Ty, as well as to attempt to besmirch Carter's reputation with a view toward interfering not only with his marriage but with his career and livelihood. That wasn't exactly rocket science.

He awarded Ty and Carter a hefty sum, more than they'd asked for on the grounds that their behavior clearly constituted malice and the damages needed to be sufficiently punitive that the defendants wouldn't blow them off. However, Sebastian Britton proved to be unable to pay.

He'd been living not in his own place, but with Ed and Beau. His own assets had been tied up in the investigation into his husband's murder. The bank hadn't promoted him and returned him to the States, they'd fired him when suspicion fell on him for the murder. Sebastian was broke.

The night after the award was handed down, an older couple showed up at Ty and Carter's place. Carter didn't recognize them, but Ty introduced them as Sebastian's parents. The Brittons were pale and drawn, and they greeted Carter with a grace and kindness the Cunninghams never showed.

Sebastian's mother cleared her throat. "I have to apologize, to both of you. I had no idea that Sebastian was capable of any of this. I knew we'd spoiled him, but I think this goes beyond spoiling."

Ty bowed his head and took her hand. "I think he'd have turned out this way no matter what. I can't say for sure if he did kill Niall, I haven't seen the evidence. But I think he does have his issues, and they're not issues that can be helped."

Mr. Britton nodded somberly. "We knew he was back in the States. He asked us to buy him an apartment. We said no, obviously. He had been violent, and we weren't comfortable encouraging him. I think he was desperate."

"Your parents always did have a soft spot for him." Mrs. Britton grimaced.

Ty huffed out a little laugh. "He was always their ideal alpha son. Everything Keegan wasn't, I guess."

"What I want to know is how he got Ed and Beau to go along with all of the crazy things he was doing." Mr. Britton massaged his own temples. "I'm sorry. I know he's not your responsibility and it's not on you to figure it all out. He's put you both through enough."

Carter smiled gently. "It's natural to want to know. He's your son, even after everything." He took a deep breath. "I don't know the Cunninghams well. But they definitely have certain, ah, ideas about society."

"They're dreadful snobs," Mrs. Britton agreed.

"Right?" Carter laughed. "And we've seen that Sebastian can be extremely charismatic when he wants to be."

"That's the truth." Ty looked away. "I fell for it for years." He picked his head back up when Carter wrapped his arm around him. "Ed and Beau already adored him. It would have been pretty easy for him to manipulate them, especially if they were living with him full time."

"So you think they were brainwashed." Carter pulled Ty in a little closer.

"I can't think of another explanation, can you?" Ty rested his head on Carter's shoulder and looked over at the Brittons. "I'm sorry. I know this has to be hard to hear."

Mr. Britton took a deep breath. "Not as hard as it must have been for you both to live through. So he was going after Tyler for his money."

"Absolutely." Ty smirked then. "He'd have been desperate. And Ed and Beau would have known, and they let it happen anyway."

"That's dreadful." Mrs. Britton covered her mouth with her hand.

"It is. But again, they were brainwashed, and we weren't all that close to begin with. I'm very lucky now. I've got a husband who loves me, and a gorgeous daughter." Ty smiled.

Carter took pity on the Brittons then. "Do you want to stay for dinner? It's nothing fancy, but Ty only knows how to cook for a crowd and it seems like we could all use a little company right now."

The Brittons did stay for dinner. And they had Ty and Carter over the next time Carter had an off day. Carter felt good about pursuing the connection. The Brittons were good people, and they were grieving. They could all support each other during this process.

Carter's parents finally came to New York after the team's postseason run ended. It had taken a while for them to finally come and meet Ty, but farming was hard work and demanded a lot of time. Ty didn't seem to mind. He was a bundle of nerves before they arrived, but Carter's mom put that to rest almost as soon as she set foot in the apartment. She hugged Ty, picked up Emily, and declared that she was just "pleased as punch" to finally see this part of her family with her own two eyes. She and Ty were chatting like old friends before dinner.

Sebastian ran out of appeals to his extradition by Christmas. His trial back in London turned out to be quick. He was convicted of murder and sentenced to thirty years' imprisonment. Carter wanted to throw a party, because they were finally safe, but instead he just bought a nice bottle of champagne and a cute stuffed koala for Emily.

Sebastian had tried to destroy their family, for money. The best way to celebrate his defeat would be to enjoy some family time. He opened up the bottle of bubbly with Ty and Keegan and they watched Emily playing with her new toy.

Maybe there had been some drama, but the contract Carter had signed with Ty had been the best contract he'd signed in his life.

Preview Chapter: Game Show

Scott smashed his alarm. Today was Sunday, the one day he didn't have to get up at the crack of dawn. Why would his alarm be going off now? He wouldn't have forgotten to turn it off, would he?

He heard the clock hit the ground, but the awful buzzing continued. With a pained groan, he realized the sound wasn't the alarm clock. It was his phone. He fumbled for it and answered it before his voice mail could pick up. "Hello?"

"Hello, is Scott Thorburn available please?"

The speaker had a deep, radio-announcer type of voice. It was the kind of voice that always made Scott's skin crawl. It had always sounded creepy to him for some reason, inappropriately cheerful at weird times. Right now cheer was definitely inappropriate, since it was nine o'clock on a Sunday morning and Scott hadn't had any coffee yet. "This is Scott. Who's calling?"

"Scott, this is Amos Yates from *Make It Work,* the premiere reality show on television. You auditioned for the program approximately six months ago. Do you recall that, Scott?"

Scott scratched his belly. He did remember the audition. The whole stupid thing had been Grant's idea. People who got an audition got a hundred bucks for their time, and Grant had needed the hundred bucks back then. He could do with a hundred bucks right now, come to think of it, but it wasn't quite so dire.

"I remember." He yawned. "Is there something wrong?"

Amos Yates, the announcer for the single worst reality show on television, laughed a laugh so artificial Scott wondered if it had been computer generated. "No, Scott. Nothing is the matter. Are you available to come to the studio tomorrow at noon? We'll be filming the first episode of the new season, and you're one of the ten omegas we've selected to be part of the show. All ten candidates will receive ten thousand dollars each, exclusive of any winnings they receive as part of the show should they be selected as the omega half of the marriage."

Scott coughed. He couldn't bring himself to believe this. "Is this some kind of sick joke?"

Yates' voice turned disapproving, in spite of the omnipresent tone of inappropriate cheer. "No, Scott. It isn't a joke. And if you'll recall, you did sign a legally binding agreement to make yourself available for filming should you make it to this round. We'll email you the address and guidelines on what to wear, and of course we'll mail you a check within sixty days of filming."

Scott grimaced. "Um. Right. Yeah, tomorrow at noon. I'll be there." He remembered that agreement. He'd signed it because the chances of having to do anything about it were about nine hundred thousand to one, or something like that. He never thought, in a million years, he'd have to go through with anything like getting up on TV.

Should he get a lawyer?

He knew, without having to pay money he didn't have, exactly what the lawyer would say. He would say, "Dude, you should have read what you signed. And then you shouldn't have signed it. Moron." Nine to one odds were a lot worse than nine hundred thousand to one, right? Sure, Scott could use an extra ten grand. He didn't have a lot hanging around in the way of savings. But he didn't want to get married, either. He didn't want a temporary marriage to some guy, all to be filmed and flashed all over the TV.

He ran into the bathroom and puked. It didn't make him feel better, but he hadn't had much choice. The thought of letting some stranger touch him just made him ill. Sure, he'd get paid. He had no idea how much he'd get paid, and he didn't care either. He'd basically be getting paid for sex, and there was a word for that.

When his body had yielded everything it was going to give, he rinsed out his mouth and went to go make the coffee. He could hear Grant slurring on the phone, so Grant was obviously getting a call too. Grant wouldn't mind having to marry a stranger. He'd probably done worse in his time. Scott would probably have to find a new roommate, but whatever. That wouldn't be hard. Astoria wasn't a bad place to live and the rents weren't awful.

By the time the coffee was done, Grant had finished his conversation and shuffled into the common area. Scott considered "accidentally" spilling the hot coffee over his bare chest, but thought better of it. Grant had come up with the idea, and he'd certainly badgered Scott into it, but Scott could have said no at any time.

"Dude. Ten grand, right?" Grant grinned at him, huge and satisfied. "Think about it. Think of the things we could do with that money. Think of the beer we can buy with that money." Scott rolled his eyes. Okay, sure, he might buy a little beer. He was going to save most of it, probably put some of it toward retirement. "I'm just hoping we don't 'win.'" He sipped from his coffee. "Can you imagine?"

"Dude. Yes, I can imagine. Being married and having to be monogamous for a year will suck but you know what else sucks? Living on ramen when they cut back hours at the gym, the studio, or the shop. Having to work two jobs, both of us, and still not getting anywhere. I for one welcome the bonds of matrimony with open and loving arms." He scratched at his beard. "Besides, it means getting laid on the regular without having to go and hit up the club or whatever, and that's got a lot of appeal for me."

Scott laughed, jollied out of his mood. "Well with any luck they'll pick you and we won't have to worry about it, then. If we want that to happen..."

"What?"

"We'll have to do something about that beard. You haven't trimmed it in a while and you're starting to look like you crawled out of the Pine Barrens. Come on, I'll take care of it."

"Can't we wait until I've had some more coffee?" Grant whined. "I just woke up, and I was on the best bender last night. I think I'm still a little buzzed."

Scott rolled his eyes, but he couldn't help but laugh. "Of course you are." He wasn't a big partier, but he wasn't going to look down on Grant for cutting loose sometimes. They both worked hard. If it helped Grant to get wild every now and then, Scott wasn't going to tell him no.

He drank his coffee and went for a run. By the time he came back, Grant was ready to get cleaned up for the occasion. Scott would have stuck around to help nurse him through his hangover and go over their materials for the next day, but he had work to do. He was teaching four group fitness classes at the gym today, and he didn't want to be late.

He went through his classes - kickboxing, yoga, self defense for omegas, and Boot Camp - and spent some time working the floor in the fitness area. Sundays at this gym tended to be fairly crowded, but at least out here people were still cool. He worked for the same gym up in Midtown on Tuesdays and those customers would drive a saint to drink. Pushy and entitled, every last one of them had a long-winded explanation as to why they were the exception to every rule in the gym.

And that was without taking the alphas into consideration. Did they not see the bio with his resume? He'd broken fingers, wrists, bones, noses, and one kneecap before the company sent out a weekly reminder to its members that touching staff was not permitted under any circumstances.

When he got home, he called his boss at the martial arts studio. They would have to get someone else to cover tomorrow night's classes. Something had come up, he had an obligation he couldn't get out of without a lawsuit, and that was just it. Bob understood. He was cool like that.

He woke up the next morning with a stomach filled with lead. Part of him still thought he might be able to find a way out of this, but he knew he couldn't. The only thing he could do was to calm himself down and go through with it. Hopefully nothing would come of it, he could stash some money away and move on.

It would be a learning experience. He'd learn to read contracts before he signed them, and not to say yes to anything Grant suggested ever again.

He went through his usual workout - a run first, then through some exercises, and finally some yoga. By the time he was finished, Grant had come home. He eyed Scott as he sat on the floor, finishing his yoga practice. "It's a good thing this part isn't being filmed. They'd pick you for sure. With abs like that? The audience would riot."

Scott blushed and went to shower. He washed up and combed his hair, although he didn't pay much attention to it. The last thing he wanted was to be attractive, for crying out loud. When he was done, he and Grant headed over to the Valor Entertainment building.

This place was huge. The front lobby was elegant, more so than anyplace Scott had ever been. They had their directions, though, and neither of them wanted to be late. They didn't have time to linger and admire the artwork.

Their studio was on the tenth floor. They took the elevator up together, although neither of them spoke much. Even Grant was intimidated by the idea of filming an actual episode of television, or maybe the enormity of potentially marrying a stranger had finally penetrated his brain. Scott was afraid that if he opened his mouth he'd throw up.

They got out of the elevator and followed the signs to the sound stage, where a flurry of cameramen, sound operators, and production assistants fluttered around a group of eight guys. All of the eight guys looked to be within twelve years of Scott and Grant, if Scott had to guess. Standing in front of the other omegas, wearing a fuchsia ascot and directing everything, was a pale man with gray hair.

"Ah. Here we are." His voice made him immediately identifiable as Amos Yates. "Scott, Grant, thank you for joining us. Let's get started, shall we?"

Scott inched up to join the other omegas in the line. Grant slouched up beside him, and Yates continued to speak.

"Let me explain how this is going to go. The alpha is on site, but none of you will see him until we are on camera and we're ready for the reveal. What we're going to do now is get your hair and makeup done. Yes, makeup. You're on television, you didn't think they all looked that good naturally? We have to account for the effects of lighting and the camera but trust me, you're all beautiful.

"Now. Once we've done that, we're going to introduce each of you one at a time. You'll go and stand on the riser that has your picture from the audition on it. Then we'll introduce the alpha. We'll announce the winner, he'll cry tears of joy while the rest of you congratulate him, and then bing bang boom we'll bring out the priest. Sound like a plan?"

One of the other omegas, a beautiful young man with dark skin, raised his hand. “Wait. Where are the judges?”

“Mikkel, the decision has already been made. We’ll announce during filming, because we want everyone’s reactions to be genuine, but everything is already set. The checks for the ones who aren’t getting married have even been cut.” He smiled creepily, all teeth and gums, and clapped his hands twice. “All right! Let’s get this done!”

An army of hairdressers and makeup artists descended, and Scott knew he was done for.

***

Danny checked himself in the mirror. The makeup itched. Truth be told, he felt ridiculous. His makeup was an inch thick, and it would have to be taken off with a chisel, and a category five hurricane wouldn’t move his hair. But he wanted a husband, didn’t he? And he didn’t have time to find one. The Hellion Club was good for a lot of things - networking, for example, and casual hookups - but they couldn’t help him find a husband.

He sighed. The longer he sat back here and watched through CCTV, the more he thought this game show wasn’t the right way to find a husband either. Sure, he was going to be married at the end of the day. When he’d signed onto this project he’d thought of it like a checklist. Everything else had gone like a checklist. College at fourteen? Check. IPO at twenty? Check. First billion by twenty-five? Also check.

Married by thirty? Not so much. And responsible men were married by the time they got to a certain age. Danny was a responsible guy, a responsible alpha. He might have dedicated a lot of his life and time to building his business, but that didn’t mean he wasn’t responsible. He needed a husband.

None of these guys he saw out on that stage was a husband. None of them had made any money to speak of. They wouldn't be able to manage his household funds, or even manage his household. He'd watched all of their intro videos and heard all kinds of stories. Some had come to the US as children from horrific situations, and that was all well and good but that didn't mean they'd be good husbands for a tech mogul. Some were deeply religious, and how was that going to mesh with a man whose life had been devoted to science?

More than half of the omegas didn't even have bachelor's degrees. What in the hell would they have to talk about?

Some of them seemed smarmy and self-assured. Danny liked a guy with a certain level of confidence, but guys who got up in front of a camera and declared themselves to be God's gift to alphas had nothing to offer the world.

Well, he'd signed the contract. And plenty of guys his age had divorces under their belt. He'd stick it out for the year, they'd divorce, and he'd set up an account on MateMaker like a normal guy.

The PA sitting in the room with him froze for a few seconds. Then she tapped him on the shoulder. "Danny, you're up. Come on, I'll tell you when it's time."

She led him out to a space in the wings off of the sound stage, where he couldn't be seen by the contestants. One of them had already been selected for him, but he couldn't make himself root for any of them. They were pretty, but that was about it. None of them sounded like they had a brain in their heads.

The PA tapped his arm. "It's your cue. Go out, your lines will be on the teleprompter, just go."

Danny strode out like he knew what he was doing. He didn't know, and he didn't care. Lines? This was supposed to be reality television. He was a self-made billionaire, damn it. No one decided what he was supposed to say.

He reached his mark and turned to the camera, still smiling. The host, Yates, stood and beamed at him while his voice boomed out from speakers Danny couldn't see. "America, meet Danny Magee. Danny went to MIT at fourteen, finished his undergrad at sixteen, and took his company public before he could legally buy a beer. Yes, you could say he's done it all. Now he's ready to find love. He's committed to making it work with one of our lovely omega contestants. Here's the question - which of these charming men will be the one to share his life for the next year and more?"

Danny looked the omegas over. They all smiled big, beautiful smiles - well, all except one. That one, who stood toward the back with his jaw clenched, had wary dark eyes and a tight black tee shirt that showed an incredible body. Why would he be here if he wasn't happy about it?

Now Yates did speak into the camera. "Danny, the whole world knows what you've accomplished in your lifetime. You're here tonight to make one more incredible accomplishment - to get married. Look out there into the audience and tell everyone who the lucky omega will be."

Danny bristled when Yates put his hand on his back, but he wasn't about to give any signs of weakness away. There weren't any people in the "audience" of course. There were only cameras, and crew. He smiled into the cameras and tried not to be obvious about reading his words. Oh, for crying out loud, who wrote this stuff? "Well, Amos, you know I'm excited about this. I've given the judges a lot of input about my tastes and my needs, and I have every confidence that they'll have made the right decision." He hadn't given them any input, just a blood test to prove he didn't have any STIs.

"Before I leave here tonight, I will have joined my life, my heart, and my soul to..." He had to pause, as the monitor blanked out on him. "Scott Thorburn."

He watched the omegas as they turned around to look at the man who'd won. They'd all clustered around the man in the tight shirt and moved in to hug him. The man himself, Scott, didn't look thrilled. He certainly wasn't crying the tears of joy called for on the teleprompter. His eyes had rolled back into his head, and his knees buckled underneath him.

Danny sprang into action before he made a conscious choice to get involved. Before he knew what he was doing he was at Scott's side, catching him in his strong arms. Scott was a *solid* guy. He didn't look all that big, but everything in him was muscle. His hair was soft and silky-smooth where it brushed against Danny's arm.

He bit his lip. His mic was still live, and he didn't want to start his year off by complaining about his husband on national television. That said, they weren't exactly getting off to a good start. The guy had already looked miserable when he was up there and now he was passing out. Was he on drugs? Was he a rare straight omega?

"Well that was dramatic," Yates said in his smarmy voice. "I don't know about you, but that certainly speaks about true love to me." A pair of PAs rushed out onto the stage with smelling salts, and Yates kept speaking. "In all my years of hosting this program I've never seen an omega so overcome with emotion that he passed out right here on the stage."

Danny rolled his eyes. He noticed another omega across from him, patting Scott's cheek carefully, who seemed to have the same view. Interesting. "Do you know him?" he asked in a whisper.

"He's my roommate." The bearded omega covered his mic with one hand.

"Is he on drugs?"

The guy scoffed. "No. Not Scott. This is not what he expected." He moved his hand away from the mic. The conversation was over.

Scott's eyelashes fluttered and he opened his huge dark eyes. He looked at his roommate and relaxed. Then he recognized Danny and jumped to his feet, like Danny's touch was poison. Where did he get off acting like that, anyway?

"Excellent! If the other omegas could take a step back we've got our priest just off stage." Yates smiled, but his eyes were hard and furious. "Excellent. Let's get this show on the road."

Danny had forgotten about the priest. The man came out and ran through an abbreviated version of the wedding service, jammed rings onto their fingers, and that was it. Yates called for the cameraman to cut and the show was over.

Everyone relaxed. Scott took several steps back from Danny. He took a few deep breaths. "Okay. So that happened." He closed his eyes and collected himself. "Where do we go from here?"

Yates curled his lip. "You're twenty-two and you don't know how a marriage works? This should be fun. The cameras have already been installed in your husband's home. You'll move in for the coming year. There will be no cheating, on either of your parts. You'll have two confessional sessions per week, recorded of course. Other than that, the rest is up to you. If ratings start to slip, we might give you a little nudge here or there to stir up the pot."

"Grand." Danny felt sick. He'd made the single worst decision of his life. He was saddled with a young husband who didn't know anything, who didn't want to be here, and who didn't want him at all.

“You signed the contract.” Yates wagged a finger at him. “You both did. Scott, dear, your things have already been brought to your new home. Enjoy.”

Danny turned to Scott. “I suppose we should make the best of it.” He held out his hand.

“I guess we should.” He didn’t take the hand, but walked toward the exit alone.

* * *

Made in the USA
Middletown, DE
07 April 2018